Mr. Bedford and the Muses

Mr. Bedford
and the Muses

by
Gail Godwin

The Viking Press / New York

First published in 1983 by The Viking Press
40 West 23rd Street, New York, N.Y. 10010
Published simultaneously in Canada by
Penguin Books Canada Limited

Library of Congress Cataloging in Publication Data
Godwin, Gail.
   Mr. Bedford and the muses.
   I. Title.
PS3557.O315M7   1983   813'.54   83-47870
ISBN 0-670-49235-3

"A Cultural Exchange" appeared originally in Atlantic Monthly; "Mr.
Bedford" was published originally in condensed form under the title "The
Unlikely Family" in Redbook; "A Father's Pleasures" and "Amanuensis"
appeared originally in Cosmopolitan, and "The Angry-Year" in McCall's.
"Amanuensis" was subsequently included in the 1980 Prize
Stories/O. Henry Awards Collection.

Grateful acknowledgment is made to Warner Bros. Music, Inc., for
permission to reprint a selection from "Carolina in the Morning," lyrics
by Gus Kahn, music by Walter Donaldson. Copyright © 1922 (renewed)
Warner Bros. Inc. All rights reserved.

Printed in the United States of America
Set in CRT Janson
Designed by Ann Gold

to Gingie

Contents

Mr. Bedford

I began keeping a journal when I was thirteen. Sometimes, now, I look with incredulity at the bulk of volumes widening along my shelf and I am reminded of the old lady who confesses to a stranger that she has always had a weakness for pancakes. "There's nothing wrong with having a weakness for pancakes," the stranger says. "Really?" she cries, relieved, and takes him up to her attic to show him her hundreds and hundreds of pancakes stacked neatly in tiers.

People say, "Oh, they must be so useful to your writing. All that material." But in fact the majority of the agonies, furies, passions, and dreads, penned in various inks in a handwriting that has changed from a stiff baroque upright to a looser, loopy slant, are as cold as those pancakes in the attic. Yet I go on with my vice. I look forward to it at the end of the day as some people do to a drink. Occasionally I indulge in a retrospective read and come away wishing that girl and then that woman had paid more attention to what was going on around her rather than heaping up more cold pancakes. But once in a while I come across something still warm. It connects me to my living past and starts my imagination glowing, as in the case of Mr. Bedford's story, written down carefully one spring afternoon in the London of 1963, within an hour after that strange and memorable couple, the Eastons, had told it to me.

My life with the Eastons began when I arrived in London in the spring of 1962. I lived with them, except for one winter's defection, until the autumn of 1964. Even today, when I try to describe the Eastons to people, I end up talking for thirty or forty minutes, growing more agitated, and finally demanding of my listeners: "Who *were* the Eastons, anyway?" And, as most people are perfectly willing to pass judgment on people they've never met, the answers are as peremptory as they are varied. "Con artists," says one person. "Victims!" insists another. "Their kind is a dying breed," remarks a third. But the minute I reread Mr. Bedford's story in my old journal, I knew that the Eastons, whatever they were, are very alive in me.

Easton is not their real name, of course. For obvious reasons, I'll change all the names, including my own. Also, made-up names make it easier to invent when you come to memory gaps. And this sometimes leads to bonuses. In the middle of "inventing," you discover you are remembering. Or, even better, you discover the real truth that lay buried beneath the literal happenings.

Only Mr. Bedford's name I won't change. It was his story that reconnected me to that chunk of raw past that now quivers to be shaped into meaning. We take our Muses where we find them, and you, Mr. Bedford, are the Muse of this story. As you once carried your candle into dark rooms for the Eastons, lead me now, in your diligent, slow-footed way, through the precarious realm of fiction-in-progress. You may keep your real name; your relatives won't sue.

The ad in the *Evening Standard* offered a bed-sitter in South Kensington, two meals included, seven guineas a week, "Student or young prof. person preferred." I had to ask someone what a guinea was, and was told that it was a fancy way to ask for more money (seven guineas being seven pounds, seven shillings). But I could still afford it, and I was a "young prof. person." So I called, or "rang up," as I would learn to say, and the woman who answered the telephone had an American voice with an Eastern Seaboard drawl. Her tone was warm and cultivated. She seemed pleased I was American, too, and even more pleased when I told her I'd be working for our Embassy. "Aren't you *lucky!*" she said. She told me to get off the 74 bus at

Old Brompton Road across from the Boltons and walk around the grassy circle to Tregunter Road. "It's the big gray house. It has a brass knocker shaped like a lion's head." She laughed. "You can move in right away if you like the room," she said. "But by all means stay and have supper with us." I was impressed by her spontaneous generosity. I had been in London less than a week and was still not certain what to make of the so-called British reserve.

I really congratulated myself on my luck when I saw the Boltons. It was just the sort of London I had imagined myself living in, knowing even as I conjured it up that I could not afford it on a GS-2 salary: a sweep of grand houses banked by well-kept lawns; old trees that, even though still bare, were tall and plentiful enough to form a cordon between the Brompton Road traffic and this austere preserve. Tregunter Road was shabbier, but the big gray house with the brass knocker still retained the ghost of former grandeur, even though its portico paint was peeling badly.

Mrs. Easton also retained the ghost of her better years. She carried herself extremely well in her baggy sweater and too-long tweed skirt, and her thoroughbred outlines were still apparent. She had a classic face, though wrinkled, and wore her faded blond hair pulled back behind her ears and fastened with a tortoiseshell barrette. "I'm *so* glad you rang when you did, Carrie," she said, "because immediately afterward a lovely young man telephoned from Leeds—he's joining Reuters (you know, the news service) and they had seen our ad and teletyped it up to him—but I told him I was pretty sure we'd already rented it. I see you've brought your bag—wasn't it heavy? Let's leave it just inside the door for now. I want you to meet Mr. Easton first and then he'll show you the room." She had a way of talking and smiling through her teeth at the same time that I found both unnerving and classy. We went past a large common room where a balding young man in a three-piece suit sat on a sofa reading a newspaper and another male of indeterminate age, also wearing a suit, was playing a Bach prelude rather badly on an old upright piano painted red.

"Do you have other tenants?" I asked, following her long, neatly shod feet down a gloomy corridor filled with promising supper smells. Somehow, from the way she had talked on the phone, I had assumed it would just be the three of us.

"Oh yes," she replied in her sunny, closed-mouth way, "we can accommodate seven. One is away at the moment, however, for the Easter holidays."

We passed a purple velvet curtain behind which someone was playing a Charles Aznavour record, then turned right into another corridor. Mrs. Easton knocked softly on a tall door with carved moldings. "Whit, dear, it's us," she called in a slightly placatory tone, then allowed a moment or two to pass before she opened it. A tall man stood erectly, with his back to us, in front of a fireplace that had a gas heater in the grate instead of a real fire. He wore well-pressed cavalry twills and a Harris tweed jacket with suede patches at the elbows. Then, with rather theatrical timing, he did an about-face. His cheeks were flushed and his light-blue eyes were a little watery and his hair was mostly gone, but he, too, still carried the outlines of a former beauty. He wore a maroon-and-gray tie that looked regimental, and also some tiny decoration in his buttonhole.

"Whit, this is Carrie Ames," said Mrs. Easton. "Carrie, this is my husband, Whitmore Easton." There was pride in her voice as she drawled out those last four words. I assumed he must be someone important, and/or she was still in love with him.

Mr. Easton shook my hand and looked me over. "So you'll be working for David Bruce, huh? Well, he's a capable chap. Gives wonderful parties, so I'm told. I was fond of Winant myself. He was ambassador here during the war. Amiable fellow. Took his own life, you know. I knew him when he was governor of New Hampshire. His second term."

"Are you two from New Hampshire?" I asked.

"No, I'm from New York and Lee, here, is from Connecticut. Say, Carrie, can I get you a drink? Darling"—he turned to his wife—"how about a drink?"

"Thank you, dear. I'll have a glass of sherry."

I said, "That sounds fine."

"Wonderful." He went to a sideboard. The room was filled with lots of large, dark-stained furniture. There was the smell of a nice perfume in the overheated air. Mrs. Easton displaced a Siamese cat from the sofa, explaining to him that he must defer to their guest. "This is Enrico," she said, fondling the cat in her arms. She wore a large pear-shaped diamond with two emerald baguettes on her wedding finger. The cat wriggled and sprang out of her arms with an ill-humored meow and stalked off to a hassock.

"Poor Rico," said Mrs. Easton, "he misses Elba. He had more freedom there. And he still hasn't forgiven us for the animal quarantine. We only recently got him back."

"You lived on Elba?" I sat down in Enrico's place. The sofa was a hideous old brown horsehair, but someone had draped a beautiful sea-green mohair shawl all along the back.

Mr. Easton joined us with the drinks. "I'm having something a wee bit stronger," he said, winking at me. He had poured himself half a tumblerful of gin with a dollop of tonic water. "Here's to Carrie," he said, raising the tumbler. We all drank to me. Mrs. Easton, with the air of a confidante, told me how for seven years she and Mr. Easton had run a little *pensione* in Portoferraio. "We met so many lovely people, mostly English, and we began to get homesick for some real civilization. And then this young man, Martin Eglantine, who owns this house and the one behind, across the garden, where your room is—listen to that, Whit!"—and she laughed, screwing up her eyes—"I'm already thinking of it as Carrie's room."

"Eglantine's a real entrepreneur," said Mr. Easton. "He owns dozens of houses like this, all over London. Buys 'em up quick as I can snap my fingers." He snapped his fingers, looked surprised to see that his glass was empty, and got up to refill it. I caught a shadow of annoyance on Mrs. Easton's face.

"Anyway," she went on brightly, smiling through her teeth, "Martin was very impressed with our *pensione*, and when we said we were ready to make a change, he offered us the use of these houses."

"But how long has it been since you've been *home?*"

"Oh, about eight years," said Mr. Easton jovially from the sideboard.

"No, Whit, it'll be ten years the thirtieth of this month," Mrs. Easton corrected him.

There was a silence in the room. The gas heater sighed. A clock ticked. Mr. Easton sloshed gin into the tumber.

"But don't you miss the United States?" I asked, more to break the silence than anything else, and earned a look from Mrs. Easton that I would come to know and dread. I called it, in my journals, "the scrunch," because her whole face bunched up into a mask of wrinkles. The eyes became little slits of light— and malevolent light, at that—and the lips disappeared altogether. And you knew you had done something unforgivably *gauche.*

But this first time the apparition was mercifully brief, and the next moment she was drawling through her teeth, "Of course we miss it, but . . . well, honestly, Carrie, England has so much to offer, and, frankly, Mr. Easton and I are more English in our *values* than we are American."

"Carrie, if you look out those French windows you'll see a big white mansion to your left," said Mr. Easton. "That's Douglas Fairbanks Junior's house. I knew him in Cairo. We met at a houseboat party on the Nile. Interesting fellow, but I always thought he had terrible taste in women."

I don't think it once occurred to me that I could choose not to take "my room." Even before I saw its unprepossessing lay-out—though it was no worse than the average room perpetrated on "students and young professional persons" all over the civilized world—I knew I was going to live here. I knew it even as I followed Mr. Easton's military pace down the narrow garden path that connected the big gray house with the less impressive row house behind, and he knew it, too, because he had brought along my suitcase. In less than an hour, the Eastons had wound me fast into their net. It was a net composed of obligation, fascination, and intrigue. I liked them, didn't quite trust them, desired their approval, and knew, with the instinct of one who likes to stir life up, that wherever they were would never be dull.

"Well, no movie star's mansion on this side," said Mr. Easton, as we looked out "my window" upon a solid block of council flats, "but you get the morning sun. It'll be easier to get up for work. We furnish linen service. Three towels a week, one change of sheets. What? Oh, a bookcase. Sure, sure. Ask Lee, I'm pretty sure there's one in the attic over at the other house. What we do is, you see, we give you the basics and then you fill in the rest according to your individual taste. Jean-Louis—that's our French textile salesman—has his room all filled with velvets and brocades. Alexander—he's a turf accountant (we call it bookie back home)—he lives in that passage with the purple curtain, we passed it on the way out. He can't afford the full rent, but he's an interesting chap, so we let him fix up that passage and have his meals for a little less than you guys pay—which reminds me, rent is payable a week in advance and on Thursday, if possible. Keeps things uniform. Get Alexander to show you his passage. He's fixed it up like a Victorian brothel. Here's your gas fire. First you put in your shilling—I'll put the first one in for good luck—and then you light it." He did a deep knee bend, amazingly limber for his age, and demonstrated. Then rose again, tilting toward me as if he'd lost his balance momentarily. "Well, I expect you'll want to wash up before supper." His face was crimson as he backed out of the room. I couldn't be sure whether he had actually patted my bottom or just brushed against it with his hand in the act of getting to his feet.

Just before supper, Mrs. Easton, wearing a handsome black bib apron with thin white stripes over her clothes, emerged from the kitchen and introduced me to my fellow boarders. She reiterated that one was away for Easter. Of the present number, I was the only girl. Mrs. Easton explained that she and her husband took their meal separately, in their own quarters. "We feel you young people are less inhibited that way." Then she went back to the kitchen and served the plates, which Mr. Easton carried out two at a time. The couple took their own plates on a tray and disappeared.

"Did you know Colonel and Mrs. Easton back in America?" asked Alexander, the turf accountant who lived in the passage.

I said no, I'd met them only this afternoon.

"Pity. We were hoping you could give us the gen on them."

"Sorry. I didn't even know he was a colonel."

"He has a DSO," said a baby-faced young man with dark eyes and beautiful long lashes. "The British gave it to him for blowing up an enemy train in World War Two. He drinks too much, but she's terribly nice. And such a terrific cook. Mmm." He parodied someone licking his chops, then took a delicate forkful of lasagne.

"Even if her servings are the size of a postage stamp," said Alexander. "That's fine for Carlos here, he can sit in his room all day eating pâté and reading novels. Carlos's father is the finance minister of Mexico."

"Alexander," said Carlos, blushing deeply, "you embarrass me."

An arrogant-appearing young man in a turtleneck sweater who was reading something in his lap while he ate gave a snort of laughter. He was the best-looking of the bunch.

"I don't see why, Carlos. I'm just saving Carrie a bit of time. She's curious about us, we're curious about her. And being such a bloody international group, we don't have access to all the shortcuts one has with one's own countrymen. That's why I was hoping she could give us the gen on the Eastons. We're all keen on placing people, Carlos."

"That's not true," protested Carlos, blinking rapidly. "It's what a person is in himself that counts."

"Rubbish," said Alexander. "What am I 'in myself'? A bloody cipher. One more human being. Whereas if you can place my accent—Yorkshire, working class—and then if you can tell I'm wearing a thirty-guinea, made-to-measure suit, and if you go in my passage and if you know anything about antiques and can recognize what I've managed to accumulate on my sodding salary, *then* you're on the road to finding out who I am. And intend to become."

"A crook?" inquired a balding young man genially, without looking up from his food. He was the one in the three-piece suit I had seen reading a newspaper earlier.

"That's Colin," Alexander told me. "He's a clerk at Barclays Bank. He earns ten pounds a week. But *his* suit is off the peg."

"Oh, really, Alexander," said Colin, continuing to eat.

The arrogant man in the turtleneck gave another snort of laughter. I had retained his name from Mrs. Easton's introductions, though his had not been one she had lingered over indulgently, as in the case of Alexander and Jean-Louis the textile salesman, or with relish, as in the case of Carlos Paredes y Broncas. The antisocial man's name was Nigel Farthingale. He ate a piece of endive with his little finger sticking out and turned the page of the book on his lap.

"Oh Colin," I said, "I wonder if you could advise me. I was in the Canary Islands just before coming here and this British lady told me I would get a better rate of exchange if I cashed my American Express dollars into pounds down there. So now I'm carrying around all these loose pound notes. Would I lose a lot if I were to turn them back into traveler's checks?"

"You might lose more if you don't," said Colin.

"Nevair carry more cash than you can afford to lose," said the French textile salesman with real feeling, looking up from his meal for the first time. There was genuine alarm on his handsome, plump face. He wore his paisley silk foulard tied so high on his neck that he appeared to have no chin.

"Oh, Carrie probably comes from a very rich family," said Alexander. "All Americans are rich."

"Rubbish," I said. But in such a way that they might think he'd hit on the truth. "You must get a lot of good tips," I said, "being a turf accountant, Alexander."

"Yes, but I don't gamble. Investment is more my nature." Alexander was the thinnest grown-person I'd ever seen. His cheeks were so hollow he looked as if he were constantly sucking a sweet.

"Then why work in such a place?"

"It's as good as any, till my ship comes in. Besides, I rather enjoy watching how people of all classes can make equally bloody asses of themselves."

The Eastons reappeared. Mr. Easton cleared the table while Mrs. Easton poured coffee and served around a platter of cookies in the common room. She had taken off her apron and dabbed on a little of the nice perfume, and now, with the air of a grand lady entertaining a group of young people in her own home, she proceeded to devote herself to each of us in turn. I came first because I was new, and she explained to the group that I would be working at the Embassy on Grosvenor Square and then asked me what my duties would be, exactly, and turned things over to me with the smoothness of a talk-show hostess. I said I wasn't sure as to the exact scope of my duties, the job didn't start till Monday, but that I would be with a new program that was supposed to encourage British people to take their holidays in the United States.

"I'd adore taking a holiday in America," said Alexander. "Why not get your department to send me over as a publicity stunt? I'll go everywhere and send back good reports."

Appreciative laughter. Except for arrogant Nigel, who sat with the air of one restrained, his demitasse cup balanced upon his closed book.

Then Mrs. Easton looked fondly at Carlos and inquired whether he had *studied* any today. "Carlos is cramming for Cambridge," she explained to me.

There followed another set-to between Alexander and Carlos, in which Alexander said Carlos would be a bloody expert on the novels of Mary Renault when he got to Cambridge, and Carlos, blinking and blushing, protested that he had studied all morning and read *The Bull from the Sea* only in the afternoon. "And besides, Mrs. Easton"—he appealed to her like a favorite child—"it *is* history."

"Of course it is, Carlos, but you mustn't neglect your other subjects." Then, squaring her shoulders a little, she turned to Nigel Farthingale. "Any luck with your auditions?" she drawled, forcing her smile wider.

With a scornful glance at her, as if to say, Must we play this ridiculous farce?, he offered her his book. "I'm reading for the part of Jack next Tuesday. It won't be a very grand production, but then"—with a curl of his lip—"beggars can't be choosers, can they?"

I thought she flinched at this, but when she saw the book she cried, "Oh! *The Importance of Being Earnest.* Nigel, you're not going to believe this, but *I* once played Jack when we did this at our boarding school." She folded her hands on the book, closed her eyes for a minute, and then leaped up like a girl from her chair. She began pacing around our little circle and we watched, fascinated, as her stride grew more masculine. Then she held out the book in front of her, as if it had suddenly become much larger and taken on weight. "Is *this* the handbag, Miss Prism?" she asked, in a husky male voice. "Examine it carefully before you speak. The happiness of more than one person depends on your answer."

We were all charmed with her as she stood before us, in the tweed skirt whose length had been right about ten years before, holding out the library book as if it really were a bag large enough to hold a manuscript . . . or a baby . . . but then Nigel cruelly revoked the spell by saying, "It's 'the happiness of more than one *life*,' actually," and Mrs. Easton visibly recalled herself. You saw the years pile up again—for a moment she had been a girl, or a boy, with youth's whole life before her—and then she spoke once more through her teeth as she said, "You're right, I'm sure, Nigel. After all, it was such a long time ago." She handed him back his book. And resumed her place at the coffee-pot.

Some desultory conversation ensued. Jean-Louis described

his success on a selling trip in Bristol, from which he had returned only that day, and had complimentary things to say about the sherry of that city; Alexander described a lamp he had seen in a shop in the King's Road that would be just bloody perfect for his passage, only it cost eighteen quid. Mr. Easton joined us. He sat down at the red piano and ran his fingers over the keys, then embarked on the first few bars of the "Moonlight Sonata." "Hey, Carrie," he called over his shoulder, "ever hear of a place called Rhinebeck, New York?"

It was at this moment that Nigel Farthingale chose to acknowledge my existence for the first time. "Come, Carrie," he said, rising abruptly, "it's time someone showed you the inside of an English pub."

I was in a quandary, one that would become a staple of my association with the Eastons: that of choosing between the call of freedom and the demands of "civilization"—one of Mrs. Easton's pet words. I had been eyeing the arrogant Nigel all through dinner, fantasizing just such an invitation as this, but why did it have to come at such an inopportune time? Mrs. Easton was just now beaming her scrunched look at Nigel with a formidable intensity. But, fearsome as the scrunch was, I dreaded any encroachment on my free choice more. This was a boardinghouse, after all, not a convent.

"Well, okay," I told Nigel. I slung my purse over my arm and followed him out of the room. Just as we reached the door, Mr. Easton hurried up behind us and took Nigel aside. "Can I count on it *this* Thursday?" I heard him ask.

"They're a frightful couple, frightful. When he started on *his* act, I felt it my duty to spare you. You'll get it yet, all the new ones do. The beautiful lady at the piano in the manor house in Rhinebeck, New York, playing the 'Moonlight Sonata,' only she turns out to have a tail. They're mean, dishonest, petty people. I think they've done something awful, that's why she can't even go home to see her grandchild. And they play favorites. They blow hot and cold on you, and they're terrible snobs. They court you as long as you're useful and do things their way, but they gossip behind your back and he tells the most awful lies. It's nothing but plot and counterplot from morning till night in that house."

"But what do you think they've done—that they can't go home?"

"Oh, who knows. Embezzled money, maybe. Perhaps they were spies. One day I was alone with her—I was in their good graces then, she thought me frightfully charming—and she showed me all these photographs of a child. 'He's almost nine years old and I've never laid eyes on him,' she said, and began to sniffle. I asked why, was it a question of money, and she laid her hand on my arm in that confidential way she has and said, 'Oh, Nigel, it's much more complicated than that.' She turned nasty on me after that, probably regretted confiding even that much. I'm getting out of there as soon as possible. I'm a bit strapped at the moment, but as soon as I get something . . . I'm seeing a chap at the BBC tomorrow. . . ."

I regretted coming out with him. The beer was warm and tasted bitter, and all exhilaration of freedom had long since fled. On and on ranted Nigel, always about the Eastons, his voice rising to a whine as he catalogued their faults. He was probably angry because Mr. Easton was closing in on him about the rent; I was a mere sounding board. I said I was tired and offered to pay for our beers, since he was strapped. He gallantly refused and said he'd go along with me tomorrow and show me where the American Express office was, as it was quite near where he had his appointment.

The next morning, as soon as breakfast was over and the dining room had cleared out, I prepared to reinstate myself with the Eastons. Mr. Easton, wearing a soft blue wool shirt with his tweed jacket today (and the little decoration on his lapel), was moving briskly around the common room, humming to himself as he emptied ashtrays and gathered up stray newspapers. I went over to him with my purse and explained that I was on my way to American Express to get all my pounds changed into traveler's checks, so could I just give him my seven guineas in advance now, though it was only Wednesday.

"Sit down, sit down," he said. He himself sat down and patted a place beside him on the couch. "A man should never take money from a woman while standing up," he said jovially. I counted out seven pounds from my envelope and then added seven shillings from my change purse. "Much appreciated," he said. "And how did the inside of an English pub look to you?" I made a sour face and shrugged. "I think it's a matter of who shows it to you. I'm going to try again." There, that should make things clear and win me back into their good graces. "Poor Nigel," he said to me, slipping my rent in his wallet, "he came to London hoping to make it big as an actor and, well, he just hasn't got what it takes. He's turning bitter and blaming it on everybody else. We've been very patient with him. Lee even baked him a cake for his thirtieth birthday and he never even thanked her." "It must be terrible to turn thirty and not be what you had hoped to be," I said, truly shocked that Nigel should be that old. "He's riding with me to the American Express office to show me where it is, but only because he has to go that way, anyway." "Sure, why not?" said Mr. Easton.

Mrs. Easton came out of the kitchen, drying her hands on a dish towel.

"Carrie wasn't too impressed with the inside of an English pub," said Mr. Easton. "Seems the company left something to be desired."

"Well, I'm not surprised," said Mrs. Easton. Her manner brightened toward me. "Carrie, come into the kitchen, if you have a moment, and I'll show you something simply splendid."

An impressive-sized fish had been laid out on the chopping board. "Isn't he wonderful?" crooned Mrs. Easton. "Daphne Heathcock brought him back with her on the train. In a wooden box packed with ice. The Heathcocks have been so lovely to us. He's an M.P. Daphne is a lovely girl, I want you two to be friends. She slept in this morning, she was tired from the trip."

"What kind of fish is it?"

"Why, it's a salmon. He's one of the first of the spring run. Honestly, I admire this fish. Do you realize he's been at least twice to sea? Look, you can tell from the scales. This fellow has gone through unbelievable hardships just to get back to his hometown river and start a family."

"How do you know it's a he?"

"Why, because of the hooked jaw. The hens have a rounded jaw; also, their sides are fatter. My father was a great salmon fisherman. He fished the Restigouche, up in Canada. Have you ever heard of the Restigouche Salmon Club?" It seemed to disappoint her that I hadn't. "Well, boy," she said to the salmon, "I'll do my best for you. I'm going to poach you and serve you with a Flemish sauce. I do hope you'll be here for dinner, Carrie. I wouldn't want you to miss this treat."

Nigel Farthingale obligingly pointed out the sights to me as we rode to Piccadilly on the top deck of the bus. He did not mention the Eastons. It was as if he knew I had gone over to the enemy and he needed to preserve his strength for his own battles. His face looked gray and worried as he walked me down the Haymarket in London's muted spring sunshine, and as he talked about his appointment—he was trying to get into television commercials—his breath was not good. I pitied him as I wished him luck at the entrance to American Express, but I was relieved he planned to leave the Eastons soon. This morning he was a walking portent of all I did not want to happen to me.

I went into the brightly lit office, found the banking window, and opened my purse. The envelope was still there, but the sheaf of pounds that had been inside was gone.

"Wait a minute, sit down and start over. Lee's just gone out for some nutmeg, she won't be long. Now let's try and reconstruct what you did with your purse from the time you paid me your rent till the time you opened your purse at American Express."

I had found Mr. Easton in their room, making up the horsehair sofa, which apparently converted to a bed at night. A pair of Mrs. Easton's stockings hung over the back of a chair, and I think he had been drinking when I knocked. The gas fire was not lit in the grate and it was cold in the room.

"Well, I think I left my purse on the sofa in the common room when Mrs. Easton called me to look at the salmon. And when I came back, you and Nigel were standing there talking."

"Wait a minute," said Mr. Easton, snapping his fingers. "I was out of the room for a few seconds. I went to the dustbin. When I came back, Nigel was there, waiting for you. I hate to say this, but it sure looks like Nigel. He owes two weeks' back rent. How much did you have in the envelope, Carrie?"

To this day I can't say why I lied. It still embarrasses me to think of that lie, and I wouldn't admit it now except that it is inextricable from this story. But that will come later.

"A hundred and fifty pounds," I told Mr. Easton, when the sum had been not quite fifty.

Mrs. Easton returned. "Who let Rico out into the hall?" (She had the Siamese cat in her arms.) "Oh, Carrie. I thought you'd gone to town."

"Sorry, darling," said Mr. Easton, "he must have slipped out. . . . Carrie's had all her money stolen."

"Oh *no!*" cried Mrs. Easton. She put down the cat. Then she removed her stockings from the back of the chair and put them away in a drawer. "When did this happen? And where?"

"We've been reconstructing," Mr. Easton said. "Apparently, our out-of-work actor was in the common room with Carrie's purse. I had just stepped out to empty the—"

"But where was Carrie without her purse?" said Mrs. Easton, looking from one to the other of us.

"In the kitchen with you," he said.

"Oh dear," said Mrs. Easton vexedly.

"I'm terribly sorry this had to happen today," I said, "I mean the day of your salmon dinner."

"It's not *your* fault," she said, but looking at me as if she really thought it was. "Well, Whit, what do you think we ought to do?"

"Call Scotland Yard," he said.

"You're joking," she said.

"No I'm not. With a hundred and fifty pounds involved, we have no choice."

"A hundred and fifty pounds? You were carrying around that much in cash, Carrie?"

I nodded miserably, my misery largely a result of the lie. Had I wanted to impress upon them my distress by tripling the amount? Or to build my fake image as a rich girl? Or was I just an awful liar, as Nigel had accused Mr. Easton of being?

"But won't they come and go through everyone's *room?*" Mrs. Easton asked Mr. Easton, getting the beginnings of her scrunch. "If you two think it's Nigel—and I join you in thinking so—why not just wait until he comes back and confront him?"

"What if he never comes back?" said Mr. Easton. "He may just take the money and scram."

"And leave his things behind?"

"Tell you what," said Mr. Easton. "It's up to Carrie, of course. We'll wait and see if Nigel does come back, and if he does, *then* I'll call the Yard."

"I hate the thought of them going through the rooms," she said. "I mean, what will Carlos think? What will *Daphne* think?"

"They'll think that if it ever happens to them we'll be just as thorough. And they'll probably find it exciting," said Mr. Easton. "If it comes to that. And, frankly, I don't think it will."

Around four o'clock, Mr. Easton came and rapped on my door like a conspirator and told me that Nigel had returned and that Inspector Roper of the CID would be along shortly. I was to come and wait in the Eastons' room, where we would go over the facts with Roper, and then Mr. Easton would summon Nigel and "confront him out of the blue" with the law. He seemed animated by all the excitement, and I noticed he had changed into a clean shirt and put the regimental-looking tie back on.

When Inspector Roper arrived, he found us grouped in a cozy tableau of domestic distress. The gas fire hissing merrily in the grate. The beautiful sea-green mohair shawl draped once more over the back of the old horsehair sofa bed. Mr. Easton standing at attention; Mrs. Easton, with her good posture, sitting beside me on the sofa, making a gesture with her hands halfway between warming them and wringing them. The American *jeune fille*, eyes open abnormally wide with horror at the possibility of being discovered by Scotland Yard in an "exaggeration"—a look that passes as shock at having been robbed by the English before she's been a week on their shores. And Enrico the cat crouched elegantly on his hassock.

Poor Nigel did not have a chance. By the time he was summoned to the room, the Eastons and Roper were old friends. Roper had heard about the blown-up armament train that had got Colonel Easton his DSO, and the CID inspector had identified Mrs. Easton's perfume as Je Reviens and told us how, briefly, before the war, he had sold beauty products for Worth in the provinces. He asked me where in America I lived and said, "I've always wanted to go there and drink a mint julep in the proper surroundings."

Nigel was incensed when he found out what he was suspected of, and the more defensive he got the more hoity-toity his accent became, which did not help his case with Roper, whose vowels were more in the Alexander category. Nigel denied stealing my money and, with the condescension of an Oxford undergraduate inviting a common policeman to his room for sherry, invited Roper to "come upstairs and conduct a search."

Roper returned alone, looking sheepish, and said that of course he had found nothing. "The bloke's had ample opportunity to dispose of it," he said, "but I'm fairly certain I've put the wind up him. Of course, that doesn't help your case, Miss Ames, but quite honestly, just between us, you oughtn't to be carrying round large amounts of cash like that . . . it's just asking for it, you know. What I'm most concerned with, if you want to know, is that you don't judge England by this one bloke. We're not all of us like that, you can be sure."

"Of *course* not," said Mrs. Easton. "England is the most civilized nation on earth."

"Thank you, ma'am, which is exactly the reason why I

can't escort that insolent young liar to his just deserts: in this country a man is innocent until he's proven guilty. And I've got nothing to convict him on, you see."

"I understand," I said. Though I was a little disappointed with Scotland Yard.

"But will you be all right?" asked Roper.

"Oh, we'll take good care of her," said Mr. Easton, putting his arm around my shoulders. "And she's got a nice job at the American Embassy, starting Monday."

"Well, then," said Roper, "you're all right, then, aren't you? Mind you, this all goes down in the books. We may get him yet. But if by chance we don't, Miss Ames, try to look back on this as a learning experience. But don't judge the English by it!"

Just before the great salmon dinner, when some of us were gathered in the common room, Jean-Louis playing his bad Bach on the red upright, Alexander leafing through an old *Queen* from the magazine rack, Mr. Easton came in and took me aside.

"Flash bulletin," he said. "Farthingale's done a flit. I went up to his room after Roper left. I was going to have a man-to-man talk with him, see if I couldn't shame him into giving your money back. Not a trace. He'd cleared out. And owing two weeks' rent."

"Oh God," I said, feeling totally responsible for everything.

"I called the Yard, but Roper wasn't back yet. I left word. Listen, Carrie, do us a favor, will you? Don't mention the robbery to the others. Mrs. Easton is worried that it'll give the house a bad name. I'll just tell them he left. Okay? And I'll keep you posted on developments from the Yard."

"Okay," I agreed, feeling I'd been let off lightly.

The salmon was a success. It was the first time I'd ever eaten it fresh, and it remains to this day my favorite delicacy. Daphne, its purveyor, was much thanked, and the merits of the fish extolled by French, English, Mexican, and American consumers alike. "Jolly good," Daphne would reply, or, "I'm *so* glad." She would have been recognized as an English girl any-where in the world by her tissue-paper-thin skin (which was al-ready beginning to crinkle around the eyes, though she was only nineteen), and her expressionless features, and her inward-turning teeth. But I found her aloofness fascinating and read into her half-a-dozen stock phrases (which consisted of the two already quoted, plus variations around the adjectives "boring" and "super," and "One hopes so," and "I shouldn't be at all sur-prised") infinite nuances and levels of meaning. Like many English people of her class that I would meet, *she* seemed to find her frugal vocabulary adequate to meet the situations of a day; it was up to me to supply the shades of difference. Mrs. Easton had told me Daphne was studying shorthand and typing at a little establishment off Bond Street, and I asked Daphne if she planned to be a secretary.

"One hopes so," she replied, transporting a modest bite of salmon, her fork prongs-down, to her small mouth.

"Among Daphne's crowd, 'shorthand/typing' is shorthand for husband-hunting," put in Alexander.

"Don't be boring," said Daphne, though she blushed scar-let.

"*C'est parfait,*" murmured Jean-Louis, not looking up from his plate. "And the sauce is exquisite, as well."

"Did you get your notes changed into something safer?" inquired Colin good-naturedly.

"Mmm," I said vaguely, pretending to have a mouthful of salmon.

"I say," said Alexander. "Do you think you can get a carton of Pall Malls for me at your PX? I can advance you the money now, if you like."

"Did you hear Nigel left?" said Carlos. "Mrs. Easton said he moved out this afternoon without even giving a day's notice."

"Well, I shan't miss him," said Alexander.

"Always had his nose in the air ... or in a book," said Colin.

"And he treated Mrs. Easton badly last evening," said

Carlos. "There was no need for him to correct that one little word."

"I think he was not very—how do you put it?—solvent," said Jean-Louis.

"He was boring," said Daphne.

"Well, at least he had the decency to leave before the meal," said Alexander. "Our portions are that much larger. But you fancied him, didn't you, Carrie?"

"Not I," I said.

Thus the waters closed over Nigel Farthingale. No more was heard of him, not even via Scotland Yard, and my money was never found. (However, fifteen years would pass, and one night, back in the States, while irritably switching TV channels, I would come upon Nigel in the act of denying yet another crime. This time he was being accused of making off with his mother-in-law's bedtime novel so he could read it himself. It was not a very good program—its U.S. appearance was undoubtedly due to our current rage for "anything English"—but I stayed with it for a while in order to watch Nigel. He had aged, of course, but then who hadn't, and his hair was different and he wore a sad, droopy mustache in keeping with his farcical role. He was clad in a nightshirt that showed his potbelly, and he *had* stolen his mother-in-law's novel, and his wife, who was on Mummy's side, clobbered him with it when he was discovered red-handed with it, in his own bed. The whole thing depressed me very much and I switched it off. As Nigel's silly, puffy face shrank to a pinpoint of light, I said uselessly, "I think I owe you an apology.")

After dinner, we all adjourned to the common room and Mrs. Easton emerged without her apron, accepted our profuse compliments on the salmon, and poured coffee. She asked Daphne if she had enjoyed her Easter vacation.

"It was super, thank you very much."

Mr. Easton joined us after he had put the dishes to soak.

"So old Nigel's cleared off, has he?" said Alexander.

"Yep. Got an urgent call from Hollywood. Had to rush right off," said Mr. Easton, sitting down at the piano.

Everybody laughed.

He played a few bars of the "Moonlight Sonata" and then told us about the time he had gone "on a matter of business" from New York City to the house of a very wealthy man in Rhinebeck, New York. "While the butler went off to announce me, I wandered about the room, looking at the paintings and so on, and then I heard this same music coming from somewhere . . . only the person was playing it much better than I do, with real talent and feeling. And I found myself going in search of it. I went through one magnificent room after another until finally I reached the most beautiful room of them all. It overlooked the Hudson and at that moment the sun was just setting. A beautiful woman sat at a grand piano; she was in three-quarter profile, so I could see her but she didn't see me. Well, I stood there admiring this vision of loveliness. I was a young man, life was just beginning for me, as it is for all of you now, and that woman in those surroundings seemed the epitome of all I hoped to win for myself: love, accomplishment, beauty, elegance, wealth. I stood on the threshold of that room, watching her like a man in a dream, and then, when it came time for her to turn the page of her music, I saw a long tail whip up from under her dress, do the job for her, and then disappear under her dress again. She went right on playing, without a break. Shortly after that, the man I'd come to see on business joined me and she heard us and stopped playing and came over to be introduced. She was his daughter. Later, after he and I had done our business, he asked me to stay and dine with them. He said his daughter didn't often have the pleasure of interesting company her own age. I thanked him and explained I had to get back to New York on urgent business. I rode all the way back to the city having one martini after another in the club car."

"And what sort of a tail was it, exactly?" asked Carlos in the tones of one who knows the story well enough to move on to its subtler embellishments.

"Oh, slender, graceful, efficient," said Mr. Easton. "Everything you'd want in a tail, really."

I was practically on the floor with hilarity.

"That is, if one wanted a tail," said Alexander.

At this point, cool Daphne almost fell off her chair laughing.

"And did it," I gasped, "did it have hair on it?"

This brought a communal shriek. Now everyone was rolling and pitching and snorting. Mrs. Easton was laughing so hard she held her stomach as if in pain, Colin had his round face buried in his hands, and Jean-Louis, cackling like a madman, took out a gorgeous square of silk and mopped the tears from his eyes.

"Did it have hair?" repeated Mr. Easton, swinging around on his piano stool to face me. Like a good performer, he had kept control of himself and only a slight twitch of his mouth betrayed his mirth. "Well, Carrie, as I recollect, it had a thin layer of hair. Not that you could see bare skin or anything. Just, you know"—his right hand stroked a sensuous curve in the air—"the right amount of hair for a ladylike tail."

The London evening closed around our happy circle, and presently, still flushed from laughing, Mrs. Easton got up to turn on a lamp. Anyone happening to pass our window then would have seen such a picture as might make his heart quicken with longing . . . or nostalgia . . . or eagerness to get home: depending on his own domestic circumstances.

In the following weeks, my energies and attentions were directed more upon Grosvenor Square than upon the goings-on at "Tregunter," as all the inmates called it, even though half of us had rooms in the shabbier house, behind, on Cathcart Road. We three "travel consultants," in our temporary quarters on the fourth floor of the Embassy, were all in our early twenties: one from California, one from Missouri, one from North Carolina. We were expected to look personable and be enthusiastic and pleasant as we doled out scenic brochures and city maps and worked out timetables, if required, for the potential British visitors to the U.S. who had seen our ads and braved their way past the Marine guards to inquire further. To those who had stayed at home in Lancs or Hants or Weston super Mare or Berwick upon Tweed and penned inquiries beginning with "I am extremely sorry to bother you" from houses with picturesque names like Tidmarsh Cottage or Eel Grange, we were expected, when not busy with "live" customers, to write warm, helpful replies, enclosing the appropriate brochures. When it was discovered that the girl from Missouri had been signing all her letters "Love, Betty Ann McRae," our supervisor, an ex–airline stewardess and the bane of my workday existence, took to screening all our letters and returning them for revision if "the tone was off" or, as once or twice in my case, "they showed too much imagination."

Colleen Drury (or "Dreary," as we called her behind her back) was an earnest woman in her forties. During slow hours, she told us stories of her grim childhood in a dead Midwestern town she had been determined to escape. Her mother had told her she was ugly, and, often, when Colleen was sleeping, would come into Colleen's bedroom and snatch her pillow from under her head. When our boss, Mr. Miles, discovered Colleen, she had been "retired" from the skies by her airline and was working as a tour planner in its London office. She was not a bad-looking woman. She liked to tell us how she was once aboard a flight with JFK when he was still a senator, and he called her over and told her, "You look a lot like my wife." There was a resemblance, in the facial structure and the hair, and Colleen frankly played it up in her choice of clothes and shoes and the little pillbox hats she always wore to Embassy receptions. She even spoke in a whispery, girlish voice that sounded exactly like the parody of Jackie on a record about the Kennedys in the White House that was all the rage that year. But poor Colleen had a witch's chin and suffered from chronic conjunctivitis and from a variety of back problems that would bring her ramrod-straight to the office one day and stooping the next. She was a spinster but, as she confided to us, she had been on the verge of marriage several times, once even having left her suitcase, as required, in the rectory of a certain village to establish residence during the period of the banns. But at the last minute, she told us, she always lost her nerve and couldn't go through with it. She was a stickler for etiquette and protocol and adored poring over manuals that told you how to address nobility and who sits where and leaves when. One morning, our post brought a letter from an earl inquiring about the ninety-nine-dollars-for-ninety-nine-days bus ticket offered by Greyhound, and Colleen spent the better part of that day rushing up and down on the elevator, from and to the USIS library, consulting *Debrett's* and *Burke's* and R. W. Chapman's *Names, Designations & Appellations*. She humbly submitted her final draft to Mr. Miles, our good-humored, unflappable director, who seemed always on his way out for an appointment. He skimmed it, standing on the threshold of the exit, and said, "Seems fine to me, Colleen. Be sure and save his seal, my nephew is making a collection."

I spent a great deal of time fretting about Colleen. She could just walk through the room and make me feel guilty. Every time I talked to her, I came away feeling I had either betrayed or incriminated myself. I discussed it with the other two, who admitted they felt the same, only not as violently as I did. "It's because she's earned this job and we haven't," said the girl from California, who was secretly engaged but wanted her year of independence before she settled down. She and I had had political entrées to our Stateside interviews with Mr. Miles. "It's because this job is the center of her life, while we have other things we care about more," said the loving Betty Ann from Missouri, who was newly wed to a handsome, strapping Texan doing a year at the London School of Economics. "I guess you're right," said I, who still drifted becalmed, uncertain, upon my ocean of possibilities. I looked upon this job as a sort of glamorous lifeboat (the glamour being the London part) that would keep me financially afloat till the winds of love and accomplishment bestirred themselves and set me on my course.

/ / /

The Eastons' name does not make its initial appearance in my journal until almost a month has elapsed from the day I entered their house. Or, rather, Martin Eglantine's house. The entire Nigel-robbery episode is summed up in the scrawled rubric "Just trying to survive!," followed by a long column of pounds, shillings, and pence in which emergency expenses are worked out till the first payday. (Mr. Miles, always good about these things, advanced a loan.) "The Eastons hang their clothes over the backs of chairs when they go to bed at night" is sandwiched inauspiciously between the conclusion of a diatribe against Colleen Drury (ending with the resolution "Do not converse with her except when absolutely necessary!") and an exchange among the "inmates" that I must have found recordable:

> ALEXANDER (*throwing down the Sunday color supplement*): Just look at the Queen! Why can't she dress properly?
> COLIN: I'm afraid that's not her fault, old boy.
> ALEXANDER: You can be dowdy and elegant at the same time.
> JEAN-LOUIS: Tell me, Carrie, what is considered a gude salarie in America?

One night, very late, the door to my room had swung shut while I was in the bathroom. I ran shivering across the connecting garden to the main house to borrow the Eastons' spare key. It took several knocks to wake them. "Carrie! What's wrong?" asked Mr. Easton, in striped flannel pajamas, when he finally opened the door. He seemed relieved when he learned I only wanted the key. From the doorway, I could see Mrs. Easton under the bedclothes in their pulled-out horsehair sofa bed. "All right now, dear?" she drawled sleepily at me. I also saw his twills, the Harris tweed, and the maroon-and-gray tie laid out neatly on a chair, and her too-long skirt and the baggy sweater draped on another chair, and their shoes beneath their respective chairs. I found the sight both touching and sinister. As though they might have to get dressed in a hurry, I thought, recalling Nigel's hints at their dark past.

All the inmates of the "youth brothel," as Mr. Easton sometimes called it, were intrigued by the Eastons' friends. There were not many, but among them numbered several whose correspondence could have added to Mr. Miles's nephew's seal collection. There was an old lady with pinkish hair and a slightly soiled lavender suit that looked like an old Chanel who arrived most Saturdays to take tea with Mrs. Easton. She drove up in a wobbly, ancient Morris Minor, tooted the horn twice (which was the signal for Mr. Easton to remove Enrico to the kitchen), and first coaxed and then dragged an angry, rheumy-eyed pug from the front seat of the Morris. The pug's name was Donna Elvira; the Eastons addressed the old lady as "Principessa." The Principessa and Donna Elvira would go off to the Eastons' room to have tea with Mrs. Easton, and Mr. Easton would chop vegetables or cube meat for a curry and keep Enrico company in the kitchen. When tea was over, the Principessa would come to the kitchen (leaving Mrs. Easton outside in the hall in charge of Donna Elvira) and say in her hoarse, heavily accented English, "Dear Whit, I have come to say good-bye." Then they would chat for a minute, during which time the old lady would always remark, "That looks delicious, is that beef or pork?" or, "Oh, what a pretty cheese," and Mr. Easton would insist on wrapping some up for her. Once she went so far as to admire Enrico's stock of tins, which were kept on a shelf over the sink, and Mr. Easton persuaded her to take one for Donna Elvira, whose palate had gone off her usual brand, the Principessa said.

"She lost everything during the war and had to flee Italy," Mrs. Easton told us. "Now she's just a raggle-taggle gypsy like us, even though the blood of the Medicis flows in her veins."

"She can't afford even a full square meal a day, but she has a Goya painting hanging in her bed-sitting room," said Mr. Easton.

"Well, she'll always have a decent tea and some scraps for her Sunday lunch as long as the blood flows in *our* veins, be it ever so sluggish," said Mrs. Easton. "But it's just a drawing, darling, not a painting." Mrs. Easton almost always corrected her husband's exaggerations, even though it pained her, you could tell. "This Chelsea pensioner came up to us on the street and wanted twenty-five shillings for a postcard," he would say. "No, darling. Four shillings," she would amend.

Then there were Lord and Lady Monleigh. He was the Eastons' age, in his early sixties; she was a handsome, languid woman about twenty years younger—his second wife. She wrote novels under her maiden name, but her book-jacket photos always showed her posed inside or outside "Houndsdene Hall, the country seat of the Marquess and Marchioness of Monleigh." Once a fortnight, the Eastons left us a cold supper and took the bus to Belgrave Square to dine at the Monleighs' town house, and about that often Lord and Lady Monleigh came to Tregunter and dined off trays in the Eastons' room and then joined us for coffee. Lord Monleigh was fascinated by our ménage (he had no children) and loved to draw us out. He was a stout little man with pointed ears like a gnome's and extremely intelligent eyes that fastened on people and things, avid to extract their essences. He asked Alexander if he might visit the famous antique-filled passage he had heard so much about, and when they returned, Alexander was saying, "You're quite welcome, sir, it's a distinct improvement to show it to someone who knows what he's seeing." He wanted to know Jean-Louis's travel routes when he went selling his silks around the provinces, and insisted upon giving him names of acquaintances who might be of help. "What delights you most about the English?" he demanded of me. "And what about us disappoints you most?" "I love their subtlety," I said. "But sometimes they ... well ... lack *vigor*." (That popular Camelot word.) "Mmm," he mused, pulling at a gnomish ear. "P'raps you'll find we make up for it with durability." Mrs. Easton nodded at Lord Monleigh as if she were a schoolgirl listening to her favorite teacher.

He asked Carlos what he'd been cramming for. "Ah yes, grammar. My nephew found a good one on his entrance examination to Sandhurst. 'What is wrong with this sentence: Our Christmas turkey did not come, so we had to eat one of our friends.' "

It sometimes occurred to me to wonder why Lady Monleigh, the novelist of the two, who slouched elegantly in her chair, smoking her Russian cigarettes and cocooned in some private reverie, was not asking these questions. I studied her discreetly, for I planned to write novels, too, once everything was sorted out in my lifeboat. Well, maybe she was absorbing it silently, all this valuable human data her husband so obligingly ferreted out for her. But I took out her latest novel from the lending library and found little evidence of it.

One Sunday the Eastons invited me to their room to take tea with two young men who had boarded with them in Portoferraio, where the Eastons seemed to have acquired all their present friends. I went expecting to meet contemporaries and was disappointed to find two middle-aged men, one with graying hair and the other gone completely silver. But the tea was comforting from other aspects. The Eastons approved of me that day, and glowed every time my portion of the discourse proved lively or intelligent. They behaved like kinsmen taking credit for an American cousin they had decided to present to their select circle. One reason I was able to shine as I did was that, as soon as I entered their room and saw the other guests, I was able to relax: Eros was not among them. The other was that Mr. Easton served sherry as well as tea.

One of the topics we discussed was that of taste. Christopher, the silver-haired one, was redecorating his part of the Chelsea house he shared with Mark, the graying-haired one. Christopher owned the house, or rather had one of those ninety-nine-year leases that pass for ownership in England; and Mark, a barrister, rented the downstairs floor. Mr. Easton, who'd had a head start on the afternoon's spirits, proclaimed that if you hadn't grown up among good things, your taste was always going to be a little off. There would always be some garish lapse to trip you up and give the whole show away.

"Oh, I disagree, Whit, darling," said Mrs. Easton animatedly, looking very happy to be having just this sort of conversation in just this sort of civilized circumstance, at tea. "I think it comes down to whether a person has an innate feel for *proportion* in all the activities of life, whether it's selecting a chair to go in a room or"—she cast about in her head for a minute—"or washing the dishes."

"I'm fascinated," said Christopher, leaning forward and recrossing his ankles. (Both visitors wore identical shoes: mud-brown suede lace-ups.) "Do tell us, Mrs. Easton, how one washes the dishes in good taste."

"All right, I will! Whit does. My husband does." She beamed at Mr. Easton, who had raised his eyebrows quizzically and, under the umbrella of her compliment, took this opportunity to top everyone's glass with more sherry. "The way our little household works, here at Tregunter, is that after the main meal we all take coffee together in the big room. I attach great importance to this; I think it fosters a sense of family life; often when young people are starting out on their own, living in digs, they tend to forget . . . well . . . that there's anything but themselves. Their isolation leads them into a kind of brooding selfishness that's neither healthy nor productive." Her forehead clouded, she began to get her scrunch. (Of whom was she thinking?)

"I know exactly what you mean," put in Mark, whose round, boyish face somewhat offset the graying temples. "When I first came up to town, I took a sort of masochistic pleasure in dragging myself home each night to my dreadful North London digs and contemplating how, once again, the world had failed to recognize my genius that day. Now if I'd had *you* to pour me a reassuring cup of coffee and . . . have I said something amusing, Carrie?"

"Just your description. I love it, it's perfect." I started to add, That's just how *I* feel, but thought better of it. I was learning.

"But the dishes, the dishes!" cried Christopher, who could be somewhat shrill.

"Yes . . . Well, *after* we've all had our coffee hour, Whit insists on doing them. You see, he wants me to save my hands," Mrs. Easton went on, casting a rather critical look down at her hands and the diamond ring with the emerald baguettes. "But I always keep him company. And I must say he goes about it in such a *manly* way, sort of making it into an organized, workmanlike thing . . . like carpentry, or something. It becomes tasteful because he makes it into a perfectly appropriate task for a man like himself to be doing." The blood rose to her face, as it always did when she became emotional.

Mr. Easton put down his sherry glass and crossed the room and kissed his wife on the forehead. "A tasteful kiss," he explained to us.

I couldn't have been more surprised when, a few days later, Mark telephoned me at the office and asked me if I would like to go for a drive in his new Fiat the following Sunday. He had given no indication during tea of finding me anything more than part of the Easton "family." I stopped by the Eastons' room to report this development, and also to ask tactfully, for the third time, if it would be possible for me to have that bookcase Mr. Easton had promised.

"Oh, I'm so glad," said Mrs. Easton. "Mark is just the nicest boy. Frankly, Carrie, it's the sort of thing we were hoping for. It's so important to go out with the right kind of men, especially in England."

"With an Englishman," said Mr. Easton, "you don't even have to flirt. They're immovable for weeks and then all of a sudden they fall flat on their faces."

"But it hasn't even been a week," I said.

"Well, then, dear, he must have thought you were very special," said Mrs. Easton.

I thought this would be a good time to mention the book-case.

"Yes, of course you need one," said Mrs. Easton. "And we're going to see that you get one even if we have to buy it."

"But isn't there a lot of furniture up in the attic?" I asked. "Mr. Easton said . . ."

"Whit, shall we tell her?" said Mrs. Easton portentously.

"Might as well. Just don't say anything to the others. We were going to announce it at the coffee hour tonight," he said.

They told me Martin Eglantine had decided to put both the house on Tregunter and the house on Cathcart on the market.

"He wants us out in a month," said Mr. Easton.

"Isn't that awful?" cried Mrs. Easton. "After he practically begged us to come here!"

The prospect of eviction had a bonding effect on our household. After Mr. Easton's grim announcement at the evening coffee hour, nobody wanted to leave the common room. We all sat around decrying Mr. Eglantine's mercenary inclinations and wondering what we were going to do. Carlos and Alexander took up a collection and brought back three large bottles of cider from the corner pub. We began congregating in one another's rooms. Usually it was Carlos's room because he kept two heaters going and had such pretty pillows and decorations. Also a steady supply of delectable snacks.

"Do you know the Eastons didn't even have a bloody *lease?*" said Alexander. "How naive can you be?"

"They assumed he was a gentleman and therefore there was no need," said Carlos.

"They are a charming couple," said Jean-Louis, "but I think they are not practical people always."

"The point is," continued Alexander, "we're out on our ears in less than a month."

"But maybe they'll find something by then," I said. "They go out looking every day. Maybe they'll find an even nicer house than Tregunter. And, frankly, the rooms over in Cathcart are nothing to write home about."

"But they're rooms," said Alexander. "I can't even afford a proper room. And what if the new house they do find doesn't have a passage?"

"Don't be silly, Alexander. They'll always make a place for you," said Carlos. "You amuse them. I feel perfectly confident they will find something."

"One hopes so," sighed Daphne, who had been standing with her back to us, looking out at the delicate green that had begun to assert itself in gardens and on trees, despite the still-raw air. "There they go off now, as a matter of fact."

We all gathered at Carlos's window in time to see the Eastons sally forth on another day of house-hunting. She wore the tweed jacket that matched her old skirt and, as it was windy, had borrowed back the sea-green mohair shawl from the sofa. He was in his regimental best and carried a rolled-up newspaper section as if it were a swagger stick. He tapped it against his thigh in rhythm to their step, and, as always, she leaned on his arm. There was a poignancy in the way they assaulted the pavement with their long-legged strides; something in their attitude reminded me of a painting I had seen of Adam and Eve being ejected from the Garden, the urgency of their situation sweetened by the sharing of it. We watched them possessively out of sight. It had not occurred to any of us to go off alone and look for a place.

"It's a Procrustean bed, whichever way you make it," Mr. Easton told us one evening, as he poured coffee. Mrs. Easton was so exhausted, she had not emerged from their room after supper. "Up in Notting Hill or over in Bayswater there are lots of big houses available for groups like us. The owners figure, I guess, we can't bring the neighborhood down much lower than it already is. But who wants to live in the middle of Wogville? Whereas, we've seen several nice houses in Knightsbridge or

South Kensington or over in Chelsea that would be fine for *us*—they don't even mind Rico—but they put their foot down when it comes to boarders. Zoning regulations, you see."

"Why tell them?" asked Alexander.

Mr. Easton seemed to have considered this already. "You guys aren't exactly invisible, you know. You all go out the front door every morning and come back every evening."

"I meant why tell them we're boarders?"

"Oh? What would you be, then? My bastard children?" Mr. Easton surveyed our circle, as if testing out the visible credibility of this. Daphne, who'd had her silky reddish hair cut that day, sat placidly knitting an argyle sock; Carlos was looking particularly cherubic in a new white cashmere turtleneck from his latest buying spree in the Burlington Arcade; Jean-Louis had taken out a small notebook and was calculating figures in it while he munched an oatmeal cookie; I was still in my office clothes because I had detoured over to Better Books in Charing Cross Road in order to buy two new American novels—Richard Yates's *Revolutionary Road* and Reynolds Price's *A Long and Happy Life*—which I planned to read over the weekend; Colin, though no older than the rest of us, gave an impression of middle-aged stodginess, possibly because of his balding head and his three-piece bank-clerk suit; then we had a new boarder, Ian, who had taken Nigel's room and who *was* slightly older. His hair was already gray and his face wore a constant look of strain. He sold office furniture. And then, of course, there was Alexander, looking like a skeletal and sinister ecclesiastic these days, since he had taken to wearing a black polo shirt with his dark suit.

Alexander took out a PX cigarette from a flat silver case and lit it with an expensive-looking lighter. His sharp cheeks, slightly scarred from acne, sucked hungrily at the flame. "Why not?" he said. "Why not say we're your family?"

Several weeks passed. Martin Eglantine had granted the Eastons an extra month's grace, but Mr. Easton was obliged to conduct prospective buyers through the two houses, and movers came and took away the sofa, the rug, and the upright piano in our common room. Mrs. Easton's cooking suffered and her eyes were often red. Carlos cut his finger badly, opening a tin of pâté, and had to go to the emergency room of St. Stephen's Hospital. The girls in the office persuaded me to look for something on my own, and I went as far as telephoning several places. But I knew I wouldn't follow through. Staying in this drama was somehow more important. More important, even, than getting settled so I could write my own novel in the evenings, a task that was beginning to assume more urgency than before, since I had subtracted Reynolds Price's birth date from the date of publication of his first novel. (Ian, the new boarder, had actually seen me doing this arithmetic in the flyleaf of the book, as a few of us hung dispiritedly about the common room one gray Saturday; he surprised me by saying, "I used to do that, too." "Don't you anymore?" I asked. "Not once they all started being younger," he said. He himself was reading Trollope. He had taken a first in history at Oxford some years before, "but things just didn't work out," and now he sold metal desks and typing chairs. He ate no midday meal and walked to work in order to afford his room at Tregunter. "I like the spirit of the Eastons," he said. "And I do so hate eating alone." He had beautiful, white, manicured hands, which he clasped and unclasped as he talked.)

And then, just before supper one evening, Mr. Easton, already three sheets to the wind, told us with flushed face that there would be an important announcement after the meal.

"I have good news and bad news," began Mr. Easton, as we all clustered around on the few remaining chairs and on some hassocks and pillows Mrs. Easton had brought down from the attic during these last weeks of depletion. "The good news is, we've taken a lease on a house. It's on Old Church Street, in Chelsea, about half a block from the river . . . wait a minute . . . wait a minute"—he held up his hand in warning against our cheers and sighs of relief. "The bad news is, it's a small house.

Smaller than we'd hoped for, but, well, Mrs. Easton and I are in a little more of a bind than you people, when you come to think of it. I mean, you're young, most of you make a salary, it's not the end of the world if you have to pack your bags and start all over. To put it frankly, Mrs. Easton and I are kind of tired, and that's why we decided to go on and take this little dollhouse in Chelsea. It's one of those row houses, thin as a pencil from the outside, the rooms going one behind the other toward the back. There are four floors. There's the basement floor, which has a storage room and a small bathroom. Then there are two rooms on the ground floor, one facing the street, the other facing the back garden, which is just a walled-in patio. Then you go up the steps and on the first landing there's the kitchen. It also looks out on the garden, or patio. Then you go up a few more steps and you get to the first floor (we'd call it the second, back in the States) and that's the drawing room / dining room. Just one room running the length of the house, from back to front. You guys with me, so far?"

We were. But the light had gone out of our faces. One more floor to go and only two possible bedrooms, so far. Carlos pulled at the loose bandage on his finger. Ian's beautiful white hands were shaking, even though they were clasped on his Trollope.

"Okay. Go up some more steps, you come to the second landing. Here there's a little room that the owner's wife uses as a sewing room. Very small room, but it gets lots of light. It's the room directly above the kitchen and it also looks out over the back garden. And then we come to the top floor, where we have a large bathroom, and the master bedroom, and another small bedroom behind. The master bedroom looks toward the street and the small one toward the garden. And that's it, gang." He spread his hands in a gesture of having no more to offer. He had remained standing the whole time. Mrs. Easton sat on a pillow on the floor with her legs tucked girlishly under her skirt. She had all the coffee things spread around her. "Would anyone like more coffee or another cookie?" she asked, smiling through her teeth. Nobody did.

"Is there a passage?" inquired Alexander.

"No, Alexander," Mr. Easton said with great meaning. "There is no passage."

"Bloody hell," said Alexander. But I noticed he seemed less upset than one would have expected. Carlos looked much more upset on Alexander's behalf.

"We figure," Mr. Easton went on, "that we've got six possible bedrooms to work with."

"I count only five," said Colin, who had listened with rigid attention to the description. "Two on the ground, one on the second landing, two on the top."

"Right you are," said Mr. Easton. "But Lee and I plan to convert the basement storage room for our use. Of course, we'll have to live in one of those ground-floor rooms until we make the basement habitable, but without the rent from those rooms we couldn't hack it. It just wouldn't pay, with anything under five paying guests. As it is, we're going to be forced to raise the rent to ten guineas."

Colin's face worked strangely. Then, abruptly, the young bank clerk got up and left the room.

"I can't stand it, Whit," said Mrs. Easton, looking up beseechingly at her husband. "It's like breaking up a family. I think *I'm* going to cry."

Ian got to his feet. "This is, of course, a great disappointment for me," he said. "But why make it difficult for you, as well? I have enjoyed being in this 'family' immensely, even though it has only been for a short time. Naturally I can't scrape together the ten, but I'm warning you"—and here he took Mrs. Easton's rather yellowish freckled hand in his own two beautiful white ones—"I shall visit you whenever I'm in need of a bit of spirit . . . if that's agreeable to you."

"Oh, it certainly *is!*" she cried, emotion and relief filling her voice. She looked up at him gratefully. "You *will* come and take tea with us sometimes? *Promise* us, Ian?"

He promised, and shook Mr. Easton's hand and, in his rather effeminate way, went away to his room with his novel.

"That's what I call a real gentleman," exclaimed Mrs. Easton passionately.

"Yep," agreed Mr. Easton, "that's the genuine article. But as my commanding officer used to say after a battle, let's pause for a minute, out of respect for our fallen comrades, and then count heads for the coming fray. Daphne, you think you'd like to come to Chelsea with us?"

The girl, who had kept her eyes lowered and had continued her knitting during the entire episode, looked up and said, in an almost chastened tone, "I should like that very much. If you'll have me. My school finishes in August. But if I might stay for the summer?"

"That would please us very much," said Mrs. Easton.

"Carrie? I take it you'll join us?" asked Mr. Easton.

"Actually," said Mrs. Easton, "the room we *tentatively* have in mind for you has two built-in bookshelves, one on either side of the fireplace. And the cutest little alcoves where Mrs. Henning keeps two *very nice* porcelain figurines. Though I'm certain she'll remove those."

"Then Carrie will have a place for her Rodin and her Giacometti," said Mr. Easton, with a wink at me.

"You know you can count me in," I said. A fireplace! In the bedroom!

"In fact, Daphne, we thought you two girls could share the top floor. And then whoever was in the sewing room on the landing—we thought maybe Carlos, because he needs the light for his studying all day—would have to share the big bathroom. But I'm sure the three of you could work out a civilized arrangement."

"Just don't all try to climb in the tub at the same time," said Mr. Easton jovially. "It's not big enough."

"I'll be above the kitchen, then," said Carlos. "Shall I be able to contain myself with all those good cooking odors?"

"Not to worry, Carlos. You'll have your pâté to console you."

Everyone looked nervously toward Alexander as he spoke.

How was he "taking" it: the fact that there was no passage for him and his turf accountant's salary.

"Alexander," burst out Carlos, "you could share with me. You're out in the daytime, so I could study, and then if you don't snore, or anything, at night, we could *muddle through*, as the English say." He sank back on his floor cushion, aglow with magnanimity.

"Thank you, Carlos, but I have no intention of muddling through."

"Actually," Mrs. Easton broke in, "there's a tiny stone *shed* in the little garden area. Whit and I thought Alexander might not mind that during the summer months for a little less rent. We mentioned it to him earlier so that he wouldn't get upset when Whit made the announcement to the group, but we didn't want to say anything to Colin, because he might have thought we were playing favorites." Then she beamed at Carlos. "You see, Carlos, we feel just as you do. Life would not be the same without Alexander."

"As a matter of fact, it was Alexander who gave us the idea that—" began Mr. Easton, but Mrs. Easton interrupted him.

"And we thought Jean-Louis could take his choice of one of the ground-floor rooms. And we'll live in the other till we get the storage room fixed up. And then, of course, we'll have to get another boarder *pronto*, or Whit and I will be in debtors' prison."

So Colin and Ian were dispensable, I was thinking, while Alexander was not. And how deftly the Eastons had managed everything: in less than a half hour, the two dispensables had been eased out and the rest of us had been assigned our spaces. And yet there was a certain comfort in being stage-managed like this. I was pretty sure I had got the master bedroom, and this indicated my stock was very high indeed with the Eastons.

Then Mrs. Easton got a very mischievous look on her face and said, "Shall I tell our little anecdote, Whit, or shall you?"

"You tell it. I knew you were dying to when you stopped me a minute ago."

"No, darling, I just thought we ought to finish up where everybody would be. You tell stories much better than I do."

"Nope. You tell it or nobody does." They were playing to us now.

"Please, Mrs. Easton," we cried.

"Go on, darling," said Mr. Easton. "You tell them while I just step into the kitchen and wash the dishes 'in good taste.' " And he tiptoed ostentatiously away, relieved, I think, that his own part of the performance had gone so well.

"Well," began Mrs. Easton, "as you know, we haven't had an easy time finding a house. The ones that were easily available were exactly the ones we didn't want; and the owners of the ones we found suitable simply put their foot down when it came to paying guests. We were getting *extremely* discouraged, and I guess it showed on our faces because Lord Monleigh noticed it when we dined at Belgrave Square last Tuesday. That was how the Hennings' house happened to come up. Mrs. Henning's father and Lord Monleigh keep their horses at the same stable near Hyde Park, and one day, while the two men were waiting for their mounts, they got into conversation. It turns out *Mr.* Henning is in the foreign service and has to go to the Far East for three years. And Mrs. Henning is just sick about going—they had just bought this adorable house in Chelsea and furnished it exactly as they liked, with antiques—but Mr. Henning is a young career officer and has to go where he's told if he's to advance. They're terribly worried about letting their house to the wrong people, which is why Mrs. Henning's father was asking Lord Monleigh if he didn't have some friend who needed a pied-à-terre in London and would take care of all their nice things. Lord Monleigh said he couldn't think of anyone off hand, but he'd keep it in mind. 'I never thought to suggest you two,' he told Whit and me, 'because I knew you were looking for something larger for your charming *family*.' And then Whit told him what Alexander had said the other evening, about telling potential landlords you all were his bastard children. Lord and Lady Monleigh thought that so amusing. And then we four got into a fascinating discussion—honestly, we always have such good talk when we go to them—about what a family is. It's so many things, really. In many cultures, it includes whoever lives in a household, including the servants. The Latin word simply *means* the servants. And Lord Monleigh was telling us that in Holinshed's *Chronicles*—which mentions his own family, by the way—the term 'family' is used when describing the retinue of any nobleman. Really, when you consider all the historical and etymological possibilities, what *we* think of as 'family'—the nuclear or conjugal family—is only a very, very small corner of the pie.

"Anyway, to make a long story short, Whit and I decided to go and look at the Henning house. We telephoned them and said we'd been at Lord Monleigh's and he'd mentioned it to us. They were *very* warm to us, and she was practically in tears when Whit sat down at the little rosewood piano and played a Chopin mazurka. 'Now I know it will be taken care of,' she said. 'I've been having these awful nightmares about little boys smearing jam between the keys and carving their initials in my Duncan Phyfe table.' 'Well,' Whit told her, 'we haven't got a single little boy. On this side of the Atlantic. We have a grandchild, of course. But even he's beyond the jam-smearing stage.' And then *I* said, 'What Mr. Easton and I are looking for is a tasteful, compact house, so that I can care for it myself, but an ample enough house so that we can have various members of our family stay with us when necessary.' 'Of course,' she said, and then we all had a very nice tea in their drawing room, which is a little over-crowded with all her knickknacks, but they can be removed. We discussed terms and Whit and I asked if we could let them know today . . . and we had to plan things, you see, because the budget is going to be *very* tight. Also, we didn't want to seem too eager. Well, anyway"—and she clasped her hands together and smiled, taking us in rather closely to judge our reactions—"late this afternoon, Whit called and said we'd take it. The lease will be drawn up tomorrow by their solicitor and they will leave England on the fifteenth of next month. Mrs. Henning got on the phone to me after the men were finished and you know what she said? She said, 'I have good feelings about this, Mrs. Easton.

I can feel you love our house and that at the end of three years we shall find it even better than we left it.' And I want to tell you something . . ." Here Mrs. Easton screwed up her face in a special way she had, a sort of cousin to her scrunch, to convey she meant business. "She *shall* find it better than she left it. And that is the main thing, isn't it?" She allowed her words to sink in. Then she asked brightly, "Are there any questions?"

"When can we see the house?" asked Carlos.

"Well, you can see the *house* any time you want. It's number twenty-one Old Church Street. I see no harm in any of you walking over to see it. Just please don't go all at once and stand outside and gape like orphans. As soon as we've signed the lease and they've gone down to the country—they're spending their last fortnight with his mother—Whit and I will take you over, one or two at a time, to have a look. It's really *very* charming. I think we are all going to be happy in this house, if we pull together. I think . . . well, they will understand that Lord Monleigh did them a great favor in finding us, when they return at the end of three years."

"Have you told Lord Monleigh, then?" asked Alexander, offering Mrs. Easton a look a complicity.

She did not return it. "As a matter of fact, I'm off to write them a note this very minute. To thank them. I'm sure he'll be so pleased. He finds you all so interesting. And he'll be happy for *us*. After all," she concluded, rising a little stiffly from her floor cushion, "we are his friends. He hardly knows that Mrs. Henning's father from the stables."

And off she went in her narrow Italian walking shoes to the kitchen. "How are you doing, darling?" we heard her ask. We were supposed to hear. Meanwhile, we could imagine the triumphant unspoken relief that charged the kitchen when their eyes communicated. "Fine, fine," came his answer. "I'm off to write a *thank-you letter to the Monleighs*," she said, very audibly. "Oh! Good idea. Good idea," came the reply.

"Anyone for the pub?" asked Alexander. "Daphne?"

"No, thank you. I must go and practice my typing exercise."

"Jean-Louis?"

"Eh . . . *non*. I must make my monthly report to Monsieur Duval." Duval was his boss in Marseilles.

Alexander, Carlos, and I went out into an evening that was, at long last, beginning to feel like spring.

"Well, that was a masterful bloody performance if ever there was one," said Alexander.

"Do you think she *will* write to Lord Monleigh?" asked Carlos.

"Oh yes. It will be a masterful letter. He'll find the whole thing amusing. Lord and Lady Monleigh like to be amused. It's their last resource. And it's just the sort of thing they'd like their rum American friends to do."

"I thought Daphne's reaction was interesting," I said.

"Daphne has no reactions," said Alexander.

"Exactly!" I cried, loving everything about this evening. "But what was she thinking underneath?"

"Possibly what 'the Monleighs' will think: that it's jolly good fun and no skin off her own nose. On the contrary, Daphne's comforts will improve."

"That's not the way to the pub, Alexander," said Carlos.

"Who's going to the pub? I'm going to go and gape like an orphan at our new house. Though I don't suppose my shed will be visible from the street."

Before I lived at 21 Old Church Street, I had a vague mental concept labeled "the ideal room," composed of parts of rooms I had seen, or read about in novels. It should be ample, but not too ample to be cozy; it should be a room with a personality and history of its own, but allow space for *my* personality and history to develop. The window would offer either a view or a stimulating vista. Its prime function would be to provide a fertile site for the growth of an intricate and active imagination.

When the Eastons took me, one quiet Sunday, down the narrow little Chelsea street to show me the house (which I had already seen at night), and Mrs. Easton led me, with some ceremony, up the softly red-carpeted stairs to the top floor and into the master bedroom, I recognized it as an incarnation of my concept. It was not large, though it was the biggest bedroom in the house, corresponding to the dimensions of the drawing room directly below, but its aspect was generous. I had been prepared for the fireplace, but not for the gray-blue velvet-cushioned window seats, or the double bed with its canopy. The wallpaper depicted bygone English rural life: shepherdesses, haymaking, the occasional cavalier in plumed hat galloping by. The creamy white bookcases awaited my books; a small table desk with a leather top, my notebooks; a three-way mirror on a kidney-shaped dressing table, my self-scrutinies and vanities; and the marvelous canopied bed, my dreams and daydreams. I threw my arms around Mrs. Easton. "I'm afraid I'll die before I get to live here!" I said rapturously.

"We thought you'd appreciate it the most," she said, beaming.

Our first days in the new house were idyllic. Mrs. Easton went around smiling constantly; she planted geraniums in the window boxes; she clearly belonged in a house like this. Mr. Easton went about efficiently with his toolbox, repairing window sashes, fixing a back entrance / exit flap for Enrico's trips to and from the garden. We all went out the door in the morning (all except Carlos, who remained in his bright "sewing room" cramming for Cambridge) looking forward to our return journeys from our jobs (or, in Daphne's case, from school), when we would alight from the 19 bus or the 22 on the King's Road and come back through the bright yellow door, knowing we had four good hours of daylight and a good supper ahead of us. Mrs. Easton was extremely pleased with her new kitchen, with its quantities of afternoon and evening light and its accurate oven and American-sized refrigerator with freezer. Her culinary imagination stretched itself, and we never knew what we might be trying for the first time in our lives: I had never had cold trout in aspic; Daphne and Alexander and Jean-Louis had never tasted fried okra and tomatoes; none of us had ever had chilled grape soup—including Mrs. Easton, who scrunched her face afterward and pronounced it a "mistake." In the new house, Mrs. Easton served our plates through a little window between the dining room and the landing outside the kitchen, and she and Mr. Easton took their meals in the kitchen. When Lord and Lady Monleigh dined at Old Church Street (Alexander had been right, they seemed to think the whole thing very amusing) they now sat with us at Mrs. Henning's Duncan Phyfe table, which Mrs. Easton kept polished to such a high gloss that, as several times happened, when one of us spilled a drop of water it simply huddled docilely upon the wax till it could be wiped away with a napkin.

When Alexander had finished decorating his garden shed, he invited us all to have a look, two at a time, as it would only hold three people comfortably, and for the occasion he had a bottle of PX champagne. This event occurred on an evening in early June when Lord and Lady Monleigh were dining for the first time with us in the new house. The Marquess and Marchioness were of course the first to go in, and when they emerged from the little stone hut into the small garden, where we were all gathered, waiting our turn, Lord Monleigh said, "That boy most certainly has an eye!" and even Lady Monleigh was more aroused than usual from her habitual torpor. "Do you know," she told her husband, "it rather reminds me of Lord Salton's Chinese Room . . . on a smaller scale, of course. In an odd way, I somehow like it better." She giggled and took out a black cigarette with a gold tip, and Alexander whipped out his lighter and lit it with the expertise of a maître d'.

"But what will you do in winter, my boy?" asked Monleigh.

"Oh, I shall be quite comfortable," replied Alexander. "That wall is almost thirty centimeters thick. I shall plug in my heater in the new electrical outlet I installed and be warm as toast. The hangings provide insulation, too, you know."

"Quite so, quite so. What a pity you can't see our tapestries down in Warwickshire. I think you'd enjoy them."

"I should like very much to see them."

"Well! Well ... er ... if you are ever down our way, you must be sure to let us know. If we're not at home, our housekeeper will be glad to show them. And if we are, all the more delightful."

"Thank you, my lord. I shall remember your kind offer."

And Alexander was to do just that. In his own ripe time.

The Eastons had been doing some speedy decorating of their basement headquarters. For, any day, a Spanish secretary from Shell Oil in Madrid would be moving into the ground-floor room they had been using. They had found her through one of their connections, and Shell Oil had obligingly sent a month's rent in advance to hold the room. One evening toward the end of June, we were all invited down to drink a glass of sherry and inspect the Eastons' new bedroom, which they had christened "Le Cave Rouge." They had painted the walls of the Hennings' basement storage room a deep red (possibly to encourage an illusion of heat, because the room never lost its slight dankness) and hung some nice Piranesi etchings and a map of Elba; some of the small pieces of furniture that had crowded the rest of the house had been brought down here; Mr. Easton had installed a thin bamboo curtain over the long slit of a window high in the wall, so that what light there was could come in but passers-by could not look down and see in. Mrs. Easton, who liked to make the best of things, told us how it comforted her, late at night, to lie in bed and hear the footsteps of the two policemen walking down Old Church Street on their night beat. "You can even see their legs and feet silhouetted by the street-lamp." Enrico the cat lay curled on the pillows of the bed, where some of us sat.

"Oh," said Carlos. "Who is reading Proust?"

"I am," said Mrs. Easton. "I can't tell you, I was so thrilled when I saw the Hennings had a complete set in that big bookcase in the drawing room. I think they must have picked them up at some auction, because the nameplates inside aren't theirs. In fact, I doubt if they bought most of their books for reading.

Except for their *Debrett's* and *Burke's Peerage*—I'm sure they read *them*. It's so nice for me to be reading Proust again; it's going to be my summer entertainment. My last husband burned my Proust, along with all my other books, when I left him to marry Whit. He telephoned me and said, 'You might as well come and get your'—well, I won't use the adjective he used— 'your *books*,' and when I got to our old house, he had dumped my entire library on the front lawn and set fire to it."

"Oh no!" we cried. "How horrible of him!"

"Yes, it was," she said. "He was not usually horrible, but jealousy makes people do vile things. Oh, well"—and she reached over and touched Mr. Easton's arm. He jumped slightly; he had been gazing down at his polished shoe, in a sort of stupor. Was he drinking more since I had begun bringing their booze from the PX, where a quart of gin cost exactly one fifth of what they'd been paying at the off-license? "What, dear?" he asked. "I was just about to say," explained Mrs. Easton with a smile that stopped short of her eyes when she saw how far gone he was, "that in spite of all our setbacks, I've got what I want." "What is that? Oh. Oh!" When it dawned on him that she meant *him*, he covered the hand she had laid on his sleeve with his own hand and patted it as though he meant to protect her from something.

On the very first morning in my ideal room, I was awakened by a sound I had never heard before in my life, a ceremonial clatter in the street below that grew louder until the house rocked. I fought my way out of the canopied bed's luxurious embrace and ran to the window and saw row after row of horsemen trotting their black steeds up the narrow street. The rising sun glinted orange on the silver helmets with their tall, waving plumes. What a sight! The room had certainly lived up to its promise of a vista. It was, I would find out from the Eastons, the Queen's Household Guards: this was their ordinary exercise route, along the Embankment and up Old Church Street. On that first morning, the sight acted as a heraldic stimulus. I dressed and went out and walked by the Thames. So much to be done. And the long English summer day to get it done in. When I returned to the house, Mrs. Easton was just starting our breakfasts and I went up to my room to write down some resolutions. There was a large square of morning sun on the leather desktop. Everything about the room's aspect invited me to sit down at that desk and begin the creative task. If only I did not have to go to the office on Grosvenor Square and deal with Colleen and the British tourists. I wrote my resolutions in a round, upright script and, in doing so, had the imitative sensation of beginning a novel—which had been one of the resolutions. Then I went downstairs and sat in my customary place at the Duncan Phyfe table and Mrs. Easton passed me my poached egg and toast through the little window.

In July I received a cablegram from Arden Speer, a friend from college. It said: ARRIVING LONDON EARLY AUGUST. HOW ABOUT A ROOMMATE? The reply was prepaid. This unexpected missive put me in a quandary. Arden and I had met, our senior year, in an editorial-writing class for journalism majors. When Arden's father had died, he had left her and her mother a small empire of newspapers and radio stations in our home state, and Arden was expected to take them over eventually. She was a strikingly lovely girl, with very white skin, lively green eyes, and thick black hair with red lights in it. She smiled often, and with apparent candor, which I considered fairly heroic, given her awful luck. Two years before, she and her mother had been driving back from an ASNE convention at night when their rear tire blew out. Arden, being that rarity, a Southern belle who knows how to change a tire, got out and began jacking up the wheel while her mother stood holding a flashlight for her. Then a drunken driver had careened out of the darkness, sideswiped the kneeling girl, and dragged her a hundred and fifty yards down the highway. Her right leg was broken in three places and the left one had to be amputated just below the knee. When she came out of the anesthetic and the doctor told her this, she replied, "Well, thank you for saving my life." That was the kind of girl she was. During our last year of college, we had gotten in the habit of having lunch together after our journalism class. We would go slowly down the steps (besides her prosthesis she used a cane, as the right leg, which had not healed straight, was in a brace) to her Ford convertible, which she was permitted to park just outside the building, and we would drive out of town to a hamburger joint we liked, and sit in her car, drinking chocolate malts and eating the hamburgers and talking. She never mentioned her accident, or the fact she was crippled; I had heard the details from her aunt, my old school nurse, who had cared for her after the accident. Our conversations had a quaintly uplifting tone to them: we spoke about our goals; we talked about books we liked, or "writing"; we never gossiped or complained. I always felt on my best behavior with Arden, as if I must live up to her image of me (she had assured me that I had it in me to "do great things").

Which was one of the three reasons for my quandary: it was one thing to have twice-weekly lunches based on shared ideals and mutual respect, but I was not quite sure I could keep up the self I had presented to Arden on an around-the-clock basis.

Reason number two was that Arden knew something about me that I didn't want known here: namely, that I had been married and divorced. I had sent Arden a wedding invitation and she had mailed back a very nice silver serving dish; by the time I got around to thanking her for the dish, I was already separated, but I was too cowardly to tell her. I waited till I was out of the country and then wrote her, saying it had been a terrible mistake, but now, at least, I had embarked on my vocation. From all our talks about Thomas Wolfe and Hemingway and Henry James, she would understand it was necessary for me to go to Europe to begin. But if she came, she would want to see what I'd written, and, though she was very discreet and could be depended on to keep a secret, she would not understand why I was posing as a girl who had never been married; she might think there was something morally murky about this. Why not just be myself, who had made a mistake?

Reason number three made me the most uneasy. In my letters home I had represented myself as the brave young adventuress, living alone as I forged my craft in a strange land. Even my mother, who knew I lived in some kind of boardinghouse, did not know the full extent of the coddling I got at Old Church Street. Why, Mrs. Easton even changed our beds. I was afraid my expatriate image would be diminished when Arden saw our cozy little fellowship. And seeing it through her eyes, I felt I had shortchanged myself for not taking the plunge and living the true solitary life.

It is evidence of how bound up I was with the Eastons that I went right down to Le Cave Rouge within minutes of receiving the cablegram, scarcely having had time to think the thoughts above. And here, my motives did become murky. Mrs. Easton and I had recently had a confrontation and I wanted to get back in her good graces by offering her something. Arden— Arden's tragic story, Arden's old-fashioned manners, and Arden's income—would, I knew, catch the imagination of the Eastons. And Daphne's shorthand/typing course finished in August, when she would be vacating the room next to mine. In spite of my quandary, it would be comforting to have Arden around. Maybe with her in the next room I would be driven, out of pure shame, to produce some pages for her to read.

Mrs. Easton's and my confrontation had been over Mark, the graying barrister whom I had met in their room at Tregunter. I had seen him often since that spring day when he had taken me driving in his new Fiat. Though he was sixteen years older than I, he seemed younger, after I got to know him, mainly because of his vision of himself as a boy who still had to prove and defend himself in the arena of his peers. He had been called "Pudding Face" by his classmates at Haileybury, and he had a wry, charming way of describing his long struggle to overcome the nickname, first in the army and then at Oxford, and his triumph at reaching the pinnacle of English legal dignity, when he put on his barrister's wig for the first time—only to find he looked more pudding-faced in it than ever. Our fondness for each other was based more on camaraderie than on Eros. We drove around London taking turns deprecating ourselves, and reinforced each other's egos afterward in fashionable little restaurants such as 49 Mossup Place. He had just joined a "water-skiing club," where we went on weekends. It was about an hour's drive out of London, situated on a quarry that had been filled with water, and just large enough to accommodate two outboard motorboats going around at the same time. The American in me found this a laughable hole, considering the membership fee, but the members themselves, mostly professional people in their thirties and forties, found it a lark. Down they came, in their little Renaults and Fiats and the occasional Jaguar or Mercedes sports model, and unloaded their picnic hampers groaning with French bread and Genoa salami and ripe Brie and Fortnum's tinned pâté with truffles and the Algerian wine that was popular just then, and sat around the quarry on tartan blankets (unless it was raining, in which case they crowded into a lean-to) and waited their turn on the list for a boat. One rare warm Sunday (the sun was actually shining) a brownish-gray Bentley came bumping down the road, and everybody got funny looks on their faces and sat up straighter or rearranged their picnic items on their blankets, and a sharp-tongued member named Giles said, "Oh bloody hell, here come the Effing-Joneses."

"Who are the Effing-Joneses?" I asked.

"Shh," said Mark. "Giles means the *Joneses.* The f---ing part is because they monopolize the boats."

"Well, why should they? Make them wait their turn like everybody else."

"That's hardly possible, darling," said Mark.

A small, pale man with a limp got out on the driver's side of the Bentley and went around to open the door for a stocky, brown-haired woman wearing a cotton dress and what looked like white nursing shoes. Then the man unloaded a great deal of equipment from the back seat of the Bentley and the two of them went down the path to a little shack where the more modest members changed. The man and the woman were both frowning and looked as though they had been having a fight. Pretty soon they returned, wearing matching rubber suits that covered them to the wrists and ankles. They took turns monopolizing the best boat. He was a crack slalom skier in spite of the fact that one of his legs was shorter and thinner than the other. She kept falling into the water. At one point a carful of photographers arrived. One of them asked Mark and Giles, our two best skiers, to ski on either side of the woman, all three of them holding on to a long wooden pole; in this way she was able to stay up long enough for the photographers in the boat to snap a picture. The photograph, cropped, appeared on the front page of the next day's *Daily Mail.* She was smiling and looked as if she'd been skiing all her life. PRINCESS MEG SKIS, read the caption.

The Eastons loved this story and told it at once to the Monleighs, and to every new guest at Old Church Street.

It was not my going to the water-skiing club with Mark that raised Mrs. Easton's hackles. As I was leaving for work one morning, she called, "Can you come in the kitchen for a minute, Carrie?"

"Sure. What's up?"

"Carrie, when I went to make your bed yesterday morning, it hadn't been slept in."

"Well, no, I hadn't slept in it. I got home just before breakfast."

"But where were you *all night?*"

"I stayed over at Mark's. We got back late from the club."

Mrs. Easton's face began to assemble itself into the lineaments of a most formidable scrunch. "Well, I'm shocked. That's all."

"But why? I often stay over on the weekends."

"But we didn't *know* you did," she said.

My face felt hot. "Look, Mrs. Easton," I said, assuming an offensive defense, "it's nineteen sixty-*two.*"

"I know what year it is, I'm the same age as this century. And even if it were nineteen *seventy*-two I'd still be shocked.

And the fact that you left your door open, so Daphne and Carlos could see right in and know the bed hadn't been *touched.*"

"Ah," I said, "you're worried about appearances. I should have known." This was the first time I had ever criticized her to her face.

"That's not it," she flared. "I think it's immoral! And Mr. Easton and I will have to ask you not to do it again as long as you live in this house."

"Very well, I'll move out tomorrow," I said, and stormed down the soft-carpeted stairs and out of the house.

When I returned at the end of the day, beaten down by my boring job, having acknowledged my reluctance to give up my cushy room and Mrs. Easton's gourmet suppers, I found *Swann's Way* on my little leather-topped writing table with a note:

> It's just that we love you and feel responsible for you. After all, you're *one of us.* We think you're a lovely girl with lots of potential and we want you to set more stock on yourself. And speaking of potential, I think it's time you got to know Proust. He is, to my mind, *indispensable* to a young writer and he expresses so many of my own thoughts on the civilized life.
>
> Love,
> Lee Easton

The entry in my journal for the next day reads: "Went to PX. Was invited alone to Le Cave Rouge tonight for brandy and good talk. I was damn lucky to find the Eastons." And then there follows an extensive quote from Proust that ends with the phrase "our social personality is created by the thoughts of other people."

When I went rushing downstairs to Le Cave Rouge the afternoon I received Arden's cablegram, I found Mrs. Easton relaxing on the bed with her shoes off; Enrico was asleep on her stomach and *Within a Budding Grove* was propped on his curved back. Mr. Easton sat forward in a wing chair, his army kit of polishes and brushes open on the floor beside him: he was doing all their shoes. Their door was open, but I knocked on the molding.

"Oh, hello, Carrie," said Mrs. Easton testily, looking up at me over the tops of her reading glasses.

"Come in, come in," said Mr. Easton, too heartily. There was that in the faces and voices of both, or so I imagined, that testified to hours of their discussing me with the maledictive energy peculiar to married couples who have learned to deflect their resentments and boredoms away from each other and onto the nearest victim.

"I've just had a cablegram—" I began.

"Oh dear," said Mrs. Easton. "Not bad news, I hope."

"No, actually, it's good." I told them about Arden, emphasizing the points that would arouse their interest most. "Of course, she thinks I just have a flat somewhere and wants to share it with me," I concluded.

"She sounds like a lovely girl. But such a horrible thing to happen to someone so young, on the brink of life. It's fortunate, though, that she has the means to . . . well, make her life as comfortable as possible," said Mrs. Easton.

"Is she able to climb stairs?" asked Mr. Easton. "If not, Lee, why don't we give her the Spanish girl's room? It's on the ground floor, at least."

"No, darling, I think it's more important for her to be on the same floor with a bathroom. And the Spanish girl's room isn't one of the nicer rooms, though I'm sure it will be nice enough for her if she ever gets here. Daphne's room is the ideal choice. That way she can be near a bathroom and"—she relented and smiled at me for the first time—"near her friend."

"Didja ever hear anything like that Spanish girl?" Mr. Easton asked me. "Supposed to be here six weeks ago, but her husband doesn't want her to come, so he keeps getting sick on her."

"No, darling, only three weeks ago," Mrs. Easton characteristically corrected her exaggerating spouse. "But it *is* annoying. I rang up that man at Shell Oil again today and told him we'd have to have a deposit to hold that room any longer. I really can't understand that girl's husband. Doesn't he know what it will mean to their income—the fact that her boss is sending her here to perfect her English so she'll be more valuable to the office in Madrid?"

And I could feel the red cave of a room, always a little damp, warm toward me, as the three of us disparaged the lot of the poor Spanish girl, whose policeman husband was doing everything in his power to keep her from partaking of the debauched English life.

"Isn't that cablegram prepaid-reply?" asked Mr. Easton at last. "Arden's probably sitting down there in Carolina wondering if you want her." (Already she was "Arden.")

"If you're really sure she'd like it here, we could just word the reply right here ... oops, sorry, Rico. ..." Mrs. Easton got up to fetch a pencil, and within minutes a glowing description of our domicile stretched the limits of the allotted words.

"Gosh," I said when Mrs. Easton put the pencil down, "*you* should be a writer."

"It's too late to be anything but what I am, Carrie," she replied with a thin smile, "and even that is a full-time job. Whit will take this to the post office for you, he's going out presently. From what you say, I think Arden will fit in very well."

Before I reached the top of the stairs, I heard their voices begin: that muted, conspiratorial buzz which was constantly at work, authoring and ordering and interpreting our household— their creation, the kingdom over which they ruled.

Mark drove me out to Heathrow to meet Arden. It was a chilly, drizzling August night. The plane was late. Mark and I stood outside the barrier and watched the passengers go through customs. At last, Arden swung through a door, followed by a porter who looked quite happy to be carrying her two blue suitcases.

"That's her," I told Mark. She had given up her cane since I last saw her, and the brace had been removed from her leg. She propelled herself independently with a little lurching limp.

"What an attractive girl," said Mark. Arden had spotted me and was waving and smiling. "But I should have thought your American technology could devise a better leg than that one."

"No, no. The crooked one is her own, it didn't heal right. It's the straight, realistic-looking one that's artificial."

The Eastons had been watching for us, and no sooner had Mark's Fiat pulled to the curb than the door to 21 Old Church Street was flung open and, for a moment, the handsome older couple stood framed against the softly lit interior and the red-carpeted stairs. Then Mr. Easton marched out into the drizzle and took charge of Arden's luggage. Mrs. Easton hugged Arden on the threshold of the door. "Welcome to our house," she said feelingly, smiling broadly through her teeth. "We're so glad you're here at last." Then she turned to Mark and said, "It was so good of you to bring them. Won't you come in for a moment? It's very late, but . . ."

Mark the gentleman took the hint. "I'm sure Arden must be very tired. May I come another time?"

The glazed chintz bedspread had been turned back in Arden's room, and there was a little silver pitcher full of late-summer flowers on her dresser. Arden and I sat on the bed talking, after the Eastons had given us tea and biscuits in front of the drawing room fire and then excused themselves for bed.

"What an interesting couple," said Arden. "Very . . . picturesque. The whole thing is picturesque. The way she's furnished the house."

"No, this foreign-service couple owns the house. The Eastons just rented it furnished. In fact, I'm not quite sure the owners realized so many of us were going to live here." I thought I'd better go easy on Arden's high ideals the first night.

"How interesting. I wonder why they've chosen to live

over here. They're obviously well-bred people. He went to Exeter."

"How do you know?"

"He was wearing an Exeter tie. I once had a boyfriend who went to Exeter. He wrote me the fattest letters you ever did see. Now I realize it was probably because he was bored to death. Once he invited me to go up there to a dance. I didn't go, I've forgotten why."

There was a lull in our dialogue. From Alexander's shed below, in the garden, drifted snatches of Charles Aznavour. I wondered if Arden now regretted not going to the dance; I wondered what conclusions she would draw when she saw that Mr. Easton wore that tie almost exclusively. Arden would meet the others tomorrow. Now I gave her amusing, quick sketches of Alexander, Carlos, Jean-Louis, and Daphne (who had left only yesterday, reluctant to go at all because at the last minute she had begun going out with the heir to the biscuit company whose products we'd just been eating downstairs). The Spanish girl had at last arrived, over her husband's angry protests, and was settling into English ways, now that she had some more words and Mrs. Easton had explained to her why it was not agreeable to come to the table wearing rollers in her hair. And I described Lord and Lady Monleigh, and the old Principessa who had lost everything under Mussolini except her Goya. She had been too ill lately to come to us on her genteel scavenges, so now Mrs. Easton took a care package to her on Saturday afternoons.

"You are the smartest thing, Carrie."

"Me? Why?"

"You have an instinct for locating the action. Are you writing about these people?"

"Not yet. I still have quite a backlog before I even *get* to England. Honestly, Arden, it gets me down when I think of all I haven't written about. And there's more piling up every day."

"Well," she said, in her upbeat drawl, "you have to start somewhere."

"I *have* started. Several places. The trouble is, I'll be working on one thing and then it flags and I think of another thing I want to write, and it seems much more interesting. So I start on it, and then it bogs down, and I look at the rough drafts of both things and feel depressed because neither of them amounts to anything yet. Then I think of ten more things I want to write about and I panic and can't put one word in front of the other."

"Hmm," said Arden. She cocked her head to one side, looking at me. Arden always looked at people the whole time they were talking, and often after they'd stopped, as if she could read a kind of subtext in their faces. "Maybe the best thing for you would be to finish something. Maybe you can help *me* out some. I plan to send home a series of five-minute tapes on aspects of England, for Mother to run on our stations. I know the radio audience of Ruffin County isn't exactly what you had in mind, but there is something to be said for having a deadline . . . and *some* audience. I was going to ask you to do this, anyway. You must know all kinds of special things about London, having lived here six months."

"I don't know. When you're living in a place, you always feel there's plenty of time to see it, so you keep putting it off."

"Well," said Arden brightly, "my project will help you get started. We can go out and explore and then come home and write up our impressions and dictate them into my machine."

"So this is to be a working visit for you, then?"

"Oh," said Arden, getting a foxy look on her face, "I have several reasons for coming to England." Then, adroitly, she switched subjects and I found myself telling more than I'd meant to reveal about my short, ill-fated marriage. I stopped short of the sexual details, however, because there was something about Arden that discouraged prurience, just as there was something about Arden that discouraged too much complaining. She said, "Of course, I understand," when I told her I'd just as soon people here didn't know I was divorced, and the ease of her reply relieved me greatly.

/ / /

Arden "fitted right in" at 21 Old Church Street, as Mrs. Easton remarked about twenty times a day. Arden delighted in the household, and the household delighted in Arden. Her enthusiasm stepped up the tempo of life, especially during the first few weeks. On Arden's first "official" evening, the day after she arrived, Mrs. Easton outdid herself with a steak-and-kidney pie, Mr. Easton did his number at the piano about the lovely Rhinebeck lady with the tail, Alexander and Carlos staged one of their conversational tussles, and even I was pressed into service. ("Carrie," said Mr. Easton, "tell Arden about those friends of yours, the Effing-Joneses, you met down at the ski club.") Three nights after Arden's arrival, my journal notes, we played charades in the drawing room. Mrs. Easton, wearing a paper wig, was Justice Walk, the quaint alleyway across the street. Arden took Isabel, otherwise known as "the Spanish girl," to Madame Tussaud's with her in a taxi, and Isabel, enslaved by this kindness (it was the first time anybody had actually invited her out), began crocheting Arden a shawl. "Alexander, have you seen that new play, *The Premise?*" Arden asked one Saturday lunchtime. "Can't afford the theater on my pittance, I'm afraid," said Alexander. "Well, will you be my guest tonight?" said Arden. "I reckon I'm old-fashioned, but I like to have an escort, and also it's fun to have someone to discuss it with afterward." "I'd be honored," said Alexander. "Is this jersey all right, or shall I wear a tie?" "A tie, I think," said Arden.

When the Marquess and Marchioness of Monleigh came to dine with us, Arden amused them extremely by interviewing them on her little battery-powered tape machine ("Could you tell our listeners in Ruffin County something about your novels, Lady Monleigh? . . . Lord Monleigh, I wonder if you would explain to us exactly what a marquess *is*") and showing them the little red celluloid discs, on which their words were recorded, which would fit flat into an ordinary envelope and be mailed home to Mother the following day.

"What a game gel," exclaimed Lord Monleigh, when Arden had clumped back upstairs to put away her machine.

"Yes, we think she is just . . . well"—Mrs. Easton screwed up her face in the intensity of searching for the right superlative—"first-*rate*. She uses every minute of her day in a way you seldom see among young people. And her energy! When you consider it's twice the effort for *her* to get from one room to another . . ."

"Quite," said Lady Monleigh, sinking back languidly onto the sofa pillows and lighting up one of her gold-tipped, black, Russian cigarettes.

I excused myself and went upstairs to do some writing. Mrs. Easton's remark about using every minute of one's day had not fallen on deaf ears. Whether I imagined it or not, I was beginning to detect a coldness in their attitude toward me that seemed to increase in direct proportion to their growing warmth toward Arden. It was as though they could not have two favorite American girls at once and had chosen Arden as the superior version. And, though I had stopped staying over at Mark's (our affair, never at white heat, had begun to cool), Arden reported to me that Mr. Easton had told her, "Carrie's a great girl, but she doesn't come home at night." I explained to Arden that Mr. Easton had a bad habit of exaggerating things, and she seemed to accept the explanation. But things turned really sinister a few days later. Coming out of my room one afternoon, I heard the Eastons chatting with Arden in the kitchen below. "Say, listen, Arden," Mr. Easton was saying, "don't carry around too much cash. Carrie had a hundred and fifty pounds stolen her first day in England." "No, darling, actually it was only a hundred and fifty dollars," came Mrs. Easton's habitual correction of her husband's exaggeration.

I tiptoed back into my room, closed the door softly, and lay down on the canopied bed, where I spent more and more of my free time now. So. The evidence was in. The Eastons had stolen my money, Mrs. Easton luring me into the kitchen at Tregunter to look at the salmon while Mr. Easton rifled the envelope from which he had seen me extract bills. Mrs. Easton was right: the actual sum had been fifty pounds, or somewhere between a hundred and forty and a hundred and fifty dollars in those days. I felt queasy at the thought of those two coolly robbing me, but I felt even queasier that, all along, the two of them had known I had lied when I told them it was a hundred and fifty pounds.

"The Eastons are very charming," Arden said, when we were curled up on my bed one evening, working up a tape on Chelsea Old Church, at the foot of our street, where, Arden had found out, Henry James's funeral service had been held, "even though he drinks a little too much."

"Oh yes, they can be very charming, but all the same . . ." And I heard myself go into a tirade that carried a sense of déjà vu. How the Eastons were snobs and played favorites and blew hot and cold. How they wooed you as long as you did things their way, but how they sat down there in Le Cave Rouge and plotted and gossiped about you. I told Arden my theory about the stolen money and about how the Eastons had misrepresented themselves to get this house. Though Arden kept nodding and letting me go on, her face froze into a polite little mask. I could see that she did not want to believe anything too bad about the Eastons. Well, neither had I, that time in the pub when Nigel Farthingale was heaping accusations on them. I hadn't cared, as long as I could bask in the security of their establishment and be entertained by their strange and interesting ways. But somehow I thought Arden was being overly defensive about them; I could see it written on her face: a sort of horror that I might say more than she wanted to hear. Why?

"And I think they've done something awful because she can't go back to the States to see her daughter's little boy," I went on, unable to stop.

"Did she say she couldn't go back?"

"She's said lots of times she would *adore* to go back, only it just isn't possible. And she gets this meaningful look on her face, as if she'd like to say more but can't. And you know yourself how she whips out those photos of little Steve whenever she gets an opportunity."

"I got the impression," said Arden, after a moment's silence, "that they just don't have the money. Which would also account for their having to take in boarders, even though they represented themselves as a couple alone to the owners. There's no question in my mind that they've come down a long way from where they started ... but ... Carrie! Stealing your money! That's a serious allegation. Are you really sure?"

"Look. I left my purse beside him when she called me into the kitchen. He had only to reach in and take that wad of pounds. I even made it easier for him, because I had fastened them together with a rubber band. Of course, they tried to blame it on this out-of-work actor who got scared by the whole thing and sneaked away the same day without paying his rent."

I could see Arden doubted my theory. But I couldn't give her the real piece of evidence because it would have meant telling her about my lie and that would have undermined her belief in everything I told her after that.

So, when she frowned and said, "I guess I'm just not able to believe that about the Eastons," I said, "Oh, what does it matter now," and in a few minutes Arden's bright, upbeat voice was reading into the tape machine what we had written about the many devastations and rebuildings of Chelsea Old Church for the subsequent enlightenment of the listeners of Ruffin County.

Things got worse between me and the Eastons. Grudges compounded. One week I just did not feel like taking the long trek out to the PX in order to buy Alexander's cigarettes and Mr. Easton's gin. "Hey, Carrie," said Mr. Easton the next day, "haven't you forgotten something?" I told him I was sorry but there had been too much work at my office for me to go to the PX. "No, no," he said, a one-upping glint in his watery eyes, "I meant your rent." He'd got me. For the first time since I'd been with them, I was late with my weekly check. "More coffee, Carrie?" said Mrs. Easton one morning, screwing up her face at me as she offered the pot through the little window between the dining room and the kitchen landing. Her smile had always been through clenched teeth—on the day we met she had smiled at me like that—but now I saw it as a malevolent grimace, beamed at me.

One night, about nine, she came up to my room. The house was very quiet. Arden, Alexander, and Isabel had gone to a movie (*Viridiana*) in a taxi; Carlos was spending the evening with his mother, who had arrived in London to console him (he had not gotten into Cambridge) and was staying at the Connaught; Jean-Louis had gone back to France for a periodic report to his boss. I know all this because I had written it in my journal. "Is it my fault that tonight I feel there is absolutely no one in the world who gives a damn about me?" I had just written, in fact, when Mrs. Easton tapped softly on my door.

"Hello, Carrie. Oh, I'm disturbing you."

"No, you're not. I was just feeling sorry for myself in my journal." (Now why had I said that?)

"But you have no cause to feel sorry for yourself," she drawled. "May I?" And she dipped her graying blond head down and crawled under the canopy into bed with me. "Oh my! No wonder you spend so much time in here. It's like . . . a womb. Oh my! Don't let me fall asleep here. I might never wake up." She laid her head back on the spare pillow and smoothed her old tweed skirt over her trim legs. With her eyes closed and that smile on her face, she looked like the Cheshire Cat. "No, Carrie," she said with her eyes closed, "*you* haven't any cause to feel sorry for yourself. As I was saying to Whit only the other night, you are a very fortunate girl. You have a fabulous job, you have a nice man to take you out, and you're young and attractive. Whit thinks you're very attractive. He said you have such an infectious laugh and that you carry yourself well."

"Did he say that?" I wondered what else they had said, down there in Le Cave Rouge.

"He certainly did. Whit thinks the world of you. As I do. Why, you're practically like a daughter."

"How is your daughter, by the way?"

"Thank you, Penny is fine. I just had a letter." She sat up

and hugged her knees. I had a sudden image of us as two girls in boarding school, having a heart-to-heart on the bed. "It's hard to believe, but Penny just celebrated her fortieth birthday."

"Don't you wish you could have been there!" I said, hoping to bait her.

"Well, of course I wish it, Carrie, but there's no point brooding about the impossible." She peered approvingly over the tips of her knees at her handsome new Belgian shoes. She had ordered them from an ad in *The New Yorker*, to which her daughter had given her a five-year subscription. The Eastons devoured their *New Yorker*s. "Well, we're still okay," Mr. Easton would say, after looking at the cartoons every week. He said that if a day came when they couldn't understand any of the jokes in *The New Yorker*, they would know they had become hopeless expatriates. The whole household had been consulted about those shoes; the ad had been passed around at after-dinner coffee in the drawing room. "Seventy-five dollars, isn't that awful?" cried Mrs. Easton. "But of course they're handmade, they'll last for years." She stuck out one of her slim, long feet for us to examine. "*These* are almost ten years old. They were the first pair of shoes I bought when we got to Elba." "Buy them, buy them," encouraged Mr. Easton. "Can't skimp on shoes. My mother always used to say, 'You can tell a lady by her shoes.'" "Come on, Mrs. Easton, have them," said Alexander, in a rare moment of tenderness. "We'll all be jolly glad to eat tripe and onions for an entire month if you'll have those shoes." "Well . . . I'll have to think about it," she said. But she had ordered them. And we hadn't had tripe and onions once.

Now, looking at their sleek brown surfaces, I wondered if my stolen pounds had helped pay for them. "But why do you say it's impossible?" I went on mercilessly. "Why should it be impossible for you to go back home, once in a while, to see your daughter? And your grandson."

"Oh, Carrie . . ." And Mrs. Easton heaved such a tragic sigh that I felt ashamed of myself. "It's all so complicated."

"Complicated how?" At that moment, I felt sure I was going to find out their "secret." The atmosphere of the quiet house, the schoolgirlish coziness under my canopy, encouraged intimacy. But then (did she sense some untrustworthiness in me, some impurity of motive?) the moment passed, and she said, "Money complications. Money, or the lack of it, always makes things extremely complicated."

"But," I persisted, a bit callously (to have been so close!), "couldn't she send you the fare? I mean, you've often said how well her husband is doing in his law practice. . . ."

But she had shut down on me. "No, Carrie, life is for the young. They need their money for their own life. I've had mine, and it's been a full one. In a way, I feel sorry for the young people growing up now. I truly believe the generation to which Whit and I belong had the best years of our country. So much energy . . . and high ideals . . . and a lovely formality to things . . . and *romance.* No, I have nothing to complain about. I grew up having the best, and I had it most of my life, and now I've got my memories and . . . I've got the man I love."

"That's the most important thing," I said, picturing Mr. Easton's red face and the way he *wove,* rather than walked, into the room each evening for after-dinner coffee.

"I agree. Which reminds me, I've had a letter from Daphne. Her biscuit suitor is being *very* attentive. He writes her every day and sends flowers several times a week. Things look extremely promising."

"That's nice." I had nothing against Daphne, but I could not get too excited about her impending romantic fortunes. I frankly couldn't imagine her being passionately in love, even for the sake of all those biscuits.

"*We* think so. The thing is, Daphne would like to come back to us. In fact, she'd like to come as soon as possible. Of course, Arden has taken her old room and is likely to be in it for . . . an indefinite time . . . and the Spanish girl is due to stay through November. But I thought, when Carlos goes, Daphne might not mind his room. It's very light and cheery, even though it's rather tiny. But"—she laughed—"if things progress as they seem to be doing, Daphne won't be *in* this house for very long."

"Well, here's wishing her luck," I said, "but I thought Carlos was keeping his room till he got back from Paris. Isn't his mother taking him to Paris?"

"That's right. Carlos will need his room for his things, for six more weeks. Señora Paredes y Broncas plans to have some clothes made, and you know fittings take a while. And frankly, Carrie, here is where you can help us out, if you will."

"Help out? Me?"

"Yes, dear. Whit and I were wondering if you would be willing to share your room with Daphne. It would only be till Carlos vacates his room. And it would mean everything to Daphne. You see, she feels she has a *base* here. And . . . well . . . it's so important for a girl when she's trying . . . when the man is at the peak of his interest but hasn't declared himself yet . . . it's important for her to have the proper backdrop. Of course, the ideal backdrop at such a time is a loving family—so the man sees that she is cherished and then he doesn't try to take advantage— but Daphne's family is way up there, practically in Scotland. And so, Carrie"—she laid her left hand with the diamond-and-emerald ring persuasively on top of my hands, which were folded on top of my closed journal—"*we'll* be her family . . . till he's in the bag!"

This last caused me to snort with laughter, despite the fact that I was stunned by her proposal: *share my room?* Had I come all the way across the ocean to crawl into bed every night with an English girl? "Listen, Mrs. Easton," I said, trying to let her down without evoking the terrible scrunch, "I'd love to help, but I really need the privacy for my writing."

"We know how you feel about your writing," she said, her face compressing into the first signs of the dreaded look, "but I honestly don't see how Daphne will cramp your style. I mean, she'll be home in the daytime, while you're at work, and she'll be going out most evenings with her young man."

"What about weekends? I usually like to do something up here when I'm home on weekends."

"Well, I'm sure we can work out some sort of schedule. I hadn't noticed you were home *that much* on weekends, myself."

There was an awful stretch of silence. Both of us lay side by side on the bed looking straight ahead. My face felt numb. What I wanted most in the world was for her to go. I heard myself saying, "I know I don't please you, Mrs. Easton. I wish I could."

"Well, of course you please me, Carrie. And you'd please me more if you felt happier about yourself. You've got so much going for you, if you'd have a little courage. You have to believe in yourself. Jane Austen believed in *her*self. And she wrote her books on the dining-room table, between all her social and domestic obligations. You know, I've always believed it does people good to have limits. Limits on their time, limits on their space. It forces them to make something of themselves."

"You think so?" I was just stalling for time now. I knew she had won. At least I could give the appearance of grace in defeat.

"I really do, Carrie."

Within a few minutes, we had embraced, and she had gone over to the window and looked out, asking, "Do the guardsmen still thrill you when they come by in the morning? They do me—even though I only see their horses' hooves." And then she noticed that the velvet window-seat covers were a bit spotty, and unzipped them from the pillows and took them away with her.

I opened my journal and continued writing: "I have promised to share my room with Daphne for six weeks. Maybe it will work out. She'll get a husband and I will be *forced* into making better use of my time and finishing something."

I heard the front door slam. I went to the window and peered covertly from behind the curtain. Arm in arm, the Eastons were heading down Justice Walk to their favorite pub, where they went on select occasions when they had something to celebrate.

"She conned you!" cried the girl from California, when I told my colleagues at work the next day.

"But won't you mind sleeping in the same bed?" asked

the happily married Betty Ann, who had signed her letters "love."

"But at least," put in Colleen, who was hovering over our desks, preparing to distribute the morning letters among us, "you'll be able to *save* a little. She probably gave you a reduction, since you'll be sharing."

"She didn't actually say anything about a reduction." Just like Colleen, to put her finger unerringly on where I had been stupid.

"Then insist on one," said the girl from California. "Do it first thing, when you get back tonight. Boy, do those two know how to work their tenants. I'll bet the Mexican boy is paying full price just to keep his things in his room. They'll be *making* money on this deal."

On returning to Old Church Street, I went straight to Mrs. Easton, who was peeling potatoes in the kitchen. She greeted me with unusual warmth. To keep myself from weakening, I went gracelessly to the point. "Everything was decided so quickly last night," I said, "that I didn't get a chance to ask what kind of reduction you and Mr. Easton will give me for those six weeks when I'll be sharing my room. I mean," I went on more aggressively, "you all will be making money on this thing, specially with Carlos not even eating here for most of the time."

"Making money we will not be, Carrie. If you knew all the little expenses: that stopped-up toilet last week cost us almost ten pounds because it was on a weekend and the plumber had to come from Croydon."

"Well, that's not my fault. You told me yourself the Spanish girl was the one who flushed the sanitary napkin."

"It's not a question of whose *fault*, Carrie. This is a household. We all work together to make life as pleasant as possible. And there are other expenses that . . . well . . . Mr. Easton and I haven't liked to harp on. I mean"—and she narrowed her eyes—"we're Americans and we understand that Americans like more heat; but, between you and Arden, those upstairs heaters are going constantly on the weekend and, as Arden is home all day as well, our electric bill is becoming astronomical."

"I still think I should get some kind of discount," I said. "I didn't stop up the toilet and I don't stay home all day and run up your heating bill. And I *am* going to be inconvenienced by having to share my room."

"Very well," she said coldly. "I'll speak to Mr. Easton and we'll let you know what we can do."

They agreed to a two-pound weekly reduction, to begin the following Thursday, when Daphne would be arriving. But it was a Pyrrhic victory. In the next few days, their disapproval of me became positively hostile. They froze me out during after-dinner coffee conversations. Mrs. Easton asked me whether I would mind using a pencil when I wrote in bed, as it was hard on her hands to have to scrub the ink out of my sheets before sending them to the laundry. Every time I came out of my bedroom, it seemed they were discussing me sotto voce in the kitchen below, just loud enough for me to hear. (I was probably meant to hear.)

"I can't get over it. I mean, it's just so terribly petty when she makes thirty pounds a week." (Mrs. Easton.)

"Some people are like that. Can't bear to part with a nickel if they can avoid it." (Mr. Easton.)

One night, late, I went down to the dark kitchen to get some ice water. As luck would have it, I left the freezer door open while I emptied the cubes out of the ice tray and Mr. Easton chose that moment to materialize in his striped flannel pajamas. "Keep this thing shut, will you?" he slurred, slamming the door. From the fumes that emanated out of him, I judged he must be more gin than human and I decided to say nothing, get my ice, and leave the kitchen. I concentrated on transferring the cubes into the glass. I filled the glass with water. I refilled the ice tray. I stiffened my shoulders and got past him and replaced the tray in the freezer. "Whassa matter, cat got your tongue?" His breath came suddenly close to my ear. His hand gripped my buttock, quite intentionally, through my nightgown, gripped it so hard that the next morning when I examined myself over my shoulder in the triple mirror there were bruise marks where his fingers had been.

"You have no choice!" cried the girls at the Travel Service.

"It's time you got out of that hostel setup anyway," said the girl from California, who had spoken with an air of detached superiority ever since she had announced she would be leaving us after Christmas—first to go skiing in Zermatt, then to go home and get married.

Colleen suggested we telephone the man at Embassy housing and see what he had on the books. "I agree with the others," she said gravely, "it's time you weaned yourself from the Eastons."

By lunchtime, I was being shown through a series of ground-floor rooms in a gaunt brick row house on Green Street, a three-minute walk from the Embassy. The only trouble was, the Travel Service had recently moved to its own new office (opened with a gala party, Alistair Cooke and the Duke of Bedford in attendance) in Piccadilly. But I would still be able to walk to work from here.

"This is the situation," said the man from Embassy housing. "The old girl who owns this house wants to sell it, but she can't till next May because the two fags who live upstairs have a watertight lease till then. So she figures she may as well get what she can from these downstairs rooms."

"They certainly are partitioned off in a weird way," I said.

"Yes, well, you've got to remember this was built as a one-family dwelling. It was a nice house in its day. James Mason, the actor, owns the one like it, to the right; he's kept his in one piece."

"It's a little *dark.* . . ."

"England is dark. If you don't want it, I have a new gal with HEW who'll probably take it. . . ."

"I'll take it," I said, feeling that my honor was at stake.

/ / /

"Can we talk later?" I murmured to Arden, who sat next to me on the glazed chintz couch in the drawing room. Mrs. Easton, in her customary chair, poured after-dinner coffee into demitasse cups, adding a spoonful of sugar crystals shaped like small colored rocks for most of us. She handed me my cup with her pained smile.

"Of course we can," said Arden, "only it had better be now, because I've promised to give Isabel an English lesson this evening."

As we went upstairs, I realized the mood was wrong for what I was going to propose. Arden was happy in this house, she was becoming entrenched in its communal rituals. I had even heard the small sigh that escaped her as she put down her demitasse cup and limped ahead of me from the lamplit, people-filled room. Everyone was discussing the railway strike slated for the following day, and Alexander was trying to persuade Jean-Louis to go halves with him in renting a car so they could drive around London picking up pretty girls.

"Well," said Arden brightly, closing the door of her room rather slowly against their laughter. "What's up?"

"I've rented an apartment—a whole floor, in Mayfair—and I was wondering if you might like to share it. We could each have a bedroom, and then there's this august drawing room in the front of the house, the old lady's even left some Victorian chairs and a sofa and what they call a tallboy—"

"Carrie, I have something to tell you," she interrupted. "Of course, I was going to tell you in a few days when all the arrangements were definite. . . . We've never talked about my accident, have we?"

And she proceeded to relate a terse, objective version, almost like a combined police-and-medical report, of the story I had heard, in more human and dramatic detail, from her aunt. Her voice was the same spritely, interested voice she used when recording her "Aspects of England" reports for the listeners of

Ruffin County. It was as if the violence, although regrettable, had happened to someone else. There was, of course, no mention of the brave reply to the doctor's news.

"But as you can see, the right leg hasn't healed as it should, and after a great deal of reading up on the matter, I decided to consult the man who is considered the best in the field, Sir Rupert Wentworth-Stokes. Last week we went over the X rays and he says there's a pretty good chance of a successful operation. He'll take part of my hipbone and reshape the tibia. But we won't know for certain for two months. Half of that time, I have to stay in bed. I haven't even told Mother, and I'm not going to until I know the results. I've told the Eastons, of course, because they will have to care for me, and she has been just splendid about it. I know they have their faults, Carrie, and I'm aware that you all are on the outs. I really think you're wise to leave, things being as they are."

"What have they said to you?"

"I don't think anything can be gained by going into that," she said rather primly. Then, with more warmth, she appealed to me to keep my fingers crossed and pray for her, "and please come visit me in the hospital."

"I guess I'd better. They won't let me visit you here, once I leave."

"Oh, Carrie, they don't hate you *that* much!" she exclaimed. Then hastily revised her tactlessness: "A cooling-off period will put things in perspective on both sides."

On my first night in Green Street I imagined them discussing me over coffee in the Chelsea drawing room.

"I wonder how Carrie's getting on in her new flat." (Alexander—more to "set things up" than out of any genuine concern.)

"I'll bet she's going to miss your cooking, Mrs. Easton." (Carlos.)

"Of course we were sorry to see her go, but it's what she wanted." (Mrs. Easton.)

"The real reason was, though we don't want to shock any of you guys, Carrie felt her nightlife was too constricted here." (Mr. Easton.)

"I'm not quite sure what you mean, Mr. Easton." (Arden, who could be depended upon to be loyal.)

"Oh, nothing. Nothing." (Mr. Easton, with ominous significance.) "We were hurt, of course. She's been with us two years and then bang! Less than a week's notice."

"Six months, darling." (Mrs. Easton.) "Though in some ways it did seem like two years." (Exchanging a wry look with Alexander.)

"It cannot be cheap, having a flat in Mayfair." (Jean-Louis.)

"Oh, Carrie's got more money than she knows what to do with." (Mr. Easton.)

"Really?" (Arden, who knew better, tightrope-walking between defending her friend and placating one of the two people in England who had agreed to take care of her when she was flat on her back.)

"Personally, I'll be so glad to see Daphne again!" (Mrs. Easton.)

"Hey, Isabel. Now that your English is better, how would you like to hear a strange story? Ever heard of a place called Rhinebeck, New York?"

And Mr. Easton, breathing a little heavily from gin, would sit down at the Hennings' elegant rosewood piano and ripple his large fingers over the keys. He had a surprisingly light and accurate touch. Anyone happening to be walking along Old Church Street in the autumn dusk would look up at the lighted window, the geraniums glowing in the window boxes, and hear the opening bars of the "Moonlight Sonata," or, subsequently, the shouts of laughter, and think to himself, or herself: Ah, the family! Nothing can ever replace it!

I thought about the Chelsea house a lot, my first few weeks on Green Street. If Old Church Street had embodied domestic coziness to the point of stultifying my young soul, then Green Street certainly embodied its opposite. The Central Line ran directly beneath my bed. As I figured it—and I had plenty of long evenings to lie there and figure it—my flat was exactly the midpoint between Marble Arch and Bond Street, because, beneath me, the trains seemed to achieve their highest speed. Above me, every evening without fail, the two men upstairs took a long bath together, overflowing the drain. In the daytime, I would look down at what had once been a little courtyard but was now a swamp filled with stagnant green muck from the improper drainage. The men laughed as they bathed, and, from the cadence of their alternating voices, seemed to be telling each other about their day. And then there was the odd arrangement of the flat itself. The front room I never used, because it was on the other side of the partition and just inside the entrance to the house. Behind the partition, which is where my life began, was a hallway with first a tiny kitchen and then a tiny bathroom to the right. Edwards, the man who came to wash the windows, told me that the kitchen and bathroom had been added when the old lady had decided to turn the house into flats. My narrow little bedroom at the rear of the house, which I liked best of the rooms because of all its built-in wardrobes and cupboards and shelves, had been, he said, the butler's pantry. And the larger room next to it (which I kept locked at night, because it led—via a dark, winding passageway—to the basement, which couldn't be locked) had been the butler's bed-sitting room. Edwards told me that the little courtyard filled with stagnant drainwater had formerly been a beautiful garden where the family sat on Sundays.

Arden had to wait till mid-November for her operation, Sir Rupert's schedule was so full; she progressed so well that she was able to come to my Christmas party, which I held in the butler's bed-sitting room. She arrived looking radiant, in a long, high-necked white dress and the new shawl Isabel had crocheted for her. Her hair was piled, Gibson Girl–style, on her head, and five healthy pink toes stuck out from the cast on her right leg. In Arden's retinue were Alexander, Isabel, Jean-Louis, and the

Easton's newest boarder, a rather frail-looking young man with a large hawk nose and red cheeks, whom Arden introduced simply as "Peter, who has taken Carlos's room." Peter stuck close to Arden, anticipating her desires for a fresh drink or another sandwich. "He was awfully helpful last month," Arden told me, during one of Peter's brief absences, "he spelled the Eastons in taking care of me. He's cramming for Oxford and has been reading to me about the Hapsburgs, whom I find fascinating." When anyone asked Arden how she'd broken her leg, Peter would answer, "Had a bit of a fall on her skis," and, as soon as the person turned away, he and Arden would nudge each other and giggle.

"Well, how are things going with Daphne and her cookie heir?" I asked Alexander, who looked sleek and prosperous in his new dinner clothes. He seemed to have filled out a bit, too. Encouraged by Arden, he had a lucrative evening sideline: he had signed up with an escort service.

"Oh, Daphne's still very keen. The trouble is, *he* doesn't seem quite keen enough. The Eastons think he's starting to bolt."

"Too bad. And how are the Eastons, not that I care."

"Cunning as always. They shall ask me all about your flat, not that they care. What would you take for that horrid bamboo firescreen?"

"If it's horrid, why do you ask?"

"I know a horrid rich chap who might fancy it."

"Well, I'm sorry, but it belongs to the old lady who owns this house. All the furniture does."

"Pity. We could divide the spoils. She'd never miss half of it."

"Alexander, you're getting worse."

"That's where you're wrong. I'm getting better. One of these days I shall have perfected myself."

"For what?"

"For what I'm for." He laughed and offered me a cigarette from his case. "Still don't smoke? Good girl. I must say, I miss your PX cigarettes awfully."

"How old is that Peter, who seems to adore Arden?"

"Nineteen. The Eastons are worried."

"Why? Nineteen's old enough to take care of yourself."

"Mmm. Depends on one's circumstances, I suppose."

"Isabel's English has certainly improved," I said. (She stood not far from us, surrounded by a little circle of men. "I like the way Anglo-Saxon meng stay free like boys," she was saying. "In es-Spain, the mang, he come out from his mother and go under his wife.") "So, what *are* Peter's circumstances, then?"

"Well, Peter was entrusted to the Eastons, you might say, by their perennially useful friends, Lord and Lady Monleigh. Lady Monleigh was at school with Peter's mother. Also"—Alexander paused, relishing his role as informant—"Peter's father died last year. Which makes Peter the sixteenth Duke of Harleigh."

"Well, good for him. But the Eastons needn't worry. Arden's much too old for him, he's just good company while her leg's healing. She more or less told me so herself."

"Did she? I shall pass it on to the Eastons. It will make things less uncomfortable for Arden."

"You mean they're making her uncomfortable?"

"Cooling off, you might say."

"Those two! They'd turn on God Himself if He lived with them three months."

"They would ... unless He knew how to handle them."

"And you do?"

"Oh"—he sucked thoughtfully on his cigarette, affecting a sort of James Bond insouciance—"we rub along."

It was London's coldest winter in eighty-two years. Thirty-two people died in a fog. Out of sheer lassitude I made an omelet almost every night in my tiny kitchen. The girl from California had resigned and was skiing in Switzerland before going home to plan her wedding. The happily married Betty Ann and I sat side by side behind our counter in the new office. Behind us was a giant wooden sculpture, in orange, of the United States. The wind shrieked around the corners of the plate-glass windows of our reception room, which we called "the Fishbowl" because anybody walking along Sackville or Vigo Street could look in on us as we sat there. Anybody could *come* in—that's why we were there—and a motley assortment did, though not always to ask questions about travel in the United States of America. We had our favorites. There was the policeman we saved stamps for, who would stop by to get them and always tell us one or two stories about his profession. He gave us advice for handling lunatics: "Act interested in a disinterested way. Agree with them while walking them to the door." Then there was the nice old goldsmith who quoted Greek and Roman poets in the original and took me to see the swearing-in of the new Lord Mayor. The servants' chef at Buckingham Palace dropped in on us whenever he came from his tailor. It was he who gave me the omelet recipe: "You want to leave the middle just a wee bit runny before you fold it over." He promised—and later kept his promise—to get us inside the palace gate for the Trooping of the Colour and show us the servants' apartments afterward. Then I had befriended a hobo who had been raised in London but had traveled by boxcar to more places in the United States than I had. He brought me gifts—a plump grapefruit from Soho, an excellent penknife that I still carry—and I would type the latest pages of his memoirs while he walked up and down outside so that Mr. Miles would not worry that we had a loiterer in the reception room. The hobo wrote, he explained in a confidential voice that never rose above a hoarse whisper, standing up in the Central Post Office every night; he used the backs of telegraph forms and a pencil chained to the wall.

Colleen was out with her back a lot. It had not been a good winter for her, she was turning into an old woman overnight, she lamented to us. Her hair was going gray and two of her teeth had died.

When we had no customers, and if I had caught up with the hobo's memoirs for the day, I might get out my own manuscript and work on it. The hobo had been an inspiration as well as a reproach. I figured if he could stand up every night in the post office and write, I ought to be able to produce something sitting down in a Mies van der Rohe chair in front of a new IBM. Mr. Miles was very obliging about what we did with our spare time, as long as we answered all the letters first and stopped doing whatever we were doing when a live customer came in. I was writing about my marriage. If it came out the way I wanted, the novel would be a sort of American *Madame Bovary*. Betty Ann was reading a magazine article, one gloomy afternoon, that proved that if a divorced woman had not remarried within four years, her chances decreased sharply. I thought of poor Colleen. I thought of myself. Betty Ann confided to me that she was pregnant and her husband wanted her to quit so they could have a holiday in Greece before she was too far along.

After work I would walk home to Green Street, crack some eggs, and eat my omelet while reading and listening to the BBC. Then I would wash the dish and the fork and the pan and retreat for the night with my book and transistor to the butler's pantry, where I would feel the fast trains rumble under me and hear the men upstairs talking and splashing. I would read and write in my journal until the Home Service played "God Save the Queen" and went off the air, and sometimes after that.

Arden's cast came off and she was the possessor of a lovely straight leg. She took me to dinner to celebrate and told me she was going to splurge and order a new prosthesis as well: there was a place in New York that fashioned them so you could wear high heels. "Mother is urging me to come home, but I thought I'd stay and see the English spring," she said. Peter had promised to drive her to Oxford. "Peter has been just wonderful. Despite the difference in our ages, he's one of the most rewarding friends I've ever had. I never get tired of talking to him and it's nice just being in the same room with him." She told me how Peter could sit in a straight chair, with plugs in his ears, and read for a solid hour without once looking up. "He'll often sit in my room and read for an entire afternoon."

"And how are the Eastons taking it?"

"Taking what, Carrie?" She looked annoyed.

"I mean, his being in your room so much. Mrs. Easton can be funny about how things look."

"Well, she's welcome to come in at any time. There'll be nothing to look at. You were right about the Eastons, they do blow hot and cold on you. It's smile one minute and whisper the next, and you wonder what you've done. But *my* conscience is clear, and they'll just have to put up with me till I get ready to leave. I'm not going to let them spoil my last months in England."

"If you ever need my butler's sitting room, you're welcome to it. That awful sofa pulls out into a bed."

"Thank you, but I don't think I'll be needing it." She tilted her chin defiantly and, for some reason, blushed. "They may think what they like, but they wouldn't *dare* say it to my face. Oh no, they're too resourceful for that." She gave an uncharacteristically cynical little laugh. "*Much* too resourceful!"

The following Saturday, about four-thirty in the afternoon, my doorbell shrilled. I peeked out cautiously, keeping the chain latched, in case it was one of the local panhandlers, a seven-foot grizzled Negro, who announced himself as Yahweh. (I always gave him a half crown, but never allowed him inside the front door.) It was Arden, with a face like a death mask. She carried the smaller of her blue suitcases. "Just tell me if I'm inconveniencing you, Carrie. If I am, I can go on to a hotel, I've kept my taxi."

"Not at all! You look terrible. Here, let me run down and pay him for you."

"No, thank you, I can manage, if you'll just take the bag." She descended the few steps proudly on her straight legs and paid the driver, calling out a "Thank you" in her Southern accent as he pulled away.

She held on till we were in the inner sanctuary of my flat, behind the partition, and then she began to cry standing up, still holding her purse. I propelled her to my bed in the butler's pan-

try and then did what the English do on such occasions: made
her a cup of tea.

This is what had happened. For the past few weeks, the
Eastons had been acting "chilly." Whenever Mr. Easton, in his
tipsy states, came upon Arden alone, he would say, "Hiya,
Duchess," and wink at her. Arden said she hadn't wanted to tell
me this during our talk the week before because we were cele-
brating her successful operation and also she just didn't want to
say it aloud, hoping if she ignored it he might stop saying it.
"And it wasn't as if it were malevolent, it was just . . . presump-
tuous. But this afternoon was another matter."

She then broke down again, collected herself, and, in a
dead, even voice, with none of her usual upbeat cadences, told
how she and Peter had been reading and talking, this rainy Saturday afternoon, in her room. "Since the Eastons have been acting so funny, I always make it a point to keep my door ajar, so if
they want to creep up and look in, they are perfectly welcome,
only they never do." Arden had to go to the bathroom and excused herself to Peter and, when she got halfway down the
thickly carpeted hallway, heard Mrs. Easton talking on the telephone, which was in the hallway on the floor below. "She was
talking in that way people talk when they're really absorbed in
doing somebody in. To be perfectly honest, I probably would
have stopped to listen even if I hadn't heard my name. But, once
I heard it, I went back to the banister, where you can hear every
word. Every word comes floating up. Every horrible, fully
shaped word. She wasn't talking loudly, but she was talking
under the assumption my door upstairs was closed and I was
behind it." Arden paused and put down her teacup. She sat very
straight on the edge of my bed. With her hard, white face and
her lipsticked gash of a mouth, she looked ten years older. And
in her long-sleeved white blouse with its ruffled collar, she did
look like a duchess, though a very aggrieved one.

"But who was she talking to? What did she say, Arden?"

"She was talking to Lady Monleigh. They were discussing
Peter's 'unfortunate attachment' to me. And then Mrs. Easton
summed me up in a phrase."

"Which was . . . ?"

"I don't think I can repeat it. I'm not trying to be mysterious or make you think it was something worse than it was . . . though it was pretty bad. I can't repeat it because"—she faltered—"I don't want it to pass my lips. If it did . . . if it did, you see, it would bring me a step nearer thinking of myself like that. And if I thought of myself like that, it would make me a different person from what I am now . . . and what I am trying to be."

"Okay," I said, "I understand." Having already begun to imagine the sort of phrase that would be unspeakable for her.

"What I can't get over"—and here she began to shed tears—"is, that woman nursed me. She took complete care of me for three weeks. She had to bring me a bedpan for three whole weeks, and she did it . . . she did all of it with such grace and such kindness. There will always be gratitude in my heart for that woman who reduced me to such an unkind description. It's like being torn into two pieces. But I'll never set foot in that house again."

"But Arden, what about all your things? I mean, you're welcome to stay here, I'd love it, but won't you have to tell her something?"

"Oh, Alexander can always bring me my things. That's no problem." She laughed that harsh, cynical laugh I had heard for the first time a week before. "He'll do anything for a price. As for her, I think she already knows. After I heard . . . what I heard . . . I went back to my room and told Peter I was going to stay with you for a few days. I packed a few things and went downstairs and called a taxi. She was in the kitchen. She asked me, 'Arden, you'll be back for dinner, won't you?' And I looked her straight in the eye and said I didn't know when I would be back. I think that's when it registered. Because she looked almost stricken . . . I even felt sorry for her, Carrie. And then she said very quietly, 'Well, you will let us know you're all right, won't you?' 'Oh, yes, Mrs. Easton, we'll be in touch,' I said. I guess I sounded threatening because she flinched. She was probably thinking about how she was going to repay all that money."

"Oh God, Arden, what money?"

"The Eastons have borrowed over a hundred pounds from me."

"Oh, Arden. You'll never get it back."

"I will insist on having every penny of it back before I leave England."

"And what about Peter? He'll be sorry to see you leave the house. Of course, he can come and visit you here. I'm away at work all day, you can just pretend this is your own flat."

"Thank you, Carrie. Peter will want to come and visit me, no doubt, especially since I shall be going back to the States sooner than I'd planned. But I'd rather he came when you're home. That boy has such a simple, trusting nature. He could be so easily compromised in his position. And our friendship has been too special for me to want to do that. It's very clear to me now that the Eastons aren't even capable of understanding the kind of thing Peter and I have. It's not in their spiritual vocabulary. Because *nothing can be gained by it.* Excuse me, I just remembered I never did get to the bathroom. When I heard her talking down there—"

And Arden got up hurriedly and went to my bathroom, where I could hear her being sick.

One cold and glittery-bright March day, I was standing near the windows of our ground-floor office, "the Fishbowl," looking out. The new girl and I had already answered all the mail. She sat behind the counter, reading one of the Bollingen Foundation volumes of C. G. Jung. She was a serious, introverted person, and no one liked her very much because Mr. Miles had been about to hire a laughing, sociable girl when a telegram came from Washington telling him to hire this one because her father was a friend of the Speaker of the House. She was so cool to the customers that Colleen and I (yes, we had become friends, of a sort) played a trick on her: we wrote a letter to the Travel Service from a "customer" who felt he had been insulted by "that dark girl who's always reading the psychology books." But she turned the tables on us. She opened the letter and marched right upstairs and presented it to Mr. Miles, who, on calling Colleen and me to his office, said he recognized my style. "You can do better than this, girls," he said, dismissing us with a wave of his hand.

I was standing near the windows thinking that it would soon be exactly one year to the day since I had arrived in London. In that year, I seemed to have drifted in circles on the sea of my destiny. Neither the winds of love nor those of accomplishment had seen fit to bestir themselves and set me on my course. I had not seen Mark since Boxing Day, when, English gentleman to the end, he had stopped by with a gift, a Scotch tam-o'-shanter. The other man in my life, an ex-student of F. R. Leavis who now worked for the *Yorkshire Post*, had found me too frivolous and sent me a farewell letter that concluded with: "Your main concern should be how you're going to fill in the time between now and your funeral." As for the accomplishment department, well, the American *Madame Bovary* was bogged down at chapter nine of a projected twenty chapters. And all around me, as if to mock my unaccomplished desires, everybody else seemed to be skimming past, the wind filling their sails.

Arden had stayed three weeks with me. Peter and Alexander together had packed up her things and brought them to Green Street. Peter had come to supper a couple of times, and the two of them had had long talks in the butler's bed-sitting room, which I had turned over to her. From the looks of it, there was a sort of courtly love attachment between them. There was no doubt that he worshiped her, but they probably went no further than a few sad kisses at the end, if that. On second and third acquaintance, Peter seemed more noble to me, a bit more finely marked than the average nineteen-year-old. This was probably because I knew he was a duke. Arden also may have been influenced by this, but mainly, I believe, she liked him for himself—and because he appreciated her. She cried much of the night before she flew back to the States, but two weeks later wrote me a letter saying how invigorating it was to be home again, and how different "everything" looked from there. She mentioned twice a "very personable" man named Bruce ("just

got his M.A. in communications from our old Alma Mater"),
whom her mother had hired to manage their new TV station.

And Colleen and I had received a joint postcard from Betty
Ann saying that she and her husband were having an "ecstatic"
time in Greece. Signed "love," of course.

And my hobo had finished Book One of his memoirs. To
my surprise, several chapters had been printed in *The News of
the World.* He'd had a tentative offer to appear on a TV program. He was busy at work on Book Two, even though he had
not yet found a publisher for the first volume.

And here was I, age twenty-five, with only two more years
to go, according to Betty Ann's magazine article, before my mat-
rimonial chances plummeted; here was I, playing office pranks
with my old-maid supervisor and typing Book Two of a hobo's
manuscript.

When down the sidewalk of Vigo Street sailed a familiar
figure, her faded blond head bowed against the wind, the sea-
green mohair shawl trailing majestically in her wake. Her toes, I
noticed for the first time, turned in just a little as she took the
pavement with long-legged strides. She was wearing the Belgian
loafers. There was something portentous about her gait, as if
nothing could detain her from her mission. Could it be that she
was going to glide right by our offices? Maybe she thought I still
worked in the Embassy building on Grosvenor Square, and was
hurrying somewhere else.

I knocked urgently on the plate-glass window. She looked
up, looked in, and lifted her hand in incidental greeting as she
turned into our doorway without ever slowing. She *had* been on
her way to see me, even if I had not seen her first.

"Mrs. Easton!"

"Carrie, dear!"

We embraced. I thought of Arden watching this and felt
like Benedict Arnold.

"I had an errand on Bond Street," she said, "and I just
couldn't resist stopping in to see how you were." The winter
had roughened her complexion a bit more, but she was the same
old Mrs. Easton, smiling—genuinely, it seemed—through her

teeth. "Gosh, but it's good to see you!" she exclaimed girlishly.

"It's good to see you, too. Listen, come next door to the Thistle and have a beer. Or we could have an early lunch. They have delicious Cornish pasties and Scotch eggs and such things."

"I'd love a beer and a Cornish pasty!"

"Sydney," I called to the dark girl behind the counter, who had not even looked up from her book, "hold the fort. I'm going to lunch."

"My, but she's a dour one," murmured Mrs. Easton, pronouncing it the Scotch way as we headed next door to the pub.

"You got her immediately!" I cried, laughing a bit hysterically and hooking my arm through hers.

The Thistle was patronized mostly by Regent Street haberdashers. It was a jolly, dark place full of the smells of beer hops, pipe smoke, and its excellent hot buffet items. At first, the girls from the Travel Service had been endured as a necessary evil under the same roof. But now our lunchtime presence in a back booth had become acceptable: we ate well, drank like men, and also one strapping haberdasher who was always teasing us by flexing his muscles and announcing, "Made in England, girls," had developed a little crush on Colleen, who couldn't stand him. She thought he was vulgar. "Where's your friend?" he shouted now as Mrs. Easton and I picked our ladylike way through layers of robust pinstriped and pomade-smelling men. I called back to him that Colleen was at the dentist's.

After Mrs. Easton and I had gained our little enclave and got through the busy-ness of ordering what we wanted, an awkwardness came on both of us. Here we were, face-to-face, each of us remembering certain things that had been said and certain things that couldn't be said. What *would* we say now? That was the question. I almost ruined the whole lunch by looking down at her hands on the table and exclaiming, even in the same second I knew I could probably answer my own tactless question, "But where is your lovely *ring?*"

"Yes, it was lovely," she said, after her face had gone through an interesting series of shifts and suppressions, "but

I've had to stop wearing it. My arthritis flared up this winter. As you know, we did what we could with Le Cave Rouge, but it's never quite lost its basement dampness." She held out her hands to me for examination.

"They don't *look* too bad," I said, "but of course it's how they *feel*, probably." (I was pretty sure a ring like that could fetch a hundred pounds without much trouble.)

"Exactly," she said, massaging the fingers gingerly. Then, thank God, our beer and pasties came.

"Well, cheers," said I, raising my glass.

"Cheers, Carrie." She touched hers to mine. "Here's to . . . spring. I can't tell you how good it was to see your face when you saw me. You are one of those people whose faces show what they're feeling, and you seemed really glad to see me." She ducked her head modestly and took a big sip of beer when I assured her this was so. "It's been kind of an awful winter," I added.

"It has not been an easy winter," she said. And then she told me that the old Principessa had died at the end of January. "But, mercifully, in hospital, with all the care she needed. One of us got over to see her every day, and Whit was with her when she died. She didn't know it, of course. She was in an oxygen tent . . . pneumonia." She took a handkerchief and dabbed at the corner of each eye. "*Anyway* . . . 'The old order changeth, yielding place to new . . .' and God knows it's changing. It's going, going, *gone*, if you ask me. I just thank our lucky stars that Whit and I live here in this humane, civilized country, where if one or both of us become ill we can get decent medical care without being millionaires. We had a nice note from Arden, by the way, thanking us for taking care of her. A bit short and cool, when you consider how we waited on her hand-and-foot and how much grief she caused us. I don't know what she told you and I don't want to know. The two of you are old friends and, believe me, old friends get dearer and rarer as you get on in life. But we lost Peter over her, and Lord and Lady Monleigh haven't been the same toward us since he moved out. Arden managed to poison him against us before she went back to America, though I don't suppose I'll ever know what she said. But Lady Monleigh thinks the Dowager Duchess blames *her* for recommending us, and she in turn blames me. Though she hasn't said so in so many words. The English never do, you know." Her eyes narrowed—the beginnings of the scrunch.

"Who have you got staying with you now?" I wanted to change the subject before the great chain of blame, inevitably, reached me.

"Well, Alexander and Jean-Louis are still with us. And we have a darling new French girl, the daughter of Jean-Louis's boss in Marseilles. Monsieur Duval *delivered* her to our house, isn't that wonderfully old-fashioned? *I* think"—and she leaned forward confidentially—"that old Frenchman has it all planned. He wants his daughter and Jean-Louis, whom he'll probably make a partner in his business, to fall in love. He wants them to be close enough to get to know each other, but not *too* close, if you see what I mean. I've given her Peter's old room . . . and Carlos's . . . dear Carlos . . . we had a sweet letter, they're going to take him to the States and try to get him into Dartmouth. From now on, I'm keeping those top three rooms for girls only. They'll use the upstairs bathroom and the boys will use the lower bathroom. There'll be no excuse for all this running up and down and practically living in someone else's room. I do wish Jean-Louis would notice Anne-Marie more . . . he's always so involved in his business. So far it's Alexander who's noticing her, and though we think the world of Alexander he just wouldn't be suitable for a girl like Anne-Marie." She took a forkful of pasty and chewed it meditatively. "Young people could save themselves so much trouble if they understood who was suitable to marry and who wasn't. But who am I to preach? I shunned the fellow my parents had their hearts set on. I married a young painter who was wasting away, though at least he wasn't penniless."

"The one who burned all your Proust?"

"Heavens no!" She laughed gaily. "Gus, burn Proust? He'd

rather have set himself on fire. Poor Gus had TB—we found out shortly after our marriage. We went to a place in Switzerland: Davos. The Germans had a horrible joke, '*Letzte Grüsse aus Davos,*' they'd say. Last greetings from Davos. Unfortunately, it proved true for poor Gus—people still died from TB then, you know. But the strangest thing, Carrie: there was another American couple at Davos, only she was the sick one. But she got better and divorced that husband and remarried and, later, moved to the very next town in Connecticut to where I was living with the man I'd married after losing Gus ... *now* we're talking about the one who burned Proust. Well, this woman—Louise—and I would meet for lunch or play tennis, but years went by and I never met her husband because he was at work—he was in her father's bank in New York. Her father was an extremely wealthy, influential man—he had once run for the presidency, in the early twenties.

"Anyway! One year I told my husband, 'This has gone far enough, we're going to invite Louise and her mystery husband to our New Year's party.' And we did, and they accepted, and in walks Louise with the man I'd been looking for all my life. I knew it the minute he looked at me. That man was Whit."

"Oh, Mrs. Easton. How romantic."

"Yes, isn't it odd the way your fate comes to claim you in these roundabout little connections? Though, Lord knows, Whit and I tried to be honorable and not hurt anyone. I had my little daughter and Whit worked for his father-in-law. And then World War Two came and Whit was commissioned a colonel and sent right to the European Theater and I was sure every letter I got from him would be the last. I had to rent a post-office box in another town in order to get his letters. And it was so awful when Louise would want to have lunch and read me *her* letters from Whit. And then he came home with the DSO and they dragged on together a little longer. She was completely dependent on him—childless women often are that way. But finally Whit and I decided everyone had had their piece of us and now we wanted to have a little of each other before it was too late. I saw my daughter marry and left for Nevada the next week. Whit's divorce took longer because she fought it tooth and nail and her father more or less controlled their purse strings. But I had a little money from a cottage my father had left me, and so we made it. We burned every one of our bridges and were married by a justice of the peace in New York one morning and sailed for Elba that same afternoon on a Greek ship. We had waited for each other fifteen years. He walked into my living room on December 31, 1937."

"The year I was born."

"Was it? What a coincidence. You know, Carrie, since we seem to be having such a cozy time here and I've been spilling secrets, I must tell you what Whit said about you the other night. We were talking about the various young people who've lived with us, first at Tregunter and now at Twenty-one, and he said, 'Well, Daphne's given us the least trouble, and Arden's given us the most, but the one that had the most life in her was old Carrie.' He said to be sure and invite you for supper because he wants to hear what you've been up to. I was wondering if you'd be free this coming Saturday—I thought I'd try a real bouillabaisse in honor of Anne-Marie. Would you come?"

"Well, thank you. I think that would be nice." The old lech, I thought, did he say that or is she just making it up? I'll go, because I am free and she's the best cook in town and it will be fun to reassess the old gang from the perspective of my winter's worth of independence. "Has Daphne left you, then?"

"Oh no, poor Daphne's still with us. She's still in your old room. Her nice boy got away, I'm afraid. The timing was off somehow. It was unfortunate, because she really did care for him. She's being very subdued these days. She sits around pasting on her false fingernails and she has a part-time job typing up inventories for some Levantine who has a gift shop in Chelsea."

"And who has taken Arden's old room?"

"No one, as yet. Isabel moved in for a while, while the leak in her room was being fixed. I'm sure it was caused by Arden— she'd take hour-long baths and fill the tub so full that the water just *poured* out the drainpipe into the street. But Isabel's left us now, and, frankly, Carrie, I'm in no hurry to put just anyone in that room. It's spring now and we can afford to be choosy because the heating bills won't be so high. Do you know, Arden kept two heaters going in her room the whole time she was with us? And, as you know, she was in her room all day. I felt we would have been perfectly within our rights to raise her rent, but Whit wouldn't hear of it. Dear Whit's as scrupulous as an Eagle Scout."

The pub lunch with Mrs. Easton dominated my thoughts for the rest of that week. So often, especially when we are younger, we see other people only in relation to what they are to us; we freeze them into what they are *now*. But her story had broken the ice, or at least made a crack in it (for I am still far from "figuring out" the Eastons, which is why, I suppose, they have remained so tantalizing to my imagination), and, after the lunch, I could glimpse them as fluid creatures still moving in the auras of their colorful pasts. When she lifted her eyes from the Hennings' copy of Proust and looked across the red basement room, whose dampness had provided a perfect alibi for the missing ring (and which husband had given her the big pear-shaped diamond with the emerald baguettes, or had it been a family heirloom, or had she splurged while she waited for "Whit" to disentangle himself from the purse strings, knowing he couldn't buy her a ring and being glad she had the little legacy from her father so she could finance the burning of their bridges?)— when the Mrs. Easton I knew looked across the basement room at the alcoholic trying to fill an hour by polishing all their shoes, she saw, if not the substance, then the shadow of "the man she had been looking for all her life," the man who had written her clandestine letters, each one perhaps "the last," from the heart of all the action, and who had come home a hero. When my ex-landlady looked at my ex-landlord, who had pinched me in the kitchen and almost certainly made off with my money, she saw the man she had wanted and plotted and schemed for, as long as I had been on the earth.

But though I could now pity them their present lives, I did, a little, envy them their pasts. I could now piece together a sort of broken mosaic of the world she had pronounced "going, going, *gone,*" a world of privilege in which girls at boarding school took all the men's parts in *The Importance of Being Earnest* and boys at prep school were provided with neckties that would always grant them a certain cachet, even if their lives later went downhill. It was a world in which one's father fished at the Restigouche Salmon Club (Colleen, a Canadian, had been able to enlighten me on that one) and young artist husbands who were "not penniless" wasted away in Swiss sanatoriums. The wars were grand and revenges were grand: a husband, discovering he had been cheated of his rightful time, made a bonfire of his wife's *Remembrance of Things Past* on the lawn. You even burned your bridges in the grand style: you sailed straight for the island where Napoleon himself lay low for a while until he could rally his resources for a second assault on fortune.

It was very possibly because I was under the spell of Mrs. Easton's romance that, on the Friday before the Saturday I was to partake of her bouillabaisse, I went to a party given by some girls who lived in a mews off Green Street and convinced myself I had met the man I had been looking for all my life. Hastings Pickering was twenty-nine, "with intelligent eyes, inner calm, and manliness," as I was to write in my journal after he had left my flat. He worked as a research engineer for a spark plug company in Croydon and told me he had lost his best friend to matrimony the week before. "Now there's nothing for it but for me to find a woman and get married, too," he said, puffing at his pipe as he made me a cup of coffee in my own kitchen because I had drunk too much at the party. He was losing his hair but that was all right because he had a strong, pure, well-sculpted face and a sweet mouth. Eros quivered between us as we lay chastely together on my bed, because there were no comfortable chairs, and listened to the men taking a bath upstairs. Hastings told me his favorite pastimes were sailing and camping, and that he owned a little cottage in Rugby that he rented out. "I mean, one can't say to one's prospective father-in-law, 'Sir, I'm a good chap, I own thirty-six sweaters,' can one?" He told me that in his opinion a man should not try to sleep with a girl till after they were married.

I was in such a state of well-being on Saturday that I took an early bus to Chelsea so I could ride the extra stops and get off by the river and take my old ritual walk along the Embankment. The stretch between the Battersea and Chelsea bridges was where I came closest, I felt, to achieving a true relationship to time. During my first English summer on Old Church Street, I had often walked there to regain perspective when office gripes or Easton intrigues had got me down, and almost always I came back from the walk with a larger sense of life. Following the historic curve of the Thames from the Pleasure Gardens over on the Battersea side to the Chelsea Pensioners' Hospital on my side, I would have regathered my calm to the point of being able to see before and beyond my own existence by the time I passed the Hovis clock. Human beings had walked this bend of river before me and thought about the mutability of their individual lives, and they would still be walking and thinking after I was gone. Thus humbled, I would experience a peculiar elation, and, feeling almost weightless, as if my body had already dispersed into particles and were no longer visible, I would turn and retrace the route, wondering what all the fuss had been about. Somewhere along the way, I would take a deep breath, shuddering as the "I" and the "Now" refilled me. I would become visible again and resume the plotting of my life.

On this particular spring evening, by the time I had performed the ritual and arrived at the yellow door at 21 Old Church Street, it seemed highly possible that by the end of the summer I should have finished the American *Madame Bovary* and might even be married.

Mr. Easton, in his familiar regalia, answered the door and seemed less high than usual for almost six o'clock and heartily glad to see me.

"Carrie! You're looking wonderful. Come in, come in."

"A few contributions to the Cave Rouge cocktail hour," I

said, handing him a brown paper bag from the PX. (Mrs. Easton had invited me to come early, "so the three of us can go downstairs and have a drink and talk.")

"You shouldn't have done that, but we thank you. C'mon up to the kitchen and say hello to Lee—she's just finishing off a poor lobster. Go ahead, go ahead."

I went up the stairs in front of him, highly conscious of our previous encounter in the dark kitchen. Now the warm yellow of lengthening twilight streamed through its windows, and Mrs. Easton, wearing her handsome black bib apron with thin white stripes, turned from where she was cutting up something, put down her knife, and gave me a "cook's kiss," offering me her face but holding her wet hands aloft.

"I'm so tickled you could come, Carrie. I really think this is going to be fun. I managed to get every single ingredient except the *rascasse*, which, of course, you can't get here, as it swims only in the Mediterranean around Marseilles. But I'm sure Anne-Marie will forgive us; she's providing the wine for the evening, isn't that sweet?"

"And Carrie's providing the cocktail hour," said Mr. Easton, peering into the brown bag.

"Oh, *isn't* that nice. Sweetie, why don't you go on down and prepare our drinks while I finish with this lobster? What will you have, Carrie? We've got some medium-dry sherry and gin. And whatever you brought, of course."

"I'd love a sherry."

"Yes, so would I. Do feel free to go upstairs and use your old bathroom, if you'd like to wash up. Why don't you run upstairs anyway and say hello to your old room. Daphne's not home yet. Oh! And do me a big favor and see if you like what I've done to Arden's old room next door. I thought it needed a new personality, after being a sickroom for so long."

And so I went up, you might say, to my fate. I did not linger long at my old room, I did not even cross its threshold; Daphne's imprint was upon it, and its associations for me now were those of its latter period, when I spent more and more time in the canopied bed and no longer got up to look out the window on the mornings the Queen's Guards rode by. In the bluish evening light (for its sun was gone for the day) *it* looked rather like an opulent sickroom.

I went next door to Arden's former room. It was at its best, this time of day. The same warm yellow light that had filled the kitchen below played flatteringly upon the polished surfaces of furniture. The room's aspect had been completely changed since Arden and I lay across her bed, taping "Aspects of England" for the listeners of Ruffin County. The bed had been moved from the center of the room and pushed flush against one wall. There was a desk, by the window, which had not been here before. This room came equipped with a small washbasin, and, to the right of the basin, next to a roomy chiffonier, a narrow, old-fashioned bookcase, with brass handles on its glass doors, had been fitted in. The room now had the feeling of a study where one might also rest, rather than a boudoir where one might also write. Ah, cunning, cunning Mrs. Easton: to break up the monotonous length of mouse-gray carpeting, she had put down a small Oriental rug, with faded lions and hunters, that I had often admired in the old days when it lay, lost among too many other patterns, in the drawing room downstairs. I knew who was going to live next in this room, and the Eastons knew it, too.

I went to the window, where the desk had been placed, to try the new view. There was the tin roof of Alexander's shed, and, beyond, the greening squares of neighboring gardens, the interesting views of other people's homes, the perky London chimney pots with their crooked hats. I put my palms down upon the desk. It was still warm from the afternoon sun. Here in this alert, chaste little room (and since Hastings had expressed his views on sex before marriage, chastity was clearly going to be the order of the summer) I could begin in earnest to write. Here I could (and did) finish the American *Madame Bovary*. (I would send my only manuscript copy to an agency on Baker Street that had placed an ad in the *Evening Standard*: "Wanted: unpublished novels in which women's problems and love interests are predominant. Agreeable terms." Months would pass and I would finally ring up Directory Enquiries and discover that the agency was not listed. I went around to the address. It was an empty flat. If you ever come across a novel about an unhappy young wife named Bentley who lives on a Florida island called Gull Key—no, they might have changed the names; if you ever come across a novel that ends, "If I could do it once, I can do it again; so rises the indestructible pyramid," that's mine.) Here, at this desk, I would sit on weekend afternoons and some weekend evenings, gazing out at the gardens and houses and wondering about my future. The house of the man I would marry next was visible from this window: a dark brick building in which I would repent at leisure for the second time. But time would still, miraculously, be on my side. No crucial bridges would have been burned as yet, and I would eventually return to my own country and have an opportunity to start afresh.

And here, at this desk, in less than a month, I would sit down one warm English afternoon, after sharing drinks and spilling secrets with the Eastons at their favorite pub to celebrate my return, and write down in my journal the story they had told me, probably in exchange for my telling them all the gloomy and dramatic and salacious details of my first marriage.

Mr. Bedford

On the day Mrs. Easton sold her late father's cottage in Bedford, New York, she and Mr. Easton went walking in the fields behind and found a turtle. They named him Mr. Bedford and took him back to their rooftop flat on East Sixty-sixth Street, which a friend was lending them till Mr. Easton's divorce came through. Mr. Bedford slept in the garden in the daytime, and at night would come clunking down the stairs—a kind of combined crawl-fall—and sleep under their bed. It took him hours to follow them from room to room, and sometimes by the time he had gotten to one room, they had already left it for another. One day

Mr. E. found Mr. Bedford half buried in the hot tar on the roof. It took three hours with a bottle of turpentine, fingers, and a spoon to make him comfortable again. When they had parties, sometimes Mr. Easton would fix a lighted candle to the top of Mr. Bedford's shell and he would come marching into the dark dining room all aglow and make the ladies scream. He ate flies, lettuce leaves, and meat. When the Eastons married and left quickly for Elba, because Mr. E. could never pay the kind of alimony he had agreed to pay in order to get the divorce, they took Mr. Bedford along with them on the ship in a hatbox. The bartender on board tried to interest him in whiskey, but Mr. Bedford was not the drinking sort. The family flourished in Elba until one day Mr. Bedford fell from a second-story window during one of his prowls and cracked his shell. Mr. E. again to the rescue with iodine and adhesive tape. The shell grew back, but Mr. Bedford's legs remained slightly paralyzed despite the Eastons' faithful massages. One day some friends came to take the Eastons' picture for the front of a Christmas card. The Eastons and Mr. Bedford were all three posed looking out of a window. Afterward Mr. Bedford was left in his favorite spot on the patio to have a nap in the sun. But when he didn't come in by nighttime, Mrs. Easton got worried and went to look. But he was nowhere to be found, though they both searched for hours. It was thought that a dog had probably carried him away (as had happened before) but this time dropped him somewhere too far from home for his semiparalyzed legs to return him. Mrs. Easton cried for days because Mr. Bedford, she said, besides being an unusually faithful, intelligent character, also had been their last connection with another time and another place, neither of which could ever be returned to.

"How about it, Carrie?" asked Mr. Easton. "D'ya think you can stand it one more time?"

We were gathered together, rosy from wine and the extraordinary bouillabaisse, in the Hennings' well-appointed drawing room, with its glazed chintz sofa and armchairs, its lamps and little tea tables, its good faded Oriental rugs (one now missing), its impressive array of gilt-and-leather bindings (of which the red-and-gold *Debrett's* was placed to gleam most prominently) on the shelves. We were also rosy from laughing, for the Eastons, taking it by turns, had just retold, for my benefit, the priceless story about how, last November, Mrs. Henning had suddenly rung up to announce she was in the country for a quick visit to her ailing mother-in-law and would it be *too* silly of her to want to pop up to London and say hello to her beloved little house? "Well, thank *God* Arden was still in the hospital," said Mrs. Easton. "I could get to work de-inhabiting her room right away." And at this point Mr. Easton had taken up the story, relating in rapid, comic fashion punctuated with exaggerations how he had called an emergency meeting of the inmates. "I gave them to understand they had to have every item of personal clothing, every single sign of their existence, out of their rooms. Everyone packed themselves up in suitcases and we stored everything under a bunch of blankets down in Le Cave Rouge. And then they were under strict orders to be out of the house from two o'clock till seven o'clock on Saturday, when Mrs. Henning was coming to tea. She only stayed from four to five, but you can't be too careful." "And did she suspect?" I asked. "Well," drawled Mrs. Easton philosophically, "I think she suspected some of it, but not *all* of it. I mean, we couldn't un-paint and un-decorate Le Cave Rouge, so we told her we'd made it into a spare guest room when we had extra friends from America. And what we decided to do about Alexander's shed was tell her the truth: 'We've let a very nice boy fix up your garden shed and live there till he gets on his feet in life.' She was simply enchanted by Alexander's shed. She said it would make a perfect little guest house or study for her husband one day. All in all, she was *quite* satisfied with the state of the house." "But boy, were we glad to phone that taxi and send her back to Victoria Station!" Mr. Easton had concluded.

And then he had asked me if, for the sake of Anne-Marie, I could stand to hear the Rhinebeck story one more time.

"I hope to hear it many more times," I said, significantly. Mrs. Easton beamed at me. An unspoken agreement had already been reached between us over cocktails in Le Cave Rouge.

"Anne-Marie's English isn't so good yet, but you'll do a consecutive translation for her, won't you, Jean-Louis?"

"Eh . . . certainly." Jean-Louis looked up from his little notebook, in which he had been making a few quick calculations in the interim. He turned politely toward his boss's daughter, who sat beside Alexander on the sofa, her pretty knees close together, a beautiful girl both sultry and unawakened, as yet. (Jean-Louis would marry her, but Alexander, who brooded slyly upon her ripeness as he sucked deeply on his cigarette, would have her first.)

"Daphne? I won't be killing you with boredom, either?"

"I should quite like to hear it, actually," said poor Daphne, the only one who had not made a pig of herself over the bouillabaisse. She still mourned the loss of the biscuit heir, or perhaps felt the personal failure it implied. But she sat there bravely, examining a false fingernail that had begun to chip. (Years later I would meet Daphne at the glove counter in Bonwit's. She would be married to an American, a veterinarian specializing in Thoroughbred horses, whose profession required the couple to make frequent trips to England. "I suppose you've heard about Alexander's success," she would say, as we ran through the old guest list; no, she was ashamed to say, she was quite out of touch with the Eastons—"We had a bit of a run-in over this chap I was seeing for a while"—but she supposed they were still in London. "But they *can't* still be running a boardinghouse," I said. "They're getting near their eighties." One hoped not, she said, but had I heard of Alexander's in Berkeley Square? "It's so posh there's a waiting list for membership. He's got it furnished with all his antiques. They say the Marchioness of Monleigh set him up, after her husband died. Richard and I dined there with some friends who are members; we could never afford it. Alexander is quite changed. He's put on weight and looks really like somebody. He's the 'new' England, one might say." And she would go on to lament the other changes in the London we knew. "Remember the Boltons? Well, it's *filled* with estate-agent signs—in Arabic!")

"Well, then!" And Mr. Easton sat himself down at the rosewood piano and ran his fingers lightly over the keys. "A bit out of tune, Lee...."

"I know, darling. As soon as we get caught up, we'll have the tuner. He's so expensive," she confided to me, bending her faded blond head toward where I sat, on a silk cushion, beside her well-shod feet. (Our tenancy in that house was more limited than we knew. At the end of the summer, the Eastons would receive a terribly apologetic letter from Mrs. Henning. "... though we'd adore to have you stay on, prices have gone up so that Father feels we really must increase the rent (as allowed for in clause 14) to cover taxes and insurance rises...." That, as Mrs. Easton would say philosophically, is the way the English do things.)

Mr. Easton played the opening passages of the "Moonlight Sonata" and then told us about the time he had gone "on a matter of business" from New York City to the house of a very wealthy man in Rhinebeck, New York. But this time around, I squinted at his profile until I imagined I could see, as through a scrim, that young man winding his way innocently up the Hudson aboard the train of his convoluted destiny. There would be wives (or was he, at this time, already working for the first one's father, the one that controlled the purse strings?), a war; why, even before the day was over, he would meet a beautiful girl with a tail. Or was that—it occurs to me now—just a metaphor for something he was trying to tell us about our own futures: the contest between what we were determined to wrest from fate and what fate, in her sinuous, sporting movements, as playful and sinister as an unexpected tail, would end up wresting from us?

"... I was a young man, life was just beginning for me, as it is for all of you now, and that woman in those surroundings seemed the epitome of all I hoped to win for myself ..."

And, in a moment, Jean-Louis's translated litany of these things: ". . . *amour* . . . *accomplissement* . . . eh . . ." (Look at Anne-Marie, you fool!) ". . . *beauté* . . . *élégance* . . . *prospérité* . . ."

Now I live near Rhinebeck, New York, myself, on the other side of the bridge. I seldom drive over that bridge without scanning the rooftops of those grand riverfront houses, hidden from full view even in winter by careful forestry, and wondering if in one of them lives an old lady who by now may be reconciled to her tail. Thoughts of her inevitably lead to thoughts of the Eastons. To what have they had to reconcile themselves, since I last saw them?

I stayed with them at 21 Old Church Street till the fall and moved with them and five others to a less elegant house in Oakley Gardens, where we coexisted until the following fall, when I again left in a huff, this time (ostensibly) over a cat. They had given me the ground-floor garden room on the condition I let Enrico go in and out of my window, as this house had no back door. Enrico and I had never really got on—perhaps he smelled my ambivalence toward his owners—but when we began sharing a room the animosities bloomed on both sides. I would make him wait till I had finished doing whatever I was doing, when he yowled and scratched on the closed window; conversely, on warm mornings, when it was open, he would pounce on me while I was still asleep and wave his tail, smelling heavily of musk, in my face before demanding to be let out of the bedroom. But the real reason I was leaving was that I was just turned twenty-seven and had broken my engagement to a rugby player and felt that if I were to be an old maid like Colleen Drury I'd rather be one in the privacy of my own flat.

But fate responded with a series of capricious tail-flicks, and I had no sooner settled into my own flat on Beaufort Street than I was moving out again, across the street, to the flat of my husband. ("Colleen married that fellow you all called 'Made in England,' " Mr. Miles, who liked to keep up with his "old girls," would write to me in 1969.) As a wife, I saw Mrs. Easton occasionally, when we shopped at the same fish market on the King's Road. Sometimes she would smile and seem genuinely glad to see me; sometimes she would look in, see me buying my fish, and hurry on past, doing her other errands first.

The last time I saw Mr. Easton was on a damp night when I had been walking alone beside the Embankment and knew suddenly that I was going to leave my husband and go back to America. I decided to go and see the Eastons and tell them. I felt they, of all people, would understand. I hurried up Oakley Street and turned into Oakley Gardens, hoping they'd offer me something to drink (the husband on Beaufort Street did not believe in alcohol); but when I reached their house, the windows of the drawing room were already dark. I went up on the porch, anyway, and peered in, perhaps hoping I could make her materialize (for it was Mrs. Easton I really wanted to see), and that's when I saw him, holding on to the banister post, doing knee-bends in his striped flannel pajamas. Up and down he went, exceedingly limber for a man of his age; he was facing the front door, no doubt seeing his reflection in its glass panes, when, suddenly (I must have stepped forward, or his vision shifted), he looked perfectly horrified, as if he'd seen a ghost, and turned and bolted down the hall and away into the shadows.

Perhaps Arden knows what has become of them. She and I have been in and out of touch over the years (mostly out, I am ashamed to say), but she is the kind of person who won't let too long go by before she checks up on anyone in her life who has meant something to her. While I was writing this, I was tempted to track her down through good old 555-1212, thinking, It is entirely possible that she is not only in correspondence with them but may even be sending them money. For I've heard, through the grapevine, that Arden is now a very rich woman. (And, the last time we met, a very happy one, with her Bruce and their twin daughters. Happy people are quick to forgive: an oblation to fate?) But then I said, No, not until you finish your story.

Once I was writing a story whose whole thrust depended upon the fulcrum of a lucky cousin's idyllic marriage. Feeling closer to this cousin as I imagined her life on paper, I made the mistake of writing to her before I'd finished. Back came a torrent of anguished pages filled with lucklessness and divorce. Now her luck has changed again and things are on the upswing once more. But I never could finish that story.

One of the fascinating aspects of life is that, as long as people are in it, their stories go on, often in the most amazing ways. But another aspect of life is that, sooner or later, it kills people off.

One of the fascinating aspects of fiction is that, inside its boundaries, you can keep people alive for as long as you like. That's why I don't want to hear anything bad or sad about the Eastons, even if it exists, "out there" in life. Not until I've come to the end of my last page and have safely preserved *my* Eastons as they were to me.

In here, in the confines of my fiction, we are all still alive. Some of us are still young, plotting our favorite versions of the love, accomplishment, beauty, elegance, and wealth we hope to win for ourselves. And even for those whose main chances are now a thing of the past, nobody is friendless or destitute or *too* old or in great physical pain; nobody is even in the hospital.

The elegant drawing room is warm from the coal fire Mr. Easton has made in the grate, and Mrs. Henning's lamps play favorably on our faces, flushed from wine and good food and from laughing at the old, old story. But it was new to Anne-Marie, who laughed so hard at Jean-Louis's translation that she has the hiccups. There goes Mrs. Easton, agile as a girl in her Belgian strollers, and willing to serve her lovely young paying guest, to fetch a glass of water. Anyone happening to be walking along Old Church Street in the spring night may look up at our glowing window and sigh and think: Ah, the pleasures of a cozy, well-appointed home! Or may take an invigorating breath and declare: "Fascinating, to look unseen into a little tableau of other people's lives . . . and then move on."

A Father's
Pleasures

*R*udolf Geber loved his son with the love we reserve for those to whom we have given our best selves. Sometimes it even seemed to him that he had brought the boy into the world singlehandedly. It had been Rudolf who overcame his wife's resistance to having a baby. She was one of those people who appear to have been born sad and fearful and who go through life this way, for some inner reason nobody else can fathom. Rudolf, a man of charm, to whom life came easily, had been drawn to her because he believed he of all people could make her relaxed and happy. The pregnancy was difficult and she became more sad and fearful than ever. In her seventh month she stopped growing, and Rudolf canceled an important concert tour and stayed by her side. He rushed her to the hospital when it was learned she was toxic. He signed the papers for a cesarean and the infant was transferred straight from the womb to the incubator.

"We have a son," he told her when she came out of the anesthetic. "Only six pounds, but you should see the black fuzz all over his head, the little monkey."

She turned her face to the wall and wept softly. She knew he was lying, she knew the child had been born dead.

Rudolf never told her of the crisis that came a day later. The tiny boy, whom Rudolf already thought of as Paul, named after his own father, had developed a horrifying twitch. Rudolf stood over the incubator, watching helplessly as the little limbs jerked in spasms, as if being pulled on an invisible rack. The pediatrician was called. "Mr. Geber," she said, "this is either a simple calcium deficiency or something much more serious. At this point I cannot tell which. I shall treat him for the calcium deficiency first, as the treatment for the other thing, which involves draining spinal fluid, is dangerous in itself. And we shall pray."

She stayed with the child all night. Rudolf paced in a waiting room whose curtains he never forgot. He prayed to the deities of both his parents. With the remote, hard-nosed God of his mother, who had survived her concentration camp and now lived in Tel Aviv, he bargained Old Testament–style: "If You let the boy live, I will stop hoping for a happy marriage." Then he remembered his father as he had looked the last time Rudolf ever saw him, waving good-bye as the train pulled out of Berlin. It was the summer of 1939. Rudolf, a *Wunderkind* of twelve, was off to England to play a series of concerts. While in Leeds, Rudolf received a letter from his father, with ten English pounds enclosed, giving him the name of a family who would take him in. He stayed with this family for five years, after which he volunteered for the British forces and was sent to Africa. After the war, he visited his mother in what was then called Palestine. She was angry and bitter that what had happened in the world had been allowed to happen. She and Rudolf fell out when he said he preferred to join the forces of Art and Beauty. "You are just a dreamer, like your father," she said. Rudolf thanked her; soon afterward, he went to America. Rudolf's father had died of a heart attack at Theresienstadt, one of the "model" camps the Nazis kept for public-relations purposes. He had been carrying rocks for a rock garden to beautify the camp to which he had volunteered to accompany his wife.

Now, in the waiting room of a New York hospital, Rudolf also prayed to his father's God, the Father of Jesus. But it was his own father's face, with the high forehead and the reddish-brown mustache, he addressed: "If little Paul lives, help me to be as good a father as you were."

/ / /

When Paul was three, his father bought him a recorder. At the end of the morning's scales and arpeggios, Rudolf waited for the small voice to call through the door of his practice room: "Daddy, can we make our music now?" Their "music" consisted of little Paul's blowing boldly on his recorder and Rudolf's improvising around whatever sound the boy made. Rudolf loved this hour. He kept stealing glances at the serious child blowing for all he was worth, his dark eyes widening, his tiny nostrils flaring with the effort. Paul's face was already shaped as it would be as an adult. The funny black fuzz that had covered his head at birth had fallen out soon afterward and his hair was now the same curly russet as his father's. But Paul had inherited his mother's somber temperament.

During Paul's childhood, the mother seemed quite content to hover efficiently in the background of the love between father and son. She made their meals, worried about their health and all the possible catastrophes that might befall them. She acted as secretary for Rudolf's busy professional life. There was a satisfaction in her voice when she could tell someone, "He cannot come to the phone now, he is practicing." Or, "I am sorry, he's away on tour." She read voraciously and had grown more peaceful since Rudolf had taken the pressure off her to become a happy woman.

The summer Paul was six, the family was to have a free trip to Scandinavia. Rudolf was one of the guest artists on a cruise ship. At the last minute, the mother sprained her back. Paul was so disappointed that they decided to hire a nurse for her at home so that Rudolf could take the boy along as planned.

"Don't let him cramp your style," teased Rudolf's wife, who had grown almost jolly now that she couldn't go on the long-awaited free vacation. She came nearest to happiness during setbacks, Rudolf had learned.

"The boy is my style," he replied. He himself did not know exactly what his words meant, they simply sprang to his tongue.

The plush liner was hardly out of sight of land before Rudolf and Paul had captured the imagination of all on board. Each passenger wove his own story around the charming virtuoso and the solemn little fellow who pattered after him like a shadow. Watching the big man and the little one standing side by side at the rail, their look-alike hair blowing, engaged in intense conversation, people would make adjustments to their own memories: "Ah, my father was like that . . . or would have been, had he lived. . . ." "Yes, I, too, was a good father when my children were small. I wonder if they remember all our outings and conversations. . . ." The women on board fantasized worse fates than a sprained back for the absent mother; each imagined in her own way how she would go about making that serious little boy smile and how the attractive father would reward her with his gratitude and affection.

Both Rudolf and Paul were secretly glad to be off on their own. If his mother were here, Paul knew, she would be worrying herself sick about his falling overboard or drowning in the swimming pool or eating rotten food or staying up late to hear his father's music. As for Rudolf, he had determined this voyage should have lasting significance for his son. He himself had never got his fill of his own father. There were gaps of knowledge he would give anything to be able to fill.

"My father never carried a package," he told Paul.

"Why, was he very weak?"

"No, in that society a gentleman didn't. He didn't shave himself, either. He left the house at half-past eight and stopped at his barber's before he went on to his factory. They called him *der elegante Geber*, my father. Did you know that our name means 'the giver' in German?"

"Am I German or American?" Paul wanted to know.

"American. Third generation on your mother's side, first on mine. I am a naturalized citizen."

"Am I Jewish or just part-Jewish?"

"According to Jewish law, you're Jewish because your mother is. It's the same with me."

"What about other laws? What about American law?"

"Well, according to them, you're a mixture of your mother and father and their mothers and fathers and so on. According to American law you're also unique, you're yourself, Paul, with all the rights and privileges a free country grants an individual."

"Are there some parts of me, then, that don't come from anybody and don't belong to anybody?"

Rudolf thought for a minute, impressed by the gravity of the small boy's question. "Of course!" he answered.

One of the other entertainers on the cruise was a voluptuous, rather rowdy flamenco singer who called herself Carmen Cordero. She drank like a fish and her laugh carried clear across the ship. She had her twelve-year-old daughter with her, a quiet, slim girl who deferred to Carmen in everything yet appeared to live her real life in some remote mental kingdom. She reminded Rudolf of a medieval princess. Her name was Liane. Carmen was vague about Liane's father. Liane became attached to little Paul; she mothered him in a sweet, childish way and was teaching him how to swim. The four of them took their meals together and soon formed a makeshift family, the two sociable, talkative parents and the two quiet, withdrawn children. The available women on board thought the elegant pianist utterly wasted on the coarse Cordero.

But Carmen could not have suited Rudolf better. He liked her rowdy frankness, she was the kind of woman you could say anything to; her good humor was as endless as her capacity for Scotch. Also, she kept the other women away. Rudolf was at this time still intent upon honoring his marriage to the letter of the law. So after their respective performances were tucked away, Rudolf and Carmen sat in the bar and drank Glenfiddich—gratis for them, as was everything else on the ship—and talked music or exchanged professional anecdotes. By tacit agreement, Carmen did not bring up Rudolf's marriage and Rudolf asked no questions about the father of Liane.

"Once I was on tour with this Russian accompanist, a huge woman named Nadia Lissenko," Carmen told Rudolf. "In Medicine Hat, Alberta . . . have you ever been there? . . . we had to share a room with only one bed. In the middle of the night I dreamed I was smothering to death. I woke up and there was Nadia on top of me, naked, grinding her massive, soft body against mine. That was when I resolved to learn to accompany myself on guitar."

"It's much better with guitar, your voice is so resonant," said Rudolf. "Certainly I've been to Medicine Hat. It was there . . . no, sorry, it was Moose Jaw, where I had a small fiasco. I was playing from memory a piece by a local composer when suddenly I blanked. So I improvised. A little Scriabin, a little of my own schlock I sometimes use to warm up with. The composer was livid, but he got the best reviews of his life."

Carmen snorted so loudly with laughter that a refined couple on their honeymoon turned to stare. She put her hand on Rudolf's arm. "Your bravura playing, my dear. By the way, it went over big tonight when you dedicated your encore to little Paul. The audience ate it up."

"Yes, Paul loves the 'Kinderscenen,' " said Rudolf.

"It's funny," said Carmen. "A man alone with his little boy is like an aphrodisiac to women, but a woman alone with her little girl scares the hell out of men."

"What's the difference? Lovers come and go, but my son is always my son and your daughter is always your daughter," said Rudolf. "That's what really matters."

"I think I'll have a refill," said Carmen, with a melancholy look at Rudolf.

Little Paul flourished on the cruise. His body turned a healthy pink-brown from his swimming lessons with the patient Liane. Both of them were extremely fair-skinned and Liane saw to it that they constantly rubbed sun cream on themselves and on each other's shoulders. Liane was still perfectly flat-chested and seldom wore a top. She crooned something to Paul as she pulled him through the water and he shouted with laughter. Rudolf, watching them from the side of the pool, felt a little stab of envy.

The boy never let himself go like that, even with him. If only I could give him a sister, thought Rudolf. But the doctor had said it was inadvisable for his wife to have more children, even if Rudolf could talk her into it a second time.

Paul cried when the cruise came to an end and he hugged Liane good-bye. (But a few weeks later he started first grade and became absorbed in the interesting new world of his peers.)

"*Bonne chance!*" cried Carmen affectionately, throwing herself for the first and last time into Rudolf's arms. She gave him a wet kiss, her eyes also wet. "Maybe we'll run into each other in Medicine Hat one of these days!"

"Maybe!" echoed Rudolf pleasantly. He found a taxi for them at the pier and helped Carmen and Liane stow their suitcases on the rack above.

For many years, Rudolf kept in his wallet a snapshot of Paul as he had been on that cruise. In it Paul was wearing his little yellow swimsuit with the green fish leaping up one hip. Paul gazed up at the camera with an impatient but tolerant expression. He was eager to be off to the pool with Liane. But his father wanted to document their trip together and so here he stood, tensed on his legs, trying to oblige. The sun had dusted his aloofly arched little nose with a saddle of freckles. The unsmiling, prim little mouth tugged at Rudolf's heart.

"Dad, please. Couldn't you find something a little more up-to-date?" complained Paul when the creased snapshot, its colors slightly faded, fell out of Rudolf's wallet one day when he was lending his son his Mobil card. Paul now drove; Paul also smoked pot, Rudolf knew, and was probably trying other things that Rudolf chose not to know about. He was in his last year of high school and had been accepted by the college of his choice. The college was on the opposite side of the country. As fathers and sons went, Rudolf and Paul had what people now called a "good relationship." Paul took a genuine interest in his father's professional life, never missed a New York performance, and—though he had long ago discouraged Rudolf's attempts to turn him toward a musical career—had worked up a wicked little imitation of his father at the piano; in the opening bars of Liszt's Third Hungarian Rhapsody the son had managed to capture not only the father's romantic musical mannerisms but also some of his pet rhythmic shifts that audiences had come to identify with the Geber style.

Father and son dined out on the nights the mother went to her Yoga classes. Rudolf treasured these nights and did his best to keep them free. Each kept the other up-to-date on what he was thinking and reading and (most of) what he was doing. During one of these dinners, Paul had confided to Rudolf that he had "had sex" with a girl.

"Just before I left Berlin," said Rudolf, "my father took me for a walk and told me the facts of life. 'Whenever you feel the urge,' he said, 'take a cold shower.' Of course I was only twelve. You'll soon be eighteen. The only fatherly advice I give is, never lose the mystery and the wonder of the female."

"That's your romanticism," Paul said, but not unkindly. "Kids see things differently now."

One evening, after their bachelor meal, Rudolf and Paul stopped in at the nearest Sam Goody's. Rudolf checked from time to time to see whether all of his records were in stock. This evening he was just about to get depressed because he found only the one Chopin Nocturnes album—and that marked down for sale—when a soft woman's voice called to him, "Aren't you Rudolf Geber?"

Rudolf looked up to see an attractive, slim girl striding toward him. She wore a denim jacket embroidered with flowers and a fringed suede skirt that enhanced her long, shapely legs.

"I am," he said, rather flattered that his face should be recognizable to a member of the Rock Generation.

"It's Liane. You know, Carmen's daughter. From the ship." The girl thrust her hand into his. She was smiling at him in a dazed, happy way. "Gosh, I can't believe it. I saw you come in and I said, 'No, it can't be!' "

"But why not? We've always lived here," said Rudolf. "And here is Paul, your old shipboard playmate. Paul, you remember Liane."

"Oh yes," said Paul politely. Exactly the way he responded when his father ran into some professional colleague on the street and introduced him.

"You've grown a bit," Liane told him, with an attempt at humor. She gave him a friendly once-over. Paul was still more of an adolescent than a man; he was slightly overweight and pimply and wore his hair in the slack, unwashed ponytail that was de rigueur among his friends. "It's so *great* to see you again," Liane exclaimed, looking back at the debonair father with his rippling reddish-gray hair and his air of benevolent insouciance.

"How is Carmen?" Rudolf asked.

"Mother's dead. She killed herself in Chicago last year," said Liane in a level voice. Something in the way her body stiffened and her chin lifted brought back to Rudolf how when she was twelve he had likened her to a medieval princess, always with the option of her remote kingdom.

"How terrible! Carmen? But she was always so robust and cheerful!"

"She felt she was getting old and losing her looks. And her voice. She wasn't getting many engagements anymore. I came home from work and found her in the bathtub the night she did it." The girl's face lit suddenly with an almost malevolent brilliance as she related this. It seemed to Rudolf that she might burst into hysterical laughter any minute.

"Look," he said, laying a steadying hand on her arm, "come and have a drink with us. Or perhaps you haven't eaten? We have, but we could keep you company."

"Thank you but I can't. I just came on the floor. I work here."

"Then you live in the city now? I suppose you go to school in the daytime?"

"Oh, I finished with school a long time ago," said Liane, cocking her head at Rudolf in a familiar, rather mocking way. "I've worked since I was sixteen. After Mother died, I thought I might as well work somewhere else. She always wanted to live in this city, but we never got here."

"So you're fulfilling her dream," mused Rudolf, touched. "Poor Carmen. Do you have a phone? We'll call you. Maybe you'd like to join us for dinner some evening when you're not working."

"I'm listed under 'Marmalade,' " said Liane. "It's my cat's name."

Rudolf took her hand again. "We'll certainly call. Very soon! And meanwhile, if you should need us for anything, we're listed under my wife's maiden name, Susannah Weiss."

"Oh, yes. Because you're so famous," said the girl.

"Nonsense," said Rudolf. He kissed her hand.

As he and Paul walked home, Rudolf said, "I think you might have been a little more enthusiastic to see Liane. You once adored her. Poor kid! To find her own mother . . . well, we'll keep tabs on her. I'd like her to feel she isn't completely alone in the world."

"She's got Marmalade," said Paul.

That night Rudolf dreamed he was beside a lovely lake. On the far side of the lake rose mountains with snow on their peaks. He recognized the place, it was in Switzerland; his parents had taken him there one summer when he was a very small boy, even before he had begun his precocious career, which made it practically another life. Some children were playing in the shallow water. He wanted to join them, to laugh and splash with them, but for some reason could not. Feeling very sad, he looked closer and saw that little Paul was among them, and so was Liane, a very young Liane, even younger than the one who had played with Paul on the ship. In the dream, her hair was the same russet color as Paul's. Then it came to Rudolf that all the children playing there, at least a half-dozen children, were his and that was why he couldn't play: he was already a grown-up man, a father. This seemed unutterably sad. He turned to his wife, to say so. Perhaps if he told her his sorrow, they could reach a new understanding. But in place of his wife stood Liane, the woman Liane, looking at him in the same familiar, rather mocking way as in the record store. And he realized he was married to Liane, the woman Liane, who understood him all too well, and that all these children were theirs.

Rudolf woke in the soft spring darkness of his practice room, which had doubled these past few years as his bedroom. His wife was getting her master's in clinical psychology and liked to stay up till all hours studying in the bedroom they formerly shared. Rudolf's window was open and a slight breeze ruffled the hanging plants; voices rose from the pavement two floors below, energetic, argumentative, then faded, along with the noise of a pair of footsteps.

Rudolf recalled the weird excitement in Liane's face when she described how she had found her mother. *She felt she was getting old and losing her looks. And her voice. She wasn't getting many engagements anymore.* Poor old Carmen. What would she have been now, about fifty? She was only a few years older than himself. Rudolf would soon be forty-eight. Now it seemed to him that he had been unkind to Carmen by not making love to her on that cruise; she had wanted him and he had not been unattracted to her. No one would have been hurt; everyone had assumed they were sleeping together as it was. But at the time he had been more in love with the image of himself as the faithful, long-suffering husband. A few years later, however, the dam had broken, first with the handsome soprano Francesca Stolfi, whom he had accompanied in Boston. He was at a low point at the time: the "new music" was all the rage, and as Rudolf flatly refused to play Schumann with the evenness of a computer, or clank chains across the inside of a piano and groan and howl as part of his performance, he had fewer engagements as a soloist and more as a classical accompanist. Francesca had been dazzling in the *Frauenliebe und -Leben;* it had seemed only fitting to continue their splendid synchronization offstage. After Boston, he had become an accomplished adulterer, dividing his life mercilessly in half. One half conducted the sensual, cold-blooded liaisons in which Rudolf always made it clear from the beginning that he had no intention of leaving his wife; the other half sat lovingly across the table from his growing boy and did not even blink when Paul asked: "Well, Dad, did you have any fun at all on your tour, or was it all work?"

But the dream had changed Rudolf. He woke from it a different man. His carefully separated halves merged and his whole being seemed to be dissolving into a sea of desires and regrets. I suppose this must be middle age, he thought, letting the sweet, dark thoughts wash over him like a warm bath. If so, it's not too awful.

If Liane had been twelve when Paul was six, then she must now be . . . twenty-four?

Several months later, Rudolf stood in the door of his wife's bedroom. "Do you have a minute?"

She gave a curt nod, without looking up. The bed was covered with books and papers. Rudolf moved a large text on abnormal psychology and a Doris Lessing paperback and sat down. His wife's hair was pulled back and tied girlishly with a ribbon. Her face was shiny and intense from intellectual concentration. She looked over the tops of her reading glasses at Rudolf. For a second it seemed she was trying to remember who he was.

"Have you finished all your exams?" Rudolf asked gently.

"Oh yes. I was just making a few notes while the adrenaline is still high. And you, what's new?"

"Well, I think I'd like a divorce."

"I see. What about Paul?"

"He knows nothing. I thought we'd wait till he is safely across the country in his college. Then I could write to him."

"Very thoughtful of you. As usual. Is it anyone I know?"

"She was on that cruise years ago, the one you couldn't go on. She was just a child at the time. She and Paul played together while her mother and I drank together. I was, of course, faithful to you."

"Of course. I knew exactly when you stopped."

"You did?" Rudolf exclaimed. "How?"

"You became even kinder."

"Susannah . . ." Rudolf reached for his wife's hand. He felt like weeping.

She was regarding him calmly, as though he were one of her psychological specimens. "What is she like?"

"She's had a rough life. Always on tour with her mother. Never did learn who her father was. Now her mother is dead— slit her wrists and allowed her daughter to find her in the tub, can you imagine? And do you know, she has never lived in a real house?"

"Poor girl!" cried Susannah with so much feeling that Rudolf was astounded by her objectivity.

"You really understand, don't you?" he asked softly.

"I understand more than you think," she replied.

Dear Paul,

By now you are settled in at your college. Your mother and I were happy to hear you like your roommate. The only roommates I ever had were in the army, that was my college, but I can't tell you how much pleasure it gives me that I who never completed high school can send you to college in style! Savor *everything*, and when you have time, write me your impressions.

Paul, there is something I have to tell you. Your mother and I are getting divorced. For years now we have been just good friends, and we shall of course go on being good friends. This should not affect your happiness or security in any way. You will still have your home to come to, and your mother will be in it. She has a new job, with a testing service, and is enjoying her work. She plans to write you her own letter.

As for me, I shall not be far away. I have bought a small place in the country, within two hours' drive of the city. (You should have seen the poor Steinway being hoisted down, how it trembled, two floors above the pavement—I couldn't watch! But after a good tuning it will be recovered from its trauma and when you come—perhaps for a few days at Christmas?—it will be ready for your inimitable "Geber Impersonation.")

Paul, I hope this won't be too big a shock. Liane and I love each other and will soon marry. She is living in the house already and seems very happy, though Marmalade has not yet adjusted completely. I know this must all seem very strange to you, but always remember one thing: the love a man has for his son is like no other love in the world. It cannot be diminished or replaced by any other love.

Your Father,
Rudolf

Dear Dad,

I have suspected about you and Mom for some time. I have her letter too and you are right, she sounds fine.

The other news was a bit of a surprise but Liane was very nice to me when I was small. I hope you both will be happy together. Do you think I should write her a letter? Or not?

I probably won't get back east for Christmas. Tom has invited me to go to his parents' place in Acapulco and if it's okay with you I'd really like to go.

I dropped the Logic course and had to sign up for two hours of something to replace it, so am taking Introduction to Computers. Things are pretty hectic, will write again soon.

Love,
Paul

Rudolf found it as easy to make Liane happy as he had found it impossible to make his first wife happy. Liane had uncomplicated wants, expressed them in her quiet, cool way, and rewarded him with smiles and caresses when he fulfilled them. She wanted to live in a house with a fence around it, so Rudolf himself built the fence, even though the house sat all by itself in a little clearing in the woods. She wanted to feel she need not go anywhere for months on end, except to the village to shop, so

Rudolf cut down on his touring, except what was necessary to survive. (They didn't need much: Liane was not extravagant, Paul's college had long ago been saved for, and Susannah had accepted the house in New York in lieu of alimony payments.) Occasionally, Liane would consent to fly somewhere with Rudolf for a concert, but she tired easily and always worried about Marmalade, alone at home. Poor kid's been dragged around the world enough, thought Rudolf, and did not press her to go with him when she preferred to remain behind in their little house in the country. She was a real stay-at-home, his Liane: she liked them to dress up for dinner and light candles and sit like some elegant storybook couple at opposite ends of the dining-room table. She liked Rudolf to play Bach for her after dinner (she was not the voracious evening reader that Susannah had been) and she would recline on the sofa and close her eyes and rhythmically stroke the orange cat on her lap; she did not like Rudolf to play any of his emotional pieces or to use too much pedal, because it upset the cat, who would get up and leave the room. She had wanted an old-fashioned high bed with a canopy, and Rudolf had finally tracked one down and had it rebuilt and covered in a material Liane chose. She maintained rather touching standards of formality concerning their night dress and connubial approaches that whetted Rudolf's already romantic temperament. He marveled at his good fortune: to have this slim, affectionate, regal girl with her simple demands, and yet to be embroiled anew each night in her woman's mystery.

Meanwhile Paul, on the far side of the country, was doing well in college, though Rudolf was nonplussed when his son announced he was majoring in computer science.

"But I wouldn't know a computer if I were standing in front of one! Wait, is that it? He wants to go somewhere Dad can't follow. That's only natural. But aren't the computers enough? I don't see why he has to spend all his free time, all his vacations, going on these wilderness treks with that 'Explorer Club.' Testing his manhood, I guess. Of course, when I was his age we had the war. But when I was his age, I spent all my free time running after women. He doesn't even have a girlfriend."

"Not that he writes home about, anyway," said Liane, with a certain look, both amused and protective, she frequently gave her husband.

In the spring of the year Paul was to graduate, Rudolf was invited to go to Japan as part of a cultural exchange program. He would play a series of concerts and consult with Japanese musicians. He was elated by the prospect, and even when Liane begged off, his excitement was not really diminished. Six weeks in Japan, a mysterious country that always had fascinated him! And the timing was splendid. He could fly west to Paul's graduation, spend a few days with the boy, and then proceed to Tokyo. He read up on Japanese art and culture and commuted three times a week to New York to take a businessman's "crash course" in Japanese. "I learned a new language at twelve," he told Liane. "Wouldn't it be something if I could learn another one at fifty-one? The ideographs aren't so difficult, either; and so precise and beautiful. Did you know Japanese sacred music has a male mode, *ryo*, and a female mode, *ritsu*, in its pentatonic scale? I think I am going to love these people. Are you sure you won't change your mind and come?" But he knew she wouldn't. He had lived with her long enough to know what to stop wanting from Liane: she would not travel with him and she would not have children with him. Poor kid! Hadn't had enough of being a child herself. "Never mind, princess, you and Marmalade stay home and water the tomatoes and keep each other company!" He would miss her, but he needed this new adventure. It was just not in his nature to sit for too long inside a fence.

Liane was disoriented for several days after Rudolf left. She stayed close to the house, as she always did when Rudolf went away for a few days or a week. But this time he would be gone for six weeks. He telephoned every night from the Coast. "You should see Paul. What a metamorphosis. Hard as a rock and with a beard like Eric the Red. And everyone wants him: companies in the West, companies in the East, Alaska, Puerto Rico. He speaks the powerful, secret language of FORTRAN and COBOL. How are you? How is Marmalade? How are the tomatoes? Listen, I have a small announcement to make: I love you."

Finally Marmalade ran out of cat food and Liane made herself walk to the village. Rudolf had taken the car to the airport and left it in long-term parking, as Liane still hadn't learned to drive. She walked stiffly, leaning slightly to one side, a result of walking so often with Rudolf's arm around her; she kept close to the edge of the road and did not look up when cars passed. Even in her scuffed sneakers and long-legged jeans, she seemed not really part of the scene. By the time she reached the village and purchased the cat food, she felt victorious. She took the unprecedented step of having a Coke by herself in an open-air café. As she walked uphill, toward home again, huffing and puffing, a woman runner passed her, friendly loose breasts jogging under her T-shirt. I could do that, thought Liane, with sudden daring. It occurred to her, as though she were waking from a dream, that in two years she would be thirty years old.

Several weeks later, Liane, in shorts and a kerchief tied around her hair, came sprinting up their private road and saw a large, shiny car parked outside the house. A sunburned man with a full reddish-gold beard was sitting on one of the porch chaises, Marmalade on his lap. As Liane carefully unlatched the gate, he roared with laughter. "Who do you expect that fence to keep out? The squirrels?"

Liane looked more closely at the man. Gradually she was able to pick out Paul's finely arched nose, the soft dark eyes, the rather prim little rosebud mouth of the boy she had whispered to and taught how to float like a jellyfish.

"But . . . Rudolf's not here" was all she could think to say. "He's in Japan."

"I know. He told me to look in on you if I decided to come east for some interviews. I decided to come east for some interviews. This is a great little hideaway. I was just kidding about the fence."

"No, you weren't," said Liane.

The two of them stared at each other silently.

"Dad didn't tell me you ran," Paul at last said pleasantly. "From the way he talked, I expected to find you up in a tower, combing your hair."

"My hair does need combing," said Liane, suddenly conscious of how she must look—and smell. "Excuse me a second." She hurried through the cool house, which seemed unusually dim, and took a fast shower and put on a dress and brushed her hair. Her skin felt tingly from the running and her heart was beating rapidly.

She returned to the porch. Paul, his eyes closed, was stretched out full-length on the chaise. Marmalade was draped over his shoulder, her face against his neck, purring loudly.

"You've stolen my cat's affections," said Liane, taking in the sun-drenched scene with the orange cat and the orange man.

"Cats are fickle creatures, it didn't take much doing." Paul opened his eyes to slits and gave her a lazy smile.

"I hope you'll stay for supper. Rudolf left the freezer full of nice steaks and things," said Liane. "Also, of course, you're welcome to stay the night. The guest room has been waiting for you for four years. Or there's a daybed in your father's practice room that's quite comfortable. You might feel more at home among his things."

"Thank you," said Paul. "I always carry my sleeping bag with me. But I'll borrow a couple of square feet of your land, if it's okay. And I'll take you out to dinner. Dad says you don't go out enough."

Paul drove them through a night filled with stars. Liane sat hugging her window, like a girl on her first date. "Your car is huge. It's like a living room."

"It's a rental. One of the companies that's interviewing me is paying for it."

"It must be wonderful to be so special at something that everybody wants you," said Liane.

"Everybody is going a bit far."

"No, that's what Rudolf said on the phone. Everybody wants you and your secret language."

"That sounds exactly like my father," Paul said, laughing. "He has a way of turning everything into a romance."

As they drove home after dinner, Paul asked, "Do you remember, Liane, the night our ship started up the fjord to dock in Oslo? You came to my stateroom and woke me because you said it was a sight I would always remember. Well, I always have remembered it. Do you remember that night?"

"I . . . think so. Yes." It all came back to her: The gentle rocking of the ship. The sudden miraculous appearance of the lights against the strange greenish sky that never really went dark. Her mother in that red costume with the black trim. Carmen, of whom she always felt a little ashamed, and the elegant, sociable father of the little Paul. She remembered holding the little figure in his pajamas against her as they looked out the porthole. His neck smelled of sleep and of the sun cream they rubbed on each other all day. It seemed to her that she had, on that long-ago night, put her face against that little neck, parted her lips, and taken the soft flesh gently between her teeth for a minute. Did he remember that, too? She looked out the window of the speeding car. The stars seemed to have moved closer.

That night, for the first time, Liane found the canopied bed suffocating. She wanted air and space. She turned off the air conditioner, pulled up the shade, opened the window. There, real night air. That was better. But still she couldn't sleep. She padded barefoot through the dark house and got herself a glass of milk. From the kitchen window, she could make out the shadow of Paul, swaddled in the sleeping bag, under the big Scotch pine. On top of the shadow that was Paul's was another shadow: the fickle Marmalade, asleep on Paul's shoulder.

Liane went back to her room, pulled the silk comforter to

the floor, and made herself a cocoon by the open window, through which she could see a handful of stars.

Paul's interview was not for two more days. The next day he went running with Liane. He gave her a driving lesson in the big car. They cooked hamburgers and ate a pint of ice cream between them.

"Rudolf worries that you don't have girlfriends," Liane startled herself by saying. She added quickly, "I told him that, well, sons don't tell their fathers everything."

"Especially fathers like Rudolf. He has to be protected, my father and his ideals."

"Ah, you know that, too," said Liane.

When it came time to say goodnight, they hugged each other in a self-conscious attempt at their old shipboard camaraderie. But Paul no longer smelled like a little boy, and Liane no longer felt like a little girl.

Liane woke to a loud, urgent ringing. At first she thought that she was aboard a ship and it was going down. Then she realized she was in her makeshift silk sleeping bag on the floor of the bedroom and the phone was ringing. The luminous hands of the clock said four a.m.

"I am committing an extravagance"—Rudolf's energetic voice came clearly over the wire—"but who can blame me. You sound sleepy. What time is it? . . . Oh, sorry! I counted in the wrong direction. What an extraordinary connection this is, I can hear you breathing! . . . Yes, a marvelous time. I've got to come back here, for longer. I am going to force you to come and see for yourself. We'll hire a sitter for Marmalade if necessary. Or if Paul takes a job in New York, he might . . . What? He is? Oh, good. I told him he should look in on you. Let me speak to him. . . . What? Oh, typical! Well, go wake the outdoorsman. Tell him a man in Japan wants a word with him."

Liane stumbled through the house and out to the Scotch pine. "Paul! Wake up, Paul!" What a deep sleeper he was. She

knelt and shook him gently by the shoulders. "Paul, dear, wake
up!"

Paul woke up and took her in his arms.

"Paul, your father is on the phone! Rudolf's on the phone."

"He would be!" Paul said. He kissed her long and deeply.

After the call had been completed, Paul led Liane back to the
Scotch pine. "Do you know the last thing he said to me? 'You
two enjoy each other!' "

"He's so innocent!" cried Liane, a bittersweet joy rising in
her veins.

"This will kill him," moaned Paul, covering the trembling
Liane with his body under the canopy of stars.

But of course it did not. Rudolf was one of those people born to
survive, even cheerfully, their own worst sorrows and to build
new lives upon the ruins of their old ones. It took him time to
get over it, but get over it he did. When enough time had passed
for him to think of it philosophically, he even decided the whole
thing had been orchestrated by him, in some subterranean depth
of his psyche, so that he might, after all, attain perfect father-
hood. What more perfect gift to a son than being given the
chance to depose the father?

Rudolf rose to the occasion and did all the necessary things.
Somebody had to do them. He sold the house in the country, got
the divorce, arranged for the Steinway to go into storage. Poor
Liane could not stop bawling and Paul would not see him at all.
Both of them were quite incapacitated by their love and left
everything to him.

Not too long after their marriage, Rudolf returned to Japan
and embarked on a long love affair with that country of so much
beauty and strangeness. He married a Japanese woman of considerable intellect and loveliness and fathered two more children, a girl and a boy. The boy was a prodigy on the violin by

the time he was seven, and Rudolf, on tour, was often asked, "Are you any relation to Izumi Geber?"

But Rudolf would always love Paul the best.

Rudolf Geber played an all-Liszt program to a packed house in New Zealand on the eve of the year 2000. Liszt was "in" again; for almost two decades the world had been in the throes of a flagrant Romantic Revival. Rudolf reversed Liszt's innovation of showing one's profile to the audience: he played the "Dante Sonata" and the "Mephisto Waltz" with his back to the audience, so they could see his fingerwork.

"When a man reaches my age, people aren't interested in his face," he joked afterward, under the midnight skies of high summer in that hemisphere, at the supper of iced champagne and trout held in his honor.

During that last quiet interlude of the "Mephisto" before the storm breaks in a torrent of keys, Rudolf had experienced a moment of ecstasy. There it all is . . . the major and the minor . . . the eternal duality of life . . . the secret places . . . the grandeur of the all-imposing pattern, he thought, not entirely sure whether the words came from his brain or his fingers, or exactly what they meant.

Paul and Liane remained married and lived healthy, ordinary lives. They had no children.

Amanuensis

*J*oylessness. Deadness. *Aridity. Everything coming to a slow, dry stop.*

And on another day, after looking out of the window for an hour, she wrote: *The pond is beginning to freeze around the edges. I am beginning to freeze around the edges.*

And on still another (for she forced herself to honor her work schedule of twenty years): *Nothing.*

Then, as though keeping up the show for an invisible audience who gathered outside her study door each morning to listen for the sound of her electric typewriter, she began copying slyly from books. A passage from *Death in Venice*. The first page of an Isak Dinesen tale. Several pages from Bishop Paget's classic study on the sin of acedia. She typed quickly, in a parody of her old inspired rhythm. Then she would pull the sheet of purloined eloquence from the typewriter and squint at it, willing it to give up its secret of confidence, trying to graft onto herself the feeling of entitlement the other writer had felt when composing this page: the priceless feeling of having the *right* to say . . . precisely what one had said.

Then she gave up that pretense, too, and simply shut the door to her study every morning at nine and sat down in front of the cold machine—a stubborn priestess guarding her altar, even though its flame had gone out.

Outside, in the real world, it was deep winter. Six snowfalls lay, one on top of the other. The trees, sheathed in ice, glittered in the cold sun. The leaves of the rhododendrons she had planted were furled tight as little green cigars. And the pond,

131

the real pond as well as the image she had appropriated to describe the condition of her imagination, was frozen hard and thick.

Her name was Constance LeFevre. Through a combination of violent ambition and single-minded dedication to her talent, she had succeeded in imposing that name on the reading world. When still an undergraduate, she had taken her youth and offered it, without a second thought, to the Great God Art. He had accepted it. Then she began to accrue words that led to pages of what she determined would be a memorable first impression: a saga, based vaguely on her own family, Huguenots who had settled in an upstate New York village in the seventeenth century. From the beginning Constance had the knack of keeping one eye on her own soul and the other on the world's soul, and what resulted was a hefty novel of six hundred pages in which the reader was allowed intimate and detailed knowledge of how a family rose to financial and social and moral power, then fell again. A story the world never tires of. The world was pleased. And Constance had also managed to please herself: she had used this book, as she was to use most of her books, to further or balance her inner life. When she was twenty, her most pressing need was to discover who she was; but whereas the ordinary twenty-year-old would have focused unhesitatingly on the navel, Constance hesitated . . . for she wanted to be extraordinary . . . and then chose to use a panoply of "historical" characters to play out the drama going on in herself, where deep religious impulse warred with an attraction to frivolity, arrogance with self-doubt, a desire to be famous—notoriously famous—with the opposite desire for a private peace. Constance knew very little about her real ancestors, except for the village where they had settled. She went to that village and haunted the local Historical Society, presided over by little old ladies with old names (one of them was also a LeFevre, but from a "better" branch); Constance didn't need much, all she needed was some convincing underpinning for the saga she would build from her imagination's needs. The most memorable characters came not out of the Historical Society's files but out of Constance's head. She labored over it, this first work of hers; she wrote and rewrote; she was a stickler for details. When the "ancestor" who had made the "family fortune" began to build his fine house, Constance sought out a young architect in the village and asked him to go through the crumbling but haughtily proportioned ruin built by one Augustin DePuy in the 1760s and tell her exactly how such a house was constructed, nail by nail, plank by plank, stone by stone. The architect fell in love with Constance's masculine mind and feminine charm. Her saga came out when she was twenty-three and enjoyed exceptional success for a first novel. Movie rights were purchased, enabling Constance to buy the old DePuy ruin and adjoining acreage; and when she returned, frustrated, from Hollywood a year later, after writing the screenplay that would never be needed, she married her architect, who had created out of the old ruin the exact house built by her character in her book.

Her second book was pure fantasy. It was the kind of story her working-class parents (the "fallen" LeFevres) had neither the invention nor the time to tell her when she was a child; it was the kind of story she planned to read to her own child, as soon as it got out of the womb and became old enough to appreciate it.

Her third novel was a disillusioned account of a failed marriage and all its miscarried hopes (metaphor for Constance's lost child). It was a bit downbeat, but it restored her public's faith. They had found the "fantasy" rather cloying and self-congratulatory. This new novel spoke of the dull kind of suffering they themselves underwent daily; it did well, well enough for Constance to cash her royalties in time to purchase a round-the-world-cruise ticket for her thirtieth birthday.

The ship visited twenty-two ports. Constance talked to many passengers and crew and slept with some of them. She kept exhaustive notes. What interested her at this point in her life was the otherness of other people. She wanted to get out of herself—it was too uncomfortable being in oneself—and be able to slip into the bodies and thoughts of others, speak as they spoke, want what they wanted. She wanted to put as much distance between her writing self (which, through all, had functioned splendidly) and the self that cringed with guilt and sorrow.

Her *Ports of Folly* was proclaimed a tour de force: twenty-two people told their stories and confessed their guilts in twenty-two chapters, each labeled with the name of an exotic port. "A modern *Decameron* in which the plague is the twentieth century," wrote one reviewer.

The next few years of Constance's life sped by in a blur of twenty-pound bond sheets with carbon copies. Her love affairs, her night fears, her social life, even her writing life, she fed back into the jaws of Art, often before the experiences registered fully on her own emotions. When at thirty-five she found a dead-white patch lurking beneath the glossy dark hair on the right side of her head, she covered it over hurriedly and sat down at her typewriter and began to compose *Second Thoughts*, a novel about a playwright who wakes up one day and realizes he has fed the entire first half of his life into his art and is completely drained of all memory and feeling. She produced four hundred pages of this novel and then, suddenly sickened by it, put it away in a drawer.

One of the little old ladies in the village's upper-crust Historical Society passed away. Constance was asked to take her place. Her family's ignominious descent into poverty and ordinariness had been redeemed by her own reputation, and newcomers to the village were told by the little old ladies that Constance lived in the imposing stone house of her *other* ancestor, the grand merchant-statesman Augustin DePuy. Constance accepted the invitation to join the Historical Society. Her new duties gave her a deep satisfaction. The very boredom of having to donate one whole afternoon of her life every week to dressing nicely and sitting behind a table with fresh flowers and asking people to be sure to sign the visitors' book appealed to her. It was healthy, traditional, this once-a-week, unselfish foray into community life. But eventually she got restless, especially when

a whole afternoon would creak by without a single visitor, and
she began to rifle the old records and files, where she pounced
one afternoon on the material for a sensational short novel that,
if she drove herself, would coincide with the bicentennial. *Kull's
Kill* was written in a six-week burst of energy. It related in a
cool raconteur's voice the depraved, incestuous story of an
eighteenth-century Dutch immigrant and his daughter and was
brought out in the spring of the bicentennial. Reporters drove
up the Thruway to the little village (which was not so little anymore since the state university had opened a large branch there)
and trudged through still-frozen fields to photograph the little
kill, or stream, where poor "Kitty Kull" in sadistic mirth had
induced her father-lover to bash her head in; then they went
down to the Historical Society and photographed the author in
pre-Revolutionary costume and frilly white cap sitting de-
murely behind the desk and extending the visitors' book. Afterward they went through the files—which were, after all, open to
the public—and Xeroxed the old document that revealed the
true name of "Johannes Kull." When *Kull's Kill* became a
best-seller (Constance's first), a magazine did a feature on the
historical-novel boom: across from a close-up of Constance was a
little inset of Jonas Kip's hair-raising confession, preserved in
the photostated diary of the judge who had sentenced him to be
hanged. The little old lady who was a direct descendant of the
unfortunate Kip bore up stoically; she did not, as several other
Society members did, cut Constance dead in the supermarket.
Constance resigned from the Society, pleading pressing engagements, before they could ask her to quit. She felt a bit queasy
about the whole thing, as if she had soiled her own nest. If only
she hadn't been so desperate to get another novel out, before her
public forgot her! Now her public loved her more than ever,
whereas she despised it a little, for having granted to her most
vulgar work the popularity she had so long craved. Could it be
that, for almost twenty years, she had been courting with all the
wiles of her sensitivity a lover with a heavy, insensitive soul?

As soon as the Old Guard dropped Constance, the new
local branch of the state university picked her up. She had

snubbed its English Department when, several years before, it had approached her about teaching a Creative Writing Seminar. (Was she, Constance LeFevre, expected to appear in a catalogue that listed such "courses" as "Human Relations" and "Oral Communications" as fully accredited academic subjects?!) But now her pride was assuaged when she was invited to give the annual Rose Verplanck Memorial Lecture to the Humanities Department. She worked hard on her lecture and even drove down to New York and bought a new dress for the occasion.

A by-product of Constance's lecture was her brief affair with an associate professor in the English Department named Alan Insel. Almost as soon as she was fully into it, she realized her error in judgment. But then it took her several months to get out of it again because he had made himself so indispensable to her comforts and her vanity. Insel was an affable sort of failure who had managed to erect a civilized edifice around his short-comings. He courted Constance with formal deference. He let her know that he *knew* her financial and professional successes were far, far above *his*. He had tried and tried to get his novels published, he told her, in an amused tone of voice, as though laughing at himself, but he just hadn't been as lucky in his subject matter as she, and also, he didn't have her *technique*. But still, he let her know, there were a few points of good living he might be able to share with her, a few serendipitous delicacies she might, in her single-minded pursuit of her craft, have overlooked. He drove her, as if she were a princess, across the bridge in his renovated old brown Jaguar and bought her violets from a greenhouse in January; he always had tickets for interesting productions of rare Ibsen or Pirandello; he belonged to a local vineyard cooperative, and his wine bottles bore his own signature in gold on their pretty labels; he told her she was burning the wrong woods in her massive stone fireplace and arranged with his "man" to deliver two cords of the proper ones in early spring, "so the logs will have the whole summer to season." He liked words like *season* and *subtle* and *sensual*. When they went to bed together, he made it a point of honor never to be obvious or predictable. She never knew quite what he was going to do, but the result was ... inevitably ... satisfactory in a languid, *soothing* way. She could let herself go with him precisely because he didn't matter, but also there was something rather demonic and awful about the way his pale and oddly heavy limbs engulfed her and serviced her while his thin, satiric face gleamed at her in a curious, cold complicity.

And then, abruptly, she woke up beside him in her own bed one early spring morning and knew she loathed him and couldn't wait to get him out of the house. She felt guilty, but guilty in the way one feels guilty when about to discommode some clinging slug that has managed to attach itself to one's arm or leg. She allowed him to make their breakfast—he was an eggs Benedict and Bloody Mary man—and, cringing from him more by the minute, she sat across from him in Augustin DePuy's rustic-beamed old kitchen, whose tiny windows her architect/ex-husband had enlarged to let the morning sun in, and she allowed Insel to go on, one last time, in his snug "lecturing" voice, about how she, Constance, had been "lucky in her subject matter" and had mastered her "technique." "Now, if I had your *technique*," he said, licking a tiny drop of egg yolk from where it had fallen on his finger, "I'd be able to fly us both to Aruba ... did you see that marvelous color ad in the last *New Yorker*, the one with the Updike story ... now, *his* technique ..." And Constance, steeling herself for the strike, told him she had already been to Aruba—it was, if he recalled, the first port of call in her *Ports of Folly*. "But I must correct you, Alan, on one point," she went on, her voice dropping to a dangerous earnestness. "When you talk about technique, I think you are confusing it with talent. The two are not the same."

Several days later he sent her, inside an envelope, a postcard of Gustav Klimt's *The Kiss*. "All relationships need their breathing spells," he had typed neatly on the back. "Perhaps you ought to call me when you feel ready to see me again." At least he was tactful. He had let her off the hook and preserved his own pride in the bargain. Once or twice in the next few weeks she was tempted to call him, when she felt like sharing the leisurely courses of a gourmet meal ... or when she felt in need of oblivion, combined with caresses and flattery. I am too isolated, she told herself, I need to get out more; I would never have stooped to this "relationship"—how I loathe that word— had I not been too long alone all those months I was trying to write that wretched novel about the playwright who offered his youth to Art. And then, on top of that, when the old ladies snubbed me, that hurt, too; being loved and accepted by individual, discerning people in my everyday orbit is important to me; some dumb, anonymous mass that manifests itself in numbers of copies sold is not enough. No, I was at a particularly vulnerable juncture in my life when I took up with Associate Professor Insel, with his talk of "technique." Of course, I wasn't writing. A nonwriting Constance LeFevre is a damned Constance LeFevre, and Alan Insel was my Satan Incarnate.

And then, providentially, the State Department invited Constance to go to South America for the entire month of May. They made up a killing itinerary for her—she was to speak on "Current Fiction in the United States" in fourteen cities—and she accepted with alacrity. The trip proved exhausting, not only physically but in a curious spiritual way as well, and Constance returned feeling old and rather knocked out by life, to her Dutch-and-Huguenot-settled village in early June. Sifting through the big cardboard box of mail the post office had saved for her, she plucked out a brief, urbane note from Insel, saying that he had tried to phone her to say good-bye before he left to spend the summer in Greece.

Good riddance! thought Constance, and now I must really get back to what matters. It had been over a year since *Kull's Kill* had been published and, except for a few desultory short stories, the kind she could write with the upper half of her mind, she had not been able to get into anything that lodged at the center of her inner necessities.

She completely forgot Alan Insel.

She withdrew into herself all through that summer and into the autumn and early winter; she saw no one except for a harmless old college friend who came to visit but spent most of her time commuting to New York City for trysts with a married man. After some false starts, Constance got out all her South American notes and the State Department itineraries and began a novel about a successful American businesswoman destined to have a breakdown in Brazil. At first it went splendidly; she clocked herself at ten-page intervals and scribbled calculations: if she kept up this momentum she would be done with the book by spring! The more she thought about it, the more the idea of this novel pleased her: it was exactly right for where she was, both professionally and psychologically; it would be big and re-alistic and modern, to counterbalance the dark little romance of *Kull's Kill* in her public's eye; and it would be a way of averting her own "midlife crisis" (hateful term!) by foisting it more prof-itably on an interesting, high-powered woman character. Much more satisfactory than dealing at one remove from her sex with that tiresome male playwright character. The business angle of her new novel fascinated her. She had not done so much re-search since her Huguenot saga . . . could that really have been twenty years ago? She read up on multinationals, subscribed to three financial magazines, and sat down happily on the floor every Sunday and clipped articles from the *Times* Business Section, which formerly she had dropped, along with Sports, in the wire trash bin outside the village drugstore, to keep from weighing her bicycle down.

And then, mysteriously, without any warning, her novel died on her. She knew the signs: the sickening reluctance to begin in the mornings; the dull, heavy joylessness that spread like a greasy film over the world; the feeling that some connec-tion had been severed between herself and the book. It was ir-revocable, she knew. She had not been so sad since she had miscarried . . . could that have been fifteen years ago?

She mourned the book. She sat in her study and gazed blankly out at a world growing more still and frozen by the day and wondered, without much interest or emotion, what would happen to her next. A few days would go by and then she would be granted a flicker of false hope: where was her courage? She must just start something new—perhaps a story, something quickly finished, to give her back her confidence. Just type a sentence into the machine, see where it led, make a story from it (after all, she was Constance LeFevre, who had made her name from storytelling). "Once there was a spy," she typed, "who did not think of himself as a spy, but simply as a boy who had lost his parents and was good with languages. . . ."

And that was the end of that. Then came the short, despairing, journal-type ejaculations. And then the copying from the works of others. And then a silent Constance tending her cold altar of a typewriter, whose mechanical carriage had gone sluggish after not being turned on in weeks. Constance, barred from her Art; which returns us to the deep-winter morning on which this tale began.

Someone was knocking at the front door. The only people who used Constance's front door were the Jehovah's Witness lady with her little retarded girl and the United Parcel man bringing another bound galley of another first novel with the respectful editor's note clipped to the cover: "Just a few words from you would be of inestimable . . ."

Nonetheless, at the sound of that knock Constance sprang from her typing chair with shameful relief.

It was a young girl, slim and pretty in a piquant sort of way, with a pert face that looked like an acorn under the brown knitted cap pulled down over her ears. She wore a ratty full-length fox fur that must have been some woman's pride and joy in the 1930s, and heavy, round-toed boots like a man's.

"Yes?" said Constance. She saw a dilapidated old car parked in her circular drive.

"I was wondering if I could speak with you for a minute," said the girl, giving Constance a sudden, disarming smile. "I'm not selling anything, I promise. I'm . . . well . . . I'm offering something for free."

"Would you like to come in?" Constance could tell from the smile that the girl thought highly of herself, that she was more often asked into places than not, and that even if Constance had turned her away she would have gone on thinking highly of herself.

"Thank you," the girl said, bestowing another smile on Constance. She had small, sturdy white teeth with little spaces between them. She thrust her cold, firm hand into Constance's as she gave her big boots one last stomp on the doormat. "My name is Jesse Newbold."

"How do you do," said Constance, already impressed by the girl's precise, confident manner. She closed the door on the cold. "Mine is Constance LeFevre."

"Oh, I know who *you* are," said Jesse solemnly. "That's why I finally got up my courage to come over here. Wow, is that some fireplace!"

"The house is over two hundred years old. It's all been done over, of course. It was a ruin when we . . . I . . . Won't you sit down?" Constance sat down first on the roomy sofa and patted a place beside her. How nice this room is, she thought. Her glance passed with fresh appreciation over the massive dark-stained beams, the walls of creamy yellow, the framed drawings and old maps, the ceiling-high shelves crammed with books. It had been weeks since she had sat in this room. The impatiens plant, she noticed, had a whole sheaf of new pink buds. "Now, do tell me what it is you're offering me."

"Well," said Jesse, sitting erectly on the edge of the sofa and shrugging halfway out of the shabby fox coat, "I'm offering myself."

Under the coat she wore a long blue cotton dress sprigged with white flowers. She raised her eyes, which were the same blue as the dress, to meet Constance's puzzled look. Then, as if taking the lid off her proffered gift package, she snatched away her knitted cap. Two short brown-gold clumps of young hair fell neatly to either side of her innocent yet artful face. For a third time, Constance received the charming smile.

"But . . . I don't understand," said Constance. "You mean as a cleaning girl, or what?" She had tried several girls from the college in this capacity, but they had never worked out.

"Cleaning, if you want. Cooking, typing, fending off fans, answering letters—whatever you need. I have come to offer myself as your amanuensis," said Jesse, putting a musical lilt into the old-fashioned word. "And I wouldn't charge a penny!"

"But why?" asked Constance, who was a firm believer in the adage *nobody gets something for nothing.* "I mean, what would you get out of it?"

"Everything!" the girl exclaimed passionately, and Constance was reminded poignantly of her own younger self and how fiercely that self had wanted things. "I'll get to see how you work, how you live. . . . I'll have the satisfaction of knowing I'm freeing you from having to deal with . . . the stuff you've earned the right, through your talent, not to *have* to deal with!"

This part was probably rehearsed, thought Constance.

"Do you . . . um . . . write, yourself?" she asked, feeling depressed at the possibility that this persuasive, charming creature might write terrible prose.

"Oh, I know, I know what you're thinking," said Jesse, massaging the wool cap in her hands. "But you needn't worry, Miss LeFevre. If you'll just give me a chance, I promise you'll never be burdened by *my* paltry efforts. I've come here to relieve your burdens, not add to them."

"But . . . I don't know, Jesse . . . and please call me Constance . . . I really don't know if there's enough for you to do. Since I lost my last maid, I just run a dustcloth over things once a week, when I water the plants. . . . I've never been obsessive about housekeeping . . . how many hours a week did you have in mind?"

"As many or as few as you need," explained the smiling girl. "Let me explain. You see, I'm only taking one course this semester, Earth Science. I have to have one science course before I can transfer . . . I want to transfer to another college. . . . I've got all I can get from these people here. And . . . well . . . I hate wasting time, and since I think you're a great writer and that's what I want to be eventually, how could I spend my time any better than being around you, seeing how you do it? I don't mean I'd be snooping over your shoulder or anything, but I could sort of observe your rhythms, maybe pick up some of your discipline by osmosis."

"I couldn't possibly let you work for nothing," Constance said, "I'd feel so guilty about exploiting you, *I* couldn't work." As soon as she pronounced this lie about her own "work," the impotence of her predicament hit her anew with the force of a physical blow. She found herself dreading the moment her bright visitor would get up to go. "I would insist on paying you," she added severely. As an incentive, she added, "In cash, of course. So there wouldn't be any income tax problem."

"I'll accept whatever you say," replied Jesse. "You can make all the rules. That's the point, too, you know. I can see what rules you *will* make and be educated by that, too. I will get to observe at close hand the mental processes of a successful woman."

Constance waved this last effusion aside. "Shall we say three-fifty an hour, starting tomorrow? Come about this time? I like to have the first hours of the morning for my—" She made a gesture with her hand, rather than pronounce the lie again.

Engagingly, the girl caught Constance's hand and pressed it warmly in both of hers. "I'm thrilled!" she cried.

They smiled at each other with the joy of mutual discovery.

"By the way," said Constance, "how old are you?"

"Almost twenty," said Jesse.

"Ah, twenty was when it all began for me," said Constance with a sigh.

Constance spent the rest of that day walking around her house, seeing her life as the girl—Jesse—must see it. From the girl's view, it must look enviable. She turned over certain of Jesse's phrases with the relish she remembered from certain of her rave reviews.

That evening, Constance rearranged her study. On one table she put all her unanswered mail: the many magazines and journals still in their brown wrappers, the piles of bound galley proofs of other people's novels, with the respectful editors' notes clipped to the covers . . . yes, anyone could see from that table that Constance LeFevre was in demand. Yet, over the last frozen months, it had been all she could do to weed out the bills from the mass of correspondence and make sure they were paid on time.

She took a fresh manila file folder and wrote in large Magic Marker letters on the front: WORK IN PROGRESS, though she had never done such a thing before in her life. She put the folder, with a dozen or so sheets of yellow paper inside, to the left of her typewriter.

Then she turned on the machine and sat in front of it for a while, listening to its hum, smiling bemusedly at her lamplit reflection on the dark glass of the windowpane.

The girl was, as ladies are fond of saying about their good servants, "a gem." Not that Jesse was a mere "servant." Rather, she made you go back and reexamine the nobler uses of the verb *to serve*. Jesse served Constance. Not only that, she had the tact of one's own shadow. She fitted her movements to Constance's; Constance had been often annoyed by cleaning girls and women for no other reason than that they impinged on her space. Jesse had arrived promptly at ten-thirty on her first day. Constance heard the old car drive up, but it had been agreed the day before that Jesse would let herself in. With an uplifted mood, Constance, in her study, heard the girl take off the heavy boots and begin padding softly about the downstairs rooms. The spraying of furniture polish. The thud-*thump*, thud-*thump* of the sponge mop. Constance, in a burst of greeting, had let loose a barrage of sentences on her spy story, which she had resumed in order to pretend she was writing something. Thus the morning passed . . . thud-*thump* from downstairs . . . an answering *rackety-rackety-rack* from upstairs: like a dialogue between them.

At a little past noon, delicious lunch odors wafted upstairs.

"How did you know I adore mushroom soup?" Constance called, coming downstairs. "Mmm! Is that grilled cheese?"

"The soup was in your cabinet," said Jesse, turning to smile at Constance from her station at the stove. Today she wore a long dress of a modest squirrel-gray, with tiny pearl buttons all the way down the front, and one of Constance's old aprons tied tightly around her small waist. "And I always treat myself to a grilled-cheese sandwich when I'm in the midst of exams."

The table was laid with an indigo cloth Constance had forgotten she had. In a bud vase, Jesse had placed a cutting of the blooming impatiens. The vivid splash of fuchsia against the deep blue cloth gave Constance pleasure. "But the table's only set for one, Jesse, aren't you having anything?"

"Oh, I can get something for myself later. I thought you might like to be alone with your thoughts."

"I'd much rather eat with you," said Constance.

"In that case," replied Jesse, her pert face coloring slightly with embarrassment or delight (Constance wasn't sure which), "I'd love to."

"Are your parents alive?" Constance asked delicately, when they were having their soup. She was dying to find out more about her amanuensis.

"Yes, but they've been divorced ever since I can remember. I've always lived with my mother. She works for a dental surgeon in Queens. She's not a very happy person. My father conducts these archaeological digs. For amateurs. You've probably heard of them. Not that *he's* an amateur. He just likes to be out in the field any way he can." Jesse volunteered all this smoothly, rather glibly, as though she'd come to terms with her parents ages ago.

"And do you see much of your father?"

"Not too much," said Jesse, spooning her soup thoughtfully. "Once in a while. But we get along. He lives with someone not much older than me. She and I get along okay. Would you like more mushroom soup?"

Constance watched the girl's lithe gray-clad figure at the stove. I am old enough to be her mother, she thought. What would it have been like, to have had her all these years? Would I be what I am? Would she be as she is? Would she say, when discussing me with others, "She's not a very happy person"?

The two women soon settled into a routine. Jesse came, for five hours, on Mondays, Wednesdays, and Fridays. (Tuesdays and Thursdays were Earth Science days.) She cleaned a bit and prepared lunch. The lunches were always simple but comforting, the sort of food children might fix if the meals were left to them—sardines on toast; canned soups; bacon, lettuce, and tomato sandwiches—but Constance had not enjoyed her food so much in months. After lunch, they went to Constance's study and tackled the correspondence. Constance had been an antisocial "author" in the past, throwing in the wastebasket anything that did not directly further her career. Now, for Jesse's benefit, she found herself filling in the ballots for PEN elections, answering the questionnaires the Author's Guild was always sending about contracts, reprint rights, and so on; she dictated a brief but individual reply to every fan letter, every request to speak or teach at a college. When the correspondence table began to look threateningly bare, Constance resorted to the stacks of bound galleys of other people's novels. The publication dates had already come and gone for many of them. Of the ones still to come, Constance made two piles: the "trashy at a glance" and the "possible." For the "trashy at a glance," she dictated caustic or amusing notes designed either to instruct Jesse that one couldn't be too careful about one's integrity or simply to make the girl snort with laughter. She decided to test her protégée's budding literary acumen on the "possible" ones.

"I just don't have time to read these," she told Jesse. "Why not take one or two of these *deserving*-looking ones home with you. No big deal. Skim through them if you feel like it, scribble something if they strike a chord."

The poor girl turned pale when Constance suggested this. But then she squared her shoulders and said she'd try. Off went the galleys, under the arm of her ratty fox coat, at the end of the day; they were returned in two days' time with neatly typed notes stapled to their covers. A bit labored, thought Constance. Of course she was trying to impress me. To please Jesse, she selected the least pretentious of the girl's critiques, changed a few adjectives, and told Jesse to send it off to the publisher over the signature of Constance LeFevre. The girl seemed mildly surprised, though not as flattered as Constance would have hoped. My pretty little acorn is not an easy nut to crack, thought Constance, her curiosity piqued more each day by Jesse Newbold.

In mid-February, Constance came down with the flu. As soon as she complained of sore throat and feverishness, Jesse made her take her temperature. 102°. "Why don't I sleep over for a few days," suggested Jesse. "You go to bed and pamper yourself."

"Dear child, you can't devote your life to me," protested Constance weakly, though the idea appealed to her.

"Who said anything about life? I'll just go and pick up a few things from my place. It'll be fun for me to sleep in a two-hundred-year-old house."

Thus Constance abandoned herself to the process of her illness. She lay under her satin comforter and felt helpless and cherished. Jesse made tea and soup, lowered the shades, raised them again, ran up and down the stairs bringing Constance books she asked for. Then off the girl would go, to her Earth Science lab, to the supermarket for more cans of soup, to the drugstore for more throat lozenges and Kleenex, and Constance would lie watching the light change outside the window. Already the darkness was that of very early spring, not winter darkness anymore. In one of the panes of glass was a tiny crack that winked like a diamond. Constance lay with a book propped open on her knees, not reading but listening to the silence, waiting for the rattling sound of the old car churning its way back up the icy drive. Her thoughts—perhaps colored by her fever—turned to her old age and eventual death. Was there any sort of afterlife of the consciousness, or did you live on only through the minds of others? What others? Would any of her books outlive her? Which ones? She imagined herself leaving this house to Jesse in her will. She envisioned an elegant little memoir, published some years after her death, in which Jesse, by then an old lady herself, would tell what it had been like to live with Constance LeFevre on a day-to-day basis. She only hoped Jesse could write well enough to do justice to the material. So far, except for the "book reports," Constance had seen none of Jesse's writing. But then, the girl had vowed not to burden her with any "paltry efforts."

"You'd make a great nurse, Jesse," said Constance, who by this time was merely luxuriating in sniffles. "That is, if you didn't want to be a writer. Speaking of which . . . don't you think it's time you showed me something? You must let me help you if I can. Turnabout's fair play." For Jesse had refused, absolutely, to accept one penny for nursing Constance.

"I . . . I don't really have anything ready at the moment," stammered the girl.

"Well," pursued Constance, "show me something that's not. Maybe something you're having problems with."

"I'll see what I can come up with," said Jesse, after going very quiet for several minutes.

That night Constance dreamed Jesse was in her room, down at the other end of the hall, writing a story for her. The girl's pen scratched louder and louder, and Constance's sleep grew troubled. So abrasive! What was Jesse writing on? It sounded like a sharp instrument scratching on stone.

Constance woke up. She could still hear the repetitive scratching . . . only, it was coming from outside. She got out of bed and went to the window and pulled back the shade. A full moon gave the snowy landscape an eerie daylight quality. The amanuensis was skating on the frozen pond. Round and round, shoulders hunched forward, hands clasped behind her back. Constance could not make out her face under the knitted cap, but there was an intensity to her skating, as if she were working out her thoughts in the rhythm of it. I'd give anything to know what she is thinking, Constance thought. For one degrading moment, she was tempted to whisk down the hall to Jesse's room and go through her things. Maybe she kept a journal. Constance's heart pounded guiltily as a culprit's. No, that's not fair, she decided, perhaps she'll let me in on her life through the story she's promised to bring me. Constance went back to bed and sat in the dark, her hands laced tightly together, listening to the girl's skates cut and recut into the frozen pond.

Alas, the story Jesse brought was a disappointment. Although competently written, even with skill in places, it was weary and flat. It was about an older man, alone in some tropical climate, self-importantly reviewing his past. Also it seemed he had lost a woman, though Constance wasn't sure whether she had left him or died. Oh, poor girl, thought Constance. But I asked for it and now I must be encouraging and also very, very careful. The man is undoubtedly Jesse's attempt to "get into" her father, the distant archaeologist; she's dispensed with the father's girlfriend, I see. Besides . . . Jesse is only twenty . . . I don't want to nip any later-blooming talent in the bud. Just because I was such a ruthless, early-blooming little go-getter . . . and yet, never once in my young nights did I skate on a frozen pond in the moonlight.

"Jesse, I think it's terribly brave of you to write a story from the point of view of a man . . . and a person of an older generation, as well."

"You do?"

"Yes. And the prose is tight. Well, usually. You probably worked hard on this."

The girl blushed.

"It's an arduous business we've chosen, Jesse. I once spent four hundred pages trying to raise a character from the dead, and failed. What I'm trying to say, my dear, is—" Constance stopped. The girl's face was working in a woeful, rubbery attempt to keep back tears.

"Please," whispered Jesse, "don't call me 'dear.' "

"I'm sorry. But I didn't mean it as an affectation. You are dear to me." Now it was Constance's turn to blush.

"I'm nothing," said Jesse between her teeth, her eyes brimming. "I'm a piece of shit."

"But, Jesse, the story isn't that bad. My God, you're just

beginning. And it has a certain"—she groped for a word and found only the hated evasion Insel had used—"it has a certain tech*nique*. . . ."

"Oh, I don't give a damn about the story!" shrieked Jesse. She dashed out of Constance's study, sobbing. Constance listened to her running down the hall to her room. The door slammed. Constance realized with a strange lift of heart that if Jesse were her own daughter they might be having a scene just like this. I don't give a damn about the story, either, thought Constance. I give a damn about *her*.

At the beginning of March, Jesse insisted on moving back to her own place. "I'll miss having you in the house," Constance told her, trying to be brave, "but of course you must have your own life. I'll be all the more glad to see you on Monday, Wednesday, and Friday. And who knows, maybe next year . . . I've been thinking . . . if I knew I had someone responsible to stay in the house, I might travel a bit. I've decided I don't really get out enough."

"My plans are so uncertain," murmured the girl.

"Yes, I know. You said you might transfer. But if your new college is in easy distance, you might like to come here for weekends, or for the long vacations. You don't have to decide now. I just want you to know it's an option."

"You're great," said Jesse, but rather dispiritedly, Constance thought.

Since the day of the outburst, neither of them had mentioned the story again. Jesse arrived at the house promptly on her three working days, worked as well as, or even better than, before. Her demeanor had become more subdued and the little acorn face did not smile so readily, but she treated Constance in a new and tender way, with even more attentiveness than when she had had the flu: she asked Constance's advice about her clothes, about books she ought to read; she bought Constance a red carnation and put it in a vase in her study. One afternoon

Constance had to go to the dentist in a sleet storm; when she arrived home, she found a blazing fire in a big stone fireplace and Jesse had stayed late to prepare an "English tea" for them both. It was as if, thought Constance in bed one night, the tears springing to her eyes, the girl were making amends through these extra attentions for her lack of talent.

It was the end of March. The snow still lay on the ground, but there were hopeful patches of raw earth. Constance, up in her study, was feeling good. She could hear the drip, drip of melting snow from the gutters outside, and from downstairs were beginning to emanate the signs of one of Jesse's comforting lunches. How nice *just being* is, thought Constance, listening to the girl clattering about in the kitchen. She responded via her typewriter with some clatter of her own, to keep up the dialogue. For, although the "spy story" was by this time quite long, Constance knew it was not a real story: it was to convince Jesse that she was upstairs plying her Art; it was to give Jesse her reason for being *downstairs*.

A door slammed. A car started up. What had the girl forgotten this time? The child might not be the world's next Jane Austen, but she was a perfectionist when it came to her luncheon productions. Once before, she had rushed out at the last minute to purchase capers.

Constance decided to sneak down and see what was cooking. The table was covered with a clean cloth. In a small porcelain vase was the year's first crocus. On Constance's plate—she had already noticed with alarm that the table was set for one—was an envelope.

Constance picked up the knife beside her plate and slit open the envelope.

"Dear Constance," it said (it was the first time she had seen the girl's handwriting, wobbly and uneven like a much younger person's), "Clam chowder on LOW. Bologna sandwich in fridge. I can't keep this up anymore. You are a really good lady and I can't take any more advantage of you. Please don't try to find me, you have better things to do with your time, and besides, you won't. There is no 'Jesse Newbold.' "

She had first tried to sign herself "Your Amanuensis," but after several spelling mistakes settled for "Your Friend."

Nevertheless, Constance did try to find her. She went to all three instructors of the six sections of Earth Science at the college and described Jesse's appearance and her clothes. "You don't know her name?" they asked, wondering what this harassed woman was up to. "If you'd let me see your class lists, perhaps I could recognize it." Constance pored over girls' names on computer printouts, pouncing on the smallest clue. "How about this Jane Newburg?" she said excitedly. "No, Janie's a special student. She comes in a wheelchair."

Constance made a nuisance of herself at the registrar's office: more lists of names; Constance finally confiding in the registrar. "You might try the police," said the woman, "but otherwise ... well, frankly, you have so little to go on. Do you know how many students drop in and out of school these days like a country club? Your young secretary may be in California by now."

Constance phoned her researcher, a young man in New York who sometimes looked up things in the library for her; she asked him to call the offices of all the dental surgeons in Queens and find out if any woman who worked for them had a daughter of about twenty enrolled in this branch of the state university. But after a few days, he phoned back and said a lot of the women were suspicious and wouldn't answer until they knew why he was calling. "They're perfectly right," said Constance, suddenly seeing it from their side, and she told the young man to drop the research and how much did she owe him.

Please don't try to find me, you have better things to do with your time, and besides, you won't.

"Okay, Jesse, you win," said Constance aloud, pacing the rooms of the big old house, finding something in every room that reminded her of her vanished amanuensis. "You came out of nowhere and now you've gone back into it again." She stood looking at the bed, which Jesse herself had stripped down to the mattress, then covered neatly with a spread, when she had vacated the room. "You were a gift, and one has no right to report a vanished gift to the police."

The house began to seem like a mausoleum to her. She saw the years stretch out before her; she squinted at herself in the mirror and saw how she would be ten years from now, twenty, thirty. She saw herself as an old woman, dying alone in this house.

She telephoned her architect ex-husband, who had remarried and was living in the next village over. When they split up, she promised him she would let him know before she ever put this house on the market.

He came by that afternoon, bringing with him his small son, who was a little afraid of Constance. He had aged well, her former husband: a slim, wiry man with shaggy gray hair and, behind his steel-rimmed spectacles, a look of earnest absorption, as though he were making a constant effort to work out a floor plan of the world. Now that he belonged safely to another woman, Constance found him attractive again.

"You really mean to sell?" he asked. "Somehow I pictured you hanging on here to the very end."

"Thank you." Constance laughed dryly. "I've just pictured it myself and it's that fate I want to avoid."

"But where will you go? Donny, please don't play with those fire tongs."

"I have decided," announced Constance with significance, "to go *out*."

"Out," he echoed testily, as he had done frequently during their marriage, playing back to Constance the last words of her more ambiguous statements.

"I mean out into the world. Just to live in it. With no ulterior motive. Let things and people come and go on their own terms, without my interference, and see where they'll go *to*. I've decided to give myself a sabbatical from achievement."

"But won't you need a home to come back to when your 'sabbatical' is over?" he asked with genial concern.

"This has stopped being my home. It's more like an imposing shell that has begun to cut off my sensations and my oxygen. If you don't want to buy it, I guess I'll put it on the market."

"I always did love this house. You know that. Some of my best ideas went into this house."

"And your wife? Would she live here?"

"Would she! It's been the one bone of contention between us. How I was too soft and didn't fight you for it."

"Your softness is becoming to you," said Constance. "In fact, I think I'm going to develop *my* softness."

"Oh, Con." He laughed, with his old husband's-knowledge of her. "You say that with such *ambition.*"

Constance invested most of the house-money in securities she had learned about during her research for the aborted business-woman-novel. She banked the rest, and bought a yellow Land-Rover, some camping supplies, and traveler's checks, and she set off, with the tremulousness of a young girl, to see what was happening when she didn't interfere. She wanted to catch the outside world off-guard before it froze into her own willed conception of it. She had many adventures, some disappointments, and a few scares. Through it all, she desisted grimly from taking a single note. The active, nomadic life toughened her body and detached her mind—for a while. Then she felt she had proved her point. She felt restless to make up her own world again. Her year had made her more sensitive to the great ebbs and flows of existence: she resolved to take similar excursions in future, whenever she began to feel frozen or stale; but now, she couldn't wait to put all her fresh impressions into a huge new fiction.

She settled down, this time in a city whose energies kept pace with her own, and began to write again. The juices flowed; crosscurrents sizzled on connection; her vitality had regenerated itself. Could that have been she, poor dried-up husk rattling around in that big old house, cringing prematurely at the prospect of her own death?

It was perfectly clear now: Jesse Newbold, whatever her real name or real purpose, had been Constance's angel of release.

And Constance persisted in believing this, even after the mystery was cleared up. One day she received the bound galleys of a small novel. "Mr. Alan Insel has asked us to send you what we consider a striking first novel," wrote the editor of a second-rate publishing house. "Any comment you would care to give would be of inestimable . . ."

The novel was called *The Amanuensis.*

Constance read the novel. She recognized many things. She recognized the contents of her former medicine cabinet and wastebasket. She recognized the menus. She recognized certain conversations in which her remarks were exaggerated to seem calculating or high-flown. Certain habits and gestures of hers were spotlit in a morbid, obsessive glare. She recognized in the omniscient narrator's weary, self-satisfied voice the same voice in the bad story she had once believed Jesse to have written. She did not recognize the Lesbian encounter in which the lonely and grasping woman writer, in bed with the flu, seduces the reluctant young girl—who has taken this job, secretly, only as an "independent study" with an English professor who was cruelly spurned by the woman after he had been given cause to hope. The professor has decided to teach the woman a lesson in unrequited love.

After the girl mysteriously disappears, the woman is distraught and finally kills herself.

Ah, it was a "striking" novel, all right—but not in the sense of "technique."

When Constance had finished the book, she sat for a long time with her hands folded on her lap. He should have left himself out, she thought; it would have been a much better story if he had left himself and *his* motives out altogether. The story is the girl and the woman: all the necessary reflections and reverberations are contained within *them*. All this clutter about his broken heart and his "revenge" and about how the girl is practically illiterate but needs the one English credit to pass out of two years of college to become an airline stewardess ... that lowers the story to ... just an embarrassing personal reality. If an artist had shaped and refined this material—ah, what he might have made of it. Pity I didn't do it myself. Well, maybe I will someday. Life is long.

And also the woman shouldn't have killed herself: it's much harder to make people live.

She amused herself composing witty and malicious "blurbs" to send to Mr. Insel's editor. She even, for a minute, saw herself suing Insel, but of course that might be exactly what he was hoping for: the advance publicity. So, through herself and through Jesse, he had finally hit on a "lucky subject" and managed to get published.

In the end she opted for silence. Let his impoverished production have its short life, the poor little *clef* (so diligently compiled by Jesse) without its *roman*. Constance had her own work-in-progress and was so religiously grateful it was going well that she could pass up the triumph of having the last word. Why, in a way, she owed Insel thanks. He had, after all, provided her with her angel of release.

Had Jesse gotten the credit, the English credit she had needed for her "independent study"? The ambitious side of Constance wanted her to have got it: she had certainly earned it. But the spiritually concerned side of Constance prayed that the girl had told her shabby professor good-bye and go to hell on the same day she had scrawled her contrite farewell to Constance.

Nevertheless, when Constance flew around the country, or between countries, plying her trade, or sometimes just taking a vacation from achievement, she always looked carefully—and rather wistfully—into the faces of the stewardesses when she entered the planes.

St. John

*S*till stunned from the success of his book, Charles bought a woodland cottage in an upstate community with an artistic reputation and retreated to write his second novel.

The silence of the country surprised him almost as much as his unexpected success. Then, through the silence, especially at night, he began to hear too much: strange exploratory scufflings in last fall's leaves outside the bedroom window; the terrified cry of some animal fleeing from its assailant; a sudden single beep from the burglar alarm in the house of the absent rock singer on the other side of the woods; and, once or twice, a sibilant, rueful sigh that he did not *think* came from him.

Weekdays he worked on the book, learned for the first time the primitive masculine pleasure of chopping wood that would provide his own future warmth, and explored the small village, which combined the bohemian aura of the arts colony it had been in the 1920s and '30s with the hippie style it had picked up in the '60s. On weekends he was visited faithfully by a woman he had lived with for a while in the city. They would cook and go for hikes and, when he put her on the bus Sunday nights, he always felt sad that he wouldn't miss her more.

One morning, when he was temporarily stuck on the book and had taken time off to answer the latest packet of mail forwarded from his publisher, the phone rang. The handful of city people who had his unlisted number knew better than to call before noon.

Curious, Charles went to answer.

"Sin gin here," said a brisk, throaty female voice. At least that's what Charles thought she said.

"Hello?" repeated Charles.

"Look, I've just had a call for you," the voice went on, in a hearty English accent, distinctly upperclass. "I told him I wasn't the sin gin he wanted, but could possibly contact you, and then it would be up to you whether you wanted to ring him back."

It dawned on Charles that he and the voice on the phone had the same last name, St. John, only she pronounced hers in that funny English way. At the same time, a mystery was cleared up: a village acquaintance had recently congratulated him on his stirring letter to the local paper, and Charles hadn't the least idea what he had meant.

There were two St. Johns in town; and this other one was getting his calls.

"I'm really sorry about this," he apologized to the woman, "I know I hate to be disturbed by wrong numbers."

"Don't mind in the least, darling. Now look: got a pencil handy? Just jot down this number . . ."

As he wrote down the number, another mystery presented itself. "But how did you get my number?"

"Darling, I really *can't* say. But they were only trying to be helpful, you know, and I can assure you it is safe with me. I am always glad to be of help to an artist."

"Well, thank you," he said, more warmly. "But I'm still sorry my call interrupted your morning."

"No trouble, I assure you. But do try to call him back within the hour; he's expecting you. A nice man, he sounded. They want you to come and speak at their university."

After she hung up, Charles looked up his surname in the phone book. There she was: "S. St. John." He wondered what the *S* was for: Susanna? Serena? Sophie? Or something more English, like Samantha. Or Sybil.

Though he had no intention of flying off to speak at universities—he wanted to get on with the new work, not be admired for the one he'd finished several years ago—he did phone the man back at once. He didn't want "S. St. John" to be bothered twice in one morning. Also, he was afraid she might call back and chide him, "Look, darling, that nice man just rang again. . . ."

He dreamed more in his country life. Dense, involved dreams that left him exhausted and haunted by their rich quality of seeming fully as real as his daytime life. They caught him up in the momentum and intensity of their demands.

If his writing life were as prolific as his dream life, his book would be finished in six weeks.

Every day he plodded on, keeping faith with his idea, reminding himself of the doubts and second thoughts that had accompanied his creation of the book that was now a success. Sometimes it seemed to him he was competing with that book, and he almost resented its big, calm, assured presence out there in the world.

He chopped more wood and kept abreast of his mail: he had been brought up to answer his letters promptly. He drove each finished chapter to his typist, and jogged to the village bookstore and back for daily exercise. He had guessed that it was the bookstore couple who had given S. St. John his number (he had given it to them so they could call when books he ordered came in), but he saw no point in saying anything now that it was done.

She phoned again. "Sin gin here. Look, you just had a call from Alaska. They want you for a Midnight Sun Writers' Conference. I told them I couldn't promise I'd reach you immediately, but I was sure you'd ring them as soon as possible. Don't forget the time difference!"

On weekends, the friend from the city inveterately descended from the Trailways bus, and they drank wine in front of the fireplace, where it was chilly enough now to justify using his wood. In bed, surrounded by the mysterious night noises, he was glad of her company, even if it was no great romance on either side.

/ / /

His typist was a conversational man in his sixties. He lived in a tiny cabin atop a steep hill in the woods. He had built the cabin himself and arranged it in such a way that he could stand in the center of its one room and tend the woodstove, reach for a dictionary or thesaurus from the shelf above his bed, cook on his two-burner hotplate, or put the kettle on for tea. He told Charles he had learned the pleasures of constricted space during World War II, when he served as an officer on a destroyer. The cabin had no running water, but the typist took what he needed from a nearby stream. Once a week he bathed in a child's plastic bathtub, heating the water in shifts in the kettle. He had been many things in his life, he told Charles: an actor, a banker, a clown, a radio singer, a journalist, and an English professor. He spoke of his different professions as his "incarnations."

The typist had one peculiarity, which Charles had grown used to: he wore women's clothes while at home in his cabin. The first occasion Charles had trudged up the hill with a chapter, the typist had met him at the door in a denim skirt and a woman's red blouse. Charles shook hands with him as if he had been wearing a three-piece suit; Charles had been brought up that way. The second time, when Charles came to pick up his chapter, the typist, wearing a yellow dress and pearls, offered him tea. As the typist dipped the teabag in first one cup, then the other, he chatted in an appreciative way about Charles's chapter: he had not read Charles's first book because it was never in the library, he told Charles, who was happy that it could not yet come between the typist and this new book.

One day, S. St. John phoned with three messages. "It's that time of year," she told him in a more intimate, conspiratorial voice. "They're all making up the schedules"—she pronounced it "*shed*-ules"—"for their visiting lecturers, so we'll just have to grin and bear it, won't we?" Like an old and trusted secretary, she relayed his messages. Against his better judgment, jut as she was "ringing off," Charles asked her what the *S* stood for.

"Absolutely nothing, darling. The phone company insists one put in a first initial, that's all. *S* was just the first initial that came to mind."

"But ..." Charles waded in further. "I mean ... what should I call you?"

"Bless you, darling. I am known simply as Sin gin."

He restrained himself from asking further about a Christian name. So far, she had been brief in their conversations, in no sense encouraging loquaciousness. He said more formally: "Well, once again, thank you. I really wish this wouldn't happen, but I don't know what I can do about it."

"Not to worry," she assured him. "Actually, I don't always see fit to disturb you. Why, only the other evening a young woman from Santa Fe rang me, wanting you. She had read your book and found out from some magazine piece that you lived here now, and she wanted to talk. I explained that you weren't communicating with anyone except your Muse at the moment, but I would convey her message. She adored your book, said it gave her hope. Poor child, we talked for about an hour. The *contretemps* of some people's lives never cease to amaze me. Well, darling, I didn't mean to make a nuisance of myself. I'll ring off now."

"Do you happen to know a woman in town named St. John?" Charles asked his typist, who, despite his hermit's life, seemed to know a great deal about the village. "She pronounces it 'Sin gin.'"

"Oh, that's Magnus St. John's widow," said the typist. Today he wore the denim skirt and a sweater set, for it was cold. The outfit reminded Charles of a pair of nuns who used to visit his mother sometimes; they had just dispensed with their habits, and wore clothes much like these, and didn't know what to do with their handbags. "The one that writes letters to the paper," the typist said. "I'll bet I know why you ask: you've been getting blamed for the letters." The typist gave a low chuckle. From the neck up, with his hollow cheeks, and erudite gray eyes behind the slipping glasses, and balding gray head, he looked like a kindly professor. Well, he had been a professor in one of his previous incarnations. Charles liked him and looked forward to these visits; perhaps even wrote his chapters faster so there would be more opportunities for these sociable occasions.

The typist dipped the teabag back and forth between the steaming cups. "She's quite mad in her harmless way," he said good-humoredly.

"Who was Magnus St. John?"

"You haven't heard of him? No, I guess not. He was a fairly well-known artist in the thirties. But he had the misfortune to fall between two fashions. He came too late with his Matissean aesthetic, and the abstract expressionists considered him a fuddy-duddy. He died about five years ago. Nobody mentions him much anymore, though he exhibited right up until his death at eighty."

"Eighty! Then she's . . . she must be very old, too." Charles was shocked. The voice had sounded much younger on the phone.

"She was quite a bit younger," mused the typist. "But she's certainly no spring chicken anymore." His voice, with its bass resonances, could have been any man's in a bar, discussing a woman past her prime. Charles had been a baby when his father died, and something about the typist brought out his filial response. He tended to forget, for whole chunks of time, that the man sitting opposite him wore a skirt, blouse, and—yes—perfume (a good one, too). A round mirror hung over the china washbasin on the typist's chest of drawers. Did the typist primp before this mirror when he was alone? Solitude brought out all kinds of things in people. Charles wondered what special predilection waited to suprise *him*, some solitary evening.

"You've been getting blamed for the letter about the sewage proposal, I'll bet," said the typist, crossing a hairy leg. He wore ordinary tennis shoes and white socks.

Charles smiled obliquely. He wasn't sure why he didn't tell about St. John's telephone calls: it made an interesting anecdote. "In what way is she mad?"

"Charles, if you weren't a writer, you would make a first-rate district attorney," the typist teased him. "Though the two occupations go together, don't they? You wouldn't like it if I betrayed one client's confidences to another. I mean, what if another customer came to me and said, 'What is Charles St. John's new book about?' Would you expect me to rattle off the plot?"

"Ah, you type for her, too," said Charles, to whom it had suddenly occurred that St. John—or "Sin gin," as he thought of her—could have got his number from the typist. But hadn't the typist just been telling him how discreet he was? Charles decided to let it go.

"Occasionally," said the typist, looking at Charles over the tops of his glasses. "But now that you've gone and got me to admit it, I shall have to revise myself and say, who *doesn't* exhibit an occasional mad streak in these hills? It's part of the elixir of the place. I mean"—and with a gesture he indicated his outfit—"I frightened a lady clear down the hill the other day. She had phoned and asked if I would type up a list of raffle items for her club, and I said, 'Come right on up, I can do it while you wait.' Well!" He laughed delightedly. "The moment I saw her *hat* crest the hill I knew there would be trouble. I was in the yellow outfit . . . she took one look at me through the screen and gave a little yelp and was off in a cloud of dust."

That was the nearest they ever came to discussing the typist's predilection.

About the time the leaves fell, Charles struck a bad patch. His book reached an impasse. His dreams were wearying and confused. In one dream, his mother—dead now—was accusing him of stealing from her. He awoke in tears from that dream. He had been his mother's favorite child, born late in her life, raised by her after his brother and sister had already married and had families of their own. He switched on the bedside lamp and sat up and tried to understand why his sleeping side would punish him so. Was it because of his success? The successful book? That book, set in another era, the era of his mother's youth, could not have been written without all the stories she had told him over the years. The two of them would be walking down a street in the town and his mother would say: "Do you see that man? When he was in high school, he ran away with the band teacher. His father tracked them down and horsewhipped the man and brought his son home and he's been an exemplary citizen ever since." Then she would laugh in her special way, trying to keep her lips closed because she was sensitive about her slightly protruding teeth. And Charles would look at the red-faced old man duck-footing ahead of them in his wrinkled seersucker suit and try to imagine a boy running off with the band teacher, a man. What would it be like to have a passion for a man? Charles would try to imagine himself into the red-faced man's self—then into the man's younger self. *"Tout comprendre, c'est tout pardonner"* had been one of his mother's favorite maxims. She had come to this town years ago as the schoolteacher; that was when all eight grades were in one room, taught by one teacher. His mother had planned to save her salary for several years and go to France; then she had met his father.

After sitting awake for several hours, Charles realized that his mother would wish him only well, wherever she was; he attributed the dream to some short circuit between his uneasiness about the successful book ("his mother's book") and his difficulties with the new book, in which he was trying to "steal back" some of the flame that had propelled him—not without *its* difficulties—through the first.

Then, one Thursday, his dependable woman friend called from the city and announced she wouldn't be arriving on the Friday-evening bus. After playing it cagey for a moment, she admitted she was getting married.

"But you were here only last weekend," said Charles, baffled more than he was heartbroken.

"Yes, I know." She laughed. "I wanted to be sure."

Whatever that meant. After they had said their good-byes and Charles had wished her all the best, he went out into the crisp night and gathered some firewood and, until the crackling logs had diminished to a heap of embers, sat gazing at he scarcely knew what.

His typist finally phoned *him*. "I've been out several times this week. Buying teabags and that sort of thing. I was wondering if I'd missed your call. You're usually a chapter-every-three-weeks guy."

"I'll have something ready soon," Charles said. "I've reached a spot where there are technical problems. I know what I want, but I have to figure out how to get there. It's like ... well, I have the *impulse*, but I don't yet know how to materialize it. Can *materialize* be used as a transitive verb?"

The typist chuckled in his fatherly manner. "No, but I know what you mean."

One evening in November, Charles was coming out of the bookstore, which opened at eleven in the morning and stayed open until eight in the evening to fit in with the artistic habits of the village. There was a slight fog, which caused the streetlamps to wear fuzzy amber auras. Charles was walking slowly along the main street, enjoying the melancholy feel of the dampness against his face, when he happened to think of "Sin gin." She had not phoned in weeks. Well, what did he expect? The fact that she hadn't phoned simply meant that nobody was phoning him. Simple: after the brief flare-up of his success, the world had taken him at his word that he wanted to be left alone, and gone on to pursue newer successes.

Coming toward him on the same side of the road was the lanky silhouette of a girl, with loose, bouncy hair, pushing her bike. She was wearing jeans, of the old flare-leg variety, out of style now, and she trudged forward with a brisk, determined, quick-march step. As she passed him, he craned forward, out of simple curiosity, to see what she looked like. She was passing under the streetlamp, sheathed in its orange aura, and he saw, with some regret, that she was not a girl, but a woman no longer young, with a rather determined, lipsticked mouth. She started slightly, returned his gaze, then went on by. After they had each gone on for half-a-dozen steps more, he heard her murmur distinctly, "Hello, Charles."

He whirled around. Her silhouette receded into the fog until she became the girl with long, bouncy hair again.

He knew the voice. It was the first time she had ever used his first name. She pronounced it "Chahles."

"Have you seen your latest contribution to civic life?" Smiling, the typist handed Charles the tabloid-size local paper, folded to the letter page. Charles's stomach jolted slightly when he saw the familiar surname. He read the letter, a spirited diatribe against the new breed of town managers who were fattening their pockets by ruining the town. Though the words seemed out of proportion to what the town managers were trying to do (allow a motel to be built), they were magnificent words with a real Shakespearean bite to them: "infamous hooligans . . ." "obloquy . . . base impertinence . . ." "this rank compound of malefactors, rogues, and termagants . . ." "halcyon . . ." "dunghill . . . canker."

Charles handed the paper back to the typist. "I'd hate to get on her bad side," he quipped. But inwardly he envied the sheer energy of her passion. Over a *motel*.

The typist stood up and began making the tea preparations. The tiny woodstove was going and the cabin glowed with warmth. Today's costume consisted of a pleated skirt, which came just above the typist's pale, knobby knees; a white angora sweater; and several gold chains and ornaments. Charles tried to picture the typist, wearing the workpants and jacket that hung in the corner curtained off as a closet, going through some store's racks of skirts, fingering the fluffy sweaters: how, for instance, could he be sure things would fit when he got them home? Did he tell the saleslady he was buying them for his sister, daughter, ladyfriend, or did he just hand over his purchases with his Mastercard and professorial smile?

"Well, Charles," said the typist, with his back to him as he waited for the kettle to boil, "I finally got my turn at your book in the library. I liked it quite a lot. Of course, in the new book, you're taking more chances."

"How . . . do you mean?" inquired Charles, struggling to keep his voice nonchalant.

"Well. Of course, I'm not a fiction writer. One of the incarnations I haven't tried." The typist chuckled, lifting the kettle at the exact second it began to sing. "But it seems to me that in this new book you are trying seriously to represent the psyche of a *modern* man, and that's no easy thing."

Charles sat quite still, trying to imprint the words on his memory to replay at leisure when he got home.

"Not that I'm slighting your old book," the typist went on, performing his frugal ritual of the shared, dunked teabag. "It was a joy. You could just escape right into that earlier, safer time, when characters wore their outlines more firmly . . . like"—he turned, smiling, holding the two flowered china cups in their saucers—"well, like a good set of tailored clothes. The modern character isn't fitted so easily, and I admire you for taking the risk."

"Thank you," murmured Charles, bowing his head low over the steaming tea. He did not want the other man to see how much he had needed this encouragement. After a moment, he took a large swallow of tea and asked: "Do you happen to know if St. John rides a bike?"

"That's her mode of transportation. Keeps her slim as a sylph. Her hands are a sight, though: she refuses to wear gloves in the bitterest cold. Once I offered her a pair of mine when she was here—well, you've guessed by now who types those remarkable letters—but she turned me down. Said I was trying to undermine her toughness."

"How old did you say she was?"

"Ah, I didn't say . . . nobody knows how old St. John is. Must be pushing sixty now."

"Oh, I don't think so!" Charles protested. "I mean . . . I've only seen her once, in the fog, but she walked like a girl. Of course I could see from her face that she was a woman . . . maybe in her thirties . . . maybe even forties . . . but surely not sixty!"

"What made you so sure it was St. John?"

"The bookstore people had pointed her out to me," Charles lied. Inexplicably. Why wouldn't he confide in the only friend he had in town? But confide exactly what?

"Well, I can see that she has caught your imagination," said the typist, crossing one workboot with heavy woolen red sock over his knee. His predilection did not, apparently, take in shoes. "I'll tell you what I know about her, without betraying anything. Her legend is common knowledge around here. Another customer of mine told it to me. She came here in the late thirties as Magnus St. John's housekeeper. He was English, too, you know, his father and elder brother were peers of the realm. The story was that she—our St. John—was the daughter of an old family servant. Anyway, the story goes that she wanted to come to America and seek her fortune, and Magnus St. John paid her passage on the condition she work it off by cooking and keeping house for him. The rest is fairly commonplace: she was young and must have been very lovely—and penniless; he was a dominating old egotist used to having his way. He married her and kept her here . . . and here she sticks, living in that godforsaken shack that was part of the original arts colony compound, up on Bear Cliff Mountain. All those buildings belong to the village Craftsmen's Guild now, but Magnus St. John got it written down somewhere before he died that she could live on there. If you can call it living. Talk about primitive! The roof leaks . . . she's got pans and buckets covering half the floor to catch the drips . . . but now I am being indiscreet. I've slipped from public hearsay into personal reportage. Let's find another topic. Only I will say that the cavalier in me was wounded when she wouldn't accept my offer of gloves or my considerable carpenter's skill. I could have repaired that roof, but she said it was the Crafts-men's Guild's duty and she was going to make them do it." He laughed quietly. "St. John is a real stickler when it comes to principles."

Charles stopped by the village Copy Center on his way home from the typist's. He always duplicated his fresh chapter and sent it off at once to his editor: it gave him a feeling of progress being made. He liked the atmosphere of the little shop, with its T-shirt corner, always with several teenagers hunched over the counter watching the man iron on the slogans and epithets they had chosen for their shirts; and in another corner was a large woman in flowing robes and a turban who had set herself up with a sign in Gothic letters: VILLAGE SCRIBE. She could nota-rize documents for you, or—Charles had watched her doing it —write letters for people in the kind of language that got them fur-thest with banks, insurance companies, and collection agencies.

Charles stood slouched comfortably over the big machine, feeding in his pages and watching their doubles slide into the metal tray. At three other machines, other writers fed in their masterworks. Perhaps they had not enjoyed the fortunate noto-riety that Charles had, this past year, but in this funky room, intense with its air of self-promotion and -presentation, he was just another struggling soul, anonymous in his jeans and goose-down parka, cloning his latest visions. For many of these people, the big Xerox and Pitney-Bowes machines would be their ulti-mate printing presses; but at this moment, while flattening each page for the flashy passing eye of the camera, they all had hopes.

Sometimes Charles was sorry he had let his editor see these early chapters. Diplomatically, the man had let Charles know he was perplexed: why should Charles choose not to build on his early success with a second "bright," "humane" comedy that showed "a wisdom far beyond a young man's years"? Why had he chosen to venture into these dark, uncertain waters with who-knew-what at the bottom?

Nevertheless, Charles's spirits always lifted when he

popped a new chapter in the mail—he could just make the five o'clock collection if he hurried—and sent it on its way to the first person outside in the real world, beyond this village with its "elixir" of eccentricity.

He was counting backward through the pages of the duplicated chapter when he became aware of someone close behind him. He could hear the rapid, rather ragged breath, and—after losing count—turned, a bit irritably, to inform his successor that he could have the machine just as soon as he would kindly allow Charles to finish counting his pages in peace.

He turned and there she was, thin and frostbitten in her flare jeans and old boots and frayed pea jacket. She clutched a Guatemalan cloth bag full of papers to her chest as though they contained a matter of life and death. She was looking at him as though she had been watching him for some time and waiting for him to notice her.

"Oh, hello, St. John. It is you, isn't it?" He peered forward, an empty gesture, as he could see perfectly well that it was the woman from the foggy evening. Only, oh God, the typist was right, she was old: the dry, wispy hair that flipped up from her shoulders was a too-bright, unnatural gold under the Copy Center's fluorescent lights; the face had seen many winters, despite its structured gauntness; and the hands made him want to weep, with their red, raw joints and skin like shriveled parchment. Why in the world didn't the foolish woman wear gloves?

She surprised Charles by dropping her head shyly and mumbling something in her low British voice about being *so* glad she had run into him. Fumbling hastily in her Guatemalan bag, she brought forth an untidy sheaf of papers, which she pressed into his arms. She told him to hold those, please, while she made copies of some others.

He stood there holding her papers while she went feverishly at the Xerox machine. Then a glance at the clock impressed on him the absurdity of this scene. "Look, St. John, I have to go now," he said almost curtly. "I'll miss the five o'clock mail."

On she went, feeding the machine, her hair flying wildly as

she swooped to collect each new page fresh from the tray. "Just one more second, darling," she said, and what could he do— what could a cavalier do? as the typist would put it—but stand there holding her stuff?

He made it to the post office. He even made it with enough time left over to satisfy her other request. She had entreated him to sign his name to the copy of a letter she had written (typed by you-know-who) and buy a stamped envelope and address it to their representative in Albany.

The letter was a protest against the inhumane trapping of raccoons.

It seemed strange to Charles, who had time to mull it over while he ate supper, that, as soon as St. John had nailed him with her current cause, she was quite willing to let him go: almost eager to see him sprint out of the Copy Center for the post office. It seemed strange that neither of them had mentioned the half-dozen or more times they had spoken on the phone. She was more sure of herself on the phone, more hearty. He had been taken aback, that first time she had called him "darling" on the telephone. But that must be her style of speech; he had heard her call the Village Scribe the same thing as he had rushed from the shop. "We just have to keep trying, dah-ling," St. John had said in her breathy English voice to the large woman in flowing robes. Charles wondered if she had picked up her tony accent from the dominating old Magnus. If so, what had her own speech been like when she was young and lovely, come to seek her fortune in the New World?

And now here she was, rushing around like one possessed for the protection of raccoons, squandering words the Bard himself had used—but on sewage projects and motels.

He could weep for those hands.

By early December, Charles had finished what he estimated to be a third of his book. He felt it would be a good idea to go away. Get clear away. Though the book was at last tightening with a sense of inevitability, he himself was becoming unstrung. The village "elixir" was getting to him. How afraid he had been, a year ago, that success would ruin him, make him boasting and self-centered and trivial, as he had seen it do to others. And so he had, in a sense, exiled himself to this rural place to "keep himself honest." Oh, he was still honest, all right, more so than ever, perhaps, but the virtue was seeking new depths. When he came here, he had thought the village quaint, been tenderly amused by its artistic pretensions. So many "artists"! Everybody he met had been writing a novel or painting a canvas or transcribing the music of a different drummer. He had modestly suppressed his condescension. How, after all, was he better than they were, except in his talent and maybe discipline and luck?

But as the months of silence wrapped around him and the winter wore him down, and his social life dwindled to the book-store and his typist, he began to exist in an almost medieval anonymity. Weren't they all, in a sense, interchangeable, inter-working parts of the same divine machine that drove them on, kept them all furiously typing or sloshing paint or genuflecting in front of the Xerox machine to gather their harvests of dupli-cated pages?

Or scribbling impassioned diatribes against the mounting trash heap of brutality and greed. ("Sweep on, you fat and greasy citizens," she had written, in her most recent letter to the paper. Charles had smiled when he saw it: the Bard again.)

She had phoned him once more. This time it was about a girl he had known in high school. She had read about Charles's success in a back issue of a magazine while waiting to see her gynecologist. "But she hasn't read your book," St. John told him. "She asked me if I thought you'd mind, and I told her I really couldn't say. Anyhow, here's the number. I'm sure it would make her very happy if you called."

"I probably won't," Charles had said, "but thanks anyway, St. John. How is your raccoon campaign coming?"

But she must have picked up the slightest edge of irony in his tone, because she said defensively, "Oh, these things go

slowly, but nevertheless one feels one has to take *some* action."
She did not call him darling and rang off after a brisk goodnight.

Yes, he really had to go somewhere, take a breather away
from his reclusive life in this village. It had aroused the part of
his nature that was strange, lonely, and mad. While it had been
good for the book, he worried what it was doing to his social self.
If he didn't watch it, the first thing he knew, he would be draft-
ing petitions to be kind to mice (he had, actually, become fond
of their companionable little gnawing sounds in his garbage pail
beneath the sink) or dressing up in women's clothes.

He called an old acquaintance in the city, a gregarious fellow
who kept up with the "hot" vacation spots. The man was flattered to hear from Charles and said he would fix the whole thing
up with his own travel agent. "You mean it's not too late?"
asked Charles. "If this island is so popular, won't everything be
booked?" "They always save a block of rooms for people like
you," the man said, laughing. "People like me?" "Sure. Bache-
lors who get the heebie-jeebies right before the big holidays.
This is the kind of island that can always use a personable guy
like you. You'll make some chick's holiday, and then she'll tell
her friends. Christmas falls on a Thursday this year. When you
wanna leave?" "Better make it the Saturday before," said
Charles. "Man, you got cabin fever!" crowed the gregarious man
triumphantly.

Charles marked time through mid-December. He covered his
typewriter, as he did not want to begin pecking out another
chapter, and took a box of bakery cookies to his typist, who, he
had discovered, had a sweet tooth. Then he got out his summer
clothes and ironed them, even though they would just get wrinkled again in the suitcase. He tried to read books he had been
saving for months, but couldn't keep his mind on any of them.
He went to bed early, fell immediately into a deep sleep, and
awoke remembering the most disturbing dreams. After haunting

him all fall, his mother had faded out of his night life, to be replaced by crowds of strangers, or peripheral people from his
past. If these dream figures had anything in common, it was that
they were all discovering, and taking pains to let him know, that
he was a fraud, an impostor, or—as in one dream—an importer
of stolen animal pelts.

A week before Christmas, he was coming out of the A&P at
dusk, and a figure pedaled by on a bicycle, shrieked her brakes
to a halt, and walked the bicycle backward till she reached
Charles. "God bless you, darling, and Merry Christmas," she
said. She was wearing a red woolen muffler that made her look
like a pretty girl with a red nose in this kind half-light.

"St. John, I've missed you," he heard himself say.

"God bless you," she repeated. Then, clearly moved, she
hooked him around the neck with a freezing hand, and pulled
him to her and kissed him fervently on the cheek.

The day before Charles's plane left for the island, it began to
snow. Charles called the airline. The airline called Charles back.
The flight had been rescheduled for the following day. The following day, it snowed as if it would never quit. Charles had at
least a dozen conversations with the airline. The thing he could
not stand in life was not knowing something. Once he knew, he
could adapt. Finally, a reservations clerk told him, "Sir, you are
not the only one who wants to get home for Christmas. There
are hundreds of families waiting in this very airport to get
home."

"I am at home," said Charles. He canceled his flight.

He went to the kitchen, where the mice were having a loud
supper in the garbage pail under the sink, and poured himself a
large Scotch. He felt elated that he was not going on his trip.
Presently, he had a second Scotch, and sat smiling and shaking
his head as he drank: he felt absolutely liberated from the tyr-
anny of his "bright," "wise," social self. He went to the window

and watched the snow pile itself implacably upon the village, isolating it from the rest of the world. "The art of our necessities is strange," he murmured aloud, quoting the Bard, giving himself courage as he leafed quickly through the phone book to the page of his name.

His tires, radial though they were, would not make it up the last stretch of Bear Cliff Mountain Road. He pulled over to the side, turned the wheels inward, lifted the handbrake, and stepped out into the snowy night. All around him was the sound of clattering snowflakes. Whoever said that snow fell silently? They didn't know, didn't know firsthand. Pulling his collar closer around his neck, he climbed the hill toward the old arts colony. There were only a few lights. Not many people were willing to live here anymore.

I know we are barely acquainted, but I find myself in love with you.

Who had spoken such incredible words? They were words out of an old book, written when the world was young and innocent and the motives of characters fit closer to their skins. They were words addressed by a cavalier to a maiden, after several mutually gratifying glimpses—perhaps some hastily exchanged words—in a strict society. In this fateful snow, the old magic returned, and within the hour, Charles would clasp the woman of his imagination to his heart and speak these honorable words.

Some years later, Charles had lunch with the typist. They ate in a place the typist loved to visit whenever he came to New York. It was a replica of an English pub, only you could have your beer cold, if you wanted. Charles lived in the city now, and the typist (who had shed that incarnation) was an investment consultant for a philanthropic foundation that operated out of Philadelphia. The typist had to take the train to New York once or twice a month to take care of things to do with the foundation, or with his own affairs, and sometimes he delighted Charles by phoning him to ask if he was free.

"I love this pub," said the typist. "Did I ever tell you about the year I spent at school in England?"

"No, you never did," said Charles. The typist always seemed to have one more story to draw out of his kit bag of incarnations. Sometimes Charles would close his eyes and open them quickly and try to remember how this elderly man in the discreet, well-fitting suit had looked in the old days in the yellow outfit and pearls. Had that all been a dream? The typist's father had played him a dirty trick, as the typist put it, by dying at the age of ninety-eight and leaving him, the only surviving family member, a fortune. ("He waited until I had arthritis in my knee joints and emphysema," the typist had told Charles, "and then he knew he could drive me out of those woods and make me come back to town and play ball.")

"Well," said the typist, sipping his beer and looking kindly at Charles over the tops of his glasses, which at least had not changed, "that was just the best year of my boyhood. I loved that school. I was made their first American prefect at the end of my first year—or what I thought was to be my first year. Apparently, I had committed the crime of enjoying myself too much, because when my father met me at the dock and I told him what a dream of a year it had been, he frowned and said: 'Well, remember it, because that's the end of that.' "

"You mean, he wouldn't let you go back to England because you'd enjoyed it?"

"Something like that," said the typist. "Father had his own ideas about what my life should be like." He smiled quietly into his beer. "I had other ideas. And, I'm happy to say, I acted on them. Now I suppose I must pay my debt to the old man before I kick off myself. I'm ready any time; I've had my fun. Those years in the village, where we met, were just tops. I learned many things."

"Me, too," said Charles.

"She died, you know," said the typist.

"I know," said Charles. "It seems crazy, but I still subscribe to that mad little village paper."

"So do I," said the typist. "That's how I knew. Lungs.

Same thing that's going to get me. It was all those years in that damp cabin up there for her, first serving the needs of the great artist—who, as it turned out, wasn't so great—and then flying around town in the cold, fighting the world, without any gloves."

"I gave her a pair of gloves," said Charles, making circles with his forefinger on the table. "They were cashmere. I wanted to get kidskin, lined with rabbit fur, but I knew she wouldn't wear animal pelts. She wouldn't wear the cashmere, either. Nevertheless, I did what I could, that winter, to keep her hands warm."

That was the nearest they ever came to discussing it.

"You know, your second book remains my favorite," said the typist, after a moment. "Though I may be partial, since I got to see it come into being. It had a certain . . . elixir." He smiled.

"A definite touch of madness," Charles recalled wistfully.

He and the typist parted outside the pub, the typist taxiing downtown to the train station, and Charles walking slowly up the avenue toward the bright accoutrements of a successful novelist's, husband's, and father's life.

The
Angry-Year

*I*t was 1957, when the Big Bopper and Albert Camus still walked the earth and the Russians sent a dog into space. It was the year I was angry. The whole of my junior year, I went around angry. I had transferred at last from the modest junior college in my hometown to the big, prestigious university with the good program in English. My family was poor, they couldn't afford to send me, so I'd got there with a scholarship based on my freshman and sophomore grades. Yet, once I'd arrived where I'd slaved to get, I seethed from morning till night with a hot, unspecific anger. Everything infuriated me. I went through registration glaring at the coveys of girls with summer tans who welcomed one another back with shrill, delighted cries. I hated their skittish convertibles with the faded tops, bolting the orange traffic lights. I loathed the conformity of their Weejun loafers (though I wore them myself) and the little jeweled pins swinging saucily from their breasts. There was an enemy here who might destroy me unless I routed him out and destroyed him first, but I could not discover his identity.

I did a strange thing, under a sort of compulsion. I went out for sorority rush, although I knew perfectly well I could not afford to join one, even if asked. I dressed myself up and attended the Pan-Hellenic tea and signed the register as a rushee. I went to the first round of parties, hurrying from house to house under the autumn stars. My attitude was a queer blend of arrogance and obsequiousness. At the Chi Omega house I gulped my paper cup of cider and heard myself tell the most astonishing lies. At the Tri Delt house I ate too many cookies and insulted one of the sisters. I was calmer at the other four houses and managed to participate in the established ritual of chitchat without further incidents. Walking back to my dorm afterward, I concluded that I had done no worse than others, though—with the possible exception of the first two houses—I had not made myself memorable. I went over the evening and decided that most of the girls were shallow fools. I made out a budget in my journal to see if I could squeeze sorority dues out of the scholarship, even though there was a clause in the scholarship saying the holder could not join a fraternity or a sorority. I envisioned all six houses bidding for me, and my polite rejection of them. I would remain inscrutably independent. My roommate was a cheerful, sensible girl, a Christian Scientist. She was lying hunched on the floor of our room that evening, "working on" an injury she'd received at basketball tryouts. She said her parents had given her the choice of a sorority or a Volkswagen and she'd taken the VW, of course.

Before rush began, I had met the president of the Dekes, the big fraternity on campus, at a Get Acquainted Dance at the Armory. I was offhand and rather rude to him, and he kept asking me out. I had told him I might go through rush "just for the experience." He seemed pleased, but then Graham seemed pleased by most things. He was a slow, courtly boy from Danville, Virginia. His family owned a textile mill. I never saw him get excited about anything.

The second day of rush, he waited for me beneath a shedding oak while I ran into the Union to check my rushee mailbox. The first day, everyone got six white invitations. The second day, the serious weeding-out began. I came out of the Union enraged, my hands full of tiny bits of white paper. With Graham as my witness, I flung these into the wire trash basket beside the walk. They floated down, like languid snow, upon crumpled newsprint, paper cups, and apple cores.

"I've dropped out of rush," I said. "I've torn up all my silly invitations. There was this poor girl in there. She made me see what a cruel, stupid farce it is. There wasn't a single invitation in her box. She opened it and it was empty and there was this terrible look on her face. Sort of . . . stunned, like those newspaper pictures of people who have just been told their whole family has been wiped out. I refuse to be part of such a thing. You're looking at an Independent, Graham."

Agreeably, he hurried along the leaf-strewn path beside me. It was a splendid, crisp fall day, full of colors, the kind you breathe in exultantly if you're not preoccupied by anger. "Even though I'm a fraternity man myself," he said, "I admire you for taking a stand. Of course you must, feeling the way you do about that girl in there." He never knew how utterly alone his praise made me feel. For Graham really believed that girl existed. His world contained no necessity for inventing such lies, or for raiding a trash basket upstairs in order to have six invitations to tear up and throw away. He continued to take me out. His peaceful personality seemed to bask in the flames of my rebellion. I continued to be amazed that the president of the Dekes would want me as his girl. I never asked myself did I want him.

My second foray into the extracurricular was a visit to the student newspaper, which was published daily. I was curt and defiant. I said there were a lot of hypocrisies in the system I would love to expose. I asked for a personal column. The editor was a wild-eyed, brilliant Jewish boy from New York. He later became a well-known writer. "A mean Mary McCarthy type, that's what we need," he said. He agreed to give me a trial run: three eight-hundred-word columns a week. "And we'll run a half-column shot of you, with your hair flying, like it is now."

I worked very hard on the first three columns. They were titled, in order of appearance: "Worst of Bugs, Extracurricular-alysis" (exhorting harassed freshmen not to load themselves down with band and basketball and chorus and student politics until they'd found their true and central interests); "Spit on Me or I on Thee" (a sermon, lifted in liberal chunks from Camus, in which I cautioned fellow students to judge not that they be not judged); and "The Mythical Booked-Up Maiden" (which put forth the proposition to campus males, who outnumbered the females ten to one, that dozens of beautiful coeds sat home on Saturday evenings because the boys assumed they were dated up for months in advance).

The first two columns were ignored. The third drew an amazing barrage of fan mail from the men's dorms. They offered various, sometimes unprintable, kinds of services to these stay-at-home maidens. The editor was pleased by the response and said I could keep my column. From then on I had my weapon: the powerful Fourth Estate. I titled my column "Without Restrictions," and set about avenging my private frustrations in vitriolic prose, beneath the photo of my flying hair.

Weekends I sat on the comfortable sofa at the Deke house and studied the enemy at close hand. I drank their Scotch and smiled my Mary McCarthy smile. I was surprised to discover that all the Dekes were a little scared of me. The house read "Without Restrictions" faithfully. Graham had told them about my stand that memorable fall day. To him, I was the girl who couldn't stop for fripperies when the world was smothering under a blanket of hypocrisy. The girls who came to the Deke house were another matter. Although they were friendly and polite to me, I couldn't decipher their true feelings. Most of them came from the three top sororities out of the five that hadn't asked me back. They sat draped over the arms of their boyfriends' chairs, or, with their Weejuns tucked chastely beneath their skirts, on the rug. Their faces were composed, above their jeweled pins, shutting out all disquiet. What was their secret? I asked myself. Had their wealth bought them their unshakable serenity, as it had bought their cashmere sweaters and their perfect even teeth? Was it that simple? Or was their poise due to some secret inner powers, such as the Rosicrucians advertised, powers denied me forever because of my innately angry heart? I watched these girls, fascinated; I looked forward to the weekends not because of Graham but because of them. I sat in the circle of Graham's arm and said witty, icy things, while my eyes darted back and forth, observing their languid, seamless gestures, the way they made a special art out of lighting a cigarette, their glossy, lacquered nails cupping the flame, the charms on their bracelets faintly jingling. Were they silently, en masse, smiling at me while condemning me as a fraud?

I was never sure, and my unsureness whetted my vituperation.

"Without Restrictions" dealt with second-semester rush under the subhead *John Paul Jones Had Better Be Your Friend.* The column ran a "tape recording" of a typical rush dialogue.

SISTER: And what is *youah* name?

RUSHEE: Mary Kathleen Jones.

SISTER: Jones! Are you by any chance related to John Paul?

RUSHEE: I don't believe so. There are lots of Joneses where I come from.

SISTER: And where is that?

RUSHEE: Bent Twig.

SISTER: Bent Twig! Why didn't you say so! Then you must be good friends with the Twigs who own the bank and the funeral parlor and the newspaper and the fish market.

RUSHEE: Well, I don't know them personally, but of course everybody's heard of the Twigs.

SISTER: Uh-huh. Well, Mary Catherine—oh, excuse me, Kath*leen*—it's been just grand talking to you. I'd like you to meet Attalee Hunt, our sister from Savannah. Attie, I think Mary Catherine might like a fresh glass of ice water. She seems to have eaten all her ice.

Not long after this, I received the following letter among my fan mail:

Dear Miss Lewis,

Your farce is ridiculous and futile. Why this endless stream of poison from a girl who professes to keep late-night company with Kierkegaard and Camus? Why waste

your eye for the delicate and obscure detail on such passing, boring trivia during your short-term lease among the
stars? Where is the discrepancy? Your ambivalence haunts
me. Do you know who you are? If you did, I think you
would be less angry.

                                        Jack Krazowski
                                        211 Kerr Dorm

The letter upset me briefly. I put it out of my mind. I
sipped rum punch after the basketball game, in front of a roaring
fire at the Deke house. Suzanne Pinkerton, the Chi O who, it
was rumored, once loved Graham, studied me curiously over the
rim of her steaming mug and asked softly, "Janie, why do you
hate us so?" Graham squeezed my shoulder proudly. "Better
watch out for this one," he said. He was always saying about
me, "Look out, now," or, "Better watch out for this one." That
night, his lack of originality annoyed me.

At midterm, I got my first C. The sight of the letter-grade gave
me a shock. I remembered my former industrious scholarship,
the feeling I'd had for years that A's were my birthright. Now
my mental sharpness was blurred by this constant association
with people who demanded little of my mind. All my energy
went into planning my next printed tirade against some small or
imagined slight. Graham took me to the Interfraternity Ball. Before the dance, we were inconvenienced by a new state liquor
law that made it necessary for us to drive twenty miles into the
next county in order to purchase our bottles of J&B. Several
days later, "Without Restrictions" presented a scathing diatribe
against red-neck Baptist legislators who could not hold their liquor and therefore assumed we students at the university could
not be trusted, either.

A second letter came from Kerr Dorm.

Dear Miss Lewis,
    Have you ever read Ben Franklin's story of the tin whis-
tle? You probably have—you seem to have read every-

thing—so I won't bore you by retelling it. But your latest column put me in mind of little Ben racing about the house in manic despair, blowing stubbornly on the useless whistle for which he had given all his money.

Yours truly,
Jack Krazowski

I went to the library that evening for the first time in weeks. It was a balmy evening, almost spring, and I looked forward to browsing among shelves of books once more. In a *Benjamin Franklin Reader*, I tracked down the story of the tin whistle, how when Ben as a child had been given a gift of money and sent off to a toy store he had been "charmed" by the sound of another boy's whistle and given all his money for it at once.

I then came home and went whistling all over the house, much pleased by my whistle, but disturbing all the family. My brothers and sisters and cousins, understanding the bargain I had made, told me I had given four times as much for it as it was worth; put me in mind what good things I might have bought with the rest of my money; and laughed at me so much for my folly, that I cried with vexation; and the reflection gave me more chagrin than the whistle gave me pleasure.

I left the library and walked slowly back to my dorm. I passed students, some in groups, others solitary, whom I did not know. I wondered who they were and whether their private thoughts were poems or diatribes. Perhaps the one I had just passed would become very famous someday, and someone would say to me, "Oh did you know —— at your university? You were there at the same time." "No, I hung out mainly with the Dekes," I would answer.

I walked past Kerr Dorm nervously. It was the oldest men's dormitory, built of limestone and covered with ivy. It cost less to live there because there was no air conditioning. Which room on the second floor was 211? A pair of feet in white socks hung out of one of the lighted windows. From another came the sound of Brahms's Violin Concerto. I stood beneath the window, listening to the poignant solo of the violin. The stars were out and I was pleased I could recognize so many constellations. Then I heard footsteps and people coming along the walk laughing and I hurried away, not wanting to be discovered mooning outside Jack Krazowski's dorm.

WITHOUT RESTRICTIONS
"Night Sounds"

Last night, about nine, I walked home from the library. The air had that peculiar spring quality which clarifies a drowsy mind and conducts important sounds. As I passed my fellow students I seemed to hear the rhythms of their thoughts: some quick and angry, others slow and meditative. I heard voices out of the future speak to me and I heard my own voice, also in a future time, trying to explain, to justify, the way in which I'd used my short-term lease among the stars . . .

Dear Miss Janie Lewis,

Stick to your tirades, hon. "Night Sounds" are just not you at your best.

Your beer-drinking, frat-hating, establishment-stomping, ever-lovin' buddies from

Bingham Quad

It was Graham's twenty-first birthday. I gave up on men's stores. He had as many cuff links, sweaters, and pocket flasks as they stocked. Also, I had a limited amount to spend, and did not want to risk choosing the wrong brand, an inferior label. I went to the bookstore because here I knew I could trust my taste. Usually, for people I liked, I simply chose a book I wanted myself. Would Graham like a Kierkegaard anthology? The complete poetry of John Donne? I couldn't be sure. I went on to the hobby shelves and examined a glossy volume entitled *A Compleat Guide to the World's Firearms.*

"Looking for new ammunition for your column, Miss

Lewis?" asked an ironic male voice behind me. Somehow I knew who it was. I turned at last to see what Jack Krazowski looked like. He was tall, but otherwise a disappointment. Pale, hawklike face. Horn-rims, faded Levi's, and muddy combat boots. He was holding the Modern Library edition of *Thus Spake Zarasthustra*. His hands were surprisingly graceful and clean.

"I'm looking for a birthday present," I said. "A person I know is being given a surprise birthday party tonight."

"What sort of person?" he asked familiarly. His eyes were such a light blue, he looked as though he were perpetually squinting into the sun.

"One of those persons who have everything already." My sarcastic tone surprised me.

"Oh," he said, not very interested. He was looking at me, rather pleased about something. "You're a lot prettier than that bitchy picture of you they run," he said at last.

"I don't expect you to like my picture any better than you like my column."

"It's getting better. The one about the night sounds showed promise."

"I'm glad you think I have literary promise."

"Oh, that's never been in question. I wasn't referring to that kind of promise when I said you were getting better. Would you like a cup of coffee?"

"I can't. I have to go home and wash my hair for this party. And I haven't even bought a present."

"Let me help you. The purely impersonal shopper's guide. What is your friend like?"

"He's soft-spoken," I said, noting the flicker of disappointment at the masculine pronoun. "Well dressed," I added, looking down at his caked boots. I was being terrible, I couldn't help myself.

"Buy him this." He held up an ornate copy of the *Inferno*, with Doré engravings, on sale for $4.50. "It's a good book, if he wants to read it. And the pictures are nice if he doesn't. He'll be flattered to think that you think he'll read it, anyway."

I caught the implicit snub, but it did seem, somehow, the

perfect choice. And the price was certainly right. I bought the book.

"If he likes it, you have to go to dinner with me sometime," said Jack, who then walked me back to the dorm. He had a loping long-distance walk; I had to run along awkwardly to keep up.

"Were you in the army?" I said. "You walk like you're on a long march."

"Nope. Marines."

"For how long?"

"Four years."

"Good grief, you must be ancient."

"A decrepit twenty-seven in June. I had to get somebody to pay for law school. My old man's a miner. I have nine brothers and sisters."

"Well, I'm an only child. But my father has this problem with his temper and keeps losing jobs. I had these war bonds, luckily, my aunt and uncle used to send me every Christmas, and I cashed them in so I could go to this measly little college in my hometown as a day student. The only reason I'm here is because I made straight A's for two years and did nothing but grind, grind, grind. Now I intend to have some fun." I was shocked at myself. I had not even told my Christian Scientist roommate the whole truth.

We were standing, by this time, at the entrance to my dorm. Jack suddenly gave me a paternal pat on top of my head. "That explains a lot," he said. "Yes. Well, after all my fan mail, I guess you know where I live now. Call me when you're ready to go out to dinner. Any night except Tuesday. That's my night to collect dorm laundry."

I hurried upstairs to wash my hair. I was annoyed at Jack for telling me to call him. Where were his manners? I was sorry I had talked to him about my family, but it had poured out before I could stop it. Under the shower I closed my eyes and luxuriated in thoughts of the evening to come. I felt in control of my life here at last. And Jack had said I was pretty. Maybe we could be friends. We could go off occasionally by ourselves and have quiet conversations. He was not exactly a showpiece, but I had my showpiece already. These were those pre-"Liberation" years, before girls felt guilty about treating men like objects because turnabout is fair play.

Graham liked his present. He said, "This is one classic I have always wanted to read. This is the kind of book you can keep for a lifetime." (And I am sure Graham still has the book.)

In the days that followed I became unusually depressed. All the anger had suddenly gone out of me. I read in the newspaper about a student from Texas who had jumped from the tower due to "pressures from overwork," and every time I thought of this I cried. In fact, I tried to think about it so I could cry. I wrote a column entitled "The Pressures That Bear Us Away," a disconnected, overwrought piece that, when it was published, prompted a call to the newspaper from the Director of Student Health, who pronounced it an irresponsible romanticizing of suicide. The editor called me into his office and more or less issued an ultimatum: Get funny again, or get out. I quickly redeemed myself by "crashing" the sororities' Spring Fashion Show. My next "Without Restrictions" was called "A Visitor from Mars Reports on Pan-Hellenic Couture," and put this shallow annual event in its cosmic place. Graham telephoned, sounding uncharacteristically sad. "I know these things don't seem important to you, Janie, but Suzanne Pinkerton devoted hours of work organizing that show, and she felt your column was unfair." He was as courteous and soft-spoken as ever, but I felt the censure in his words, and imagined his alliance with Suzanne against my clumsy fury.

That afternoon, I called Kerr Dorm, second floor. The phone rang for a long time. At last a boy answered. There was a great commotion in the background, shouts echoing and shower water running. "Who is it you want?" he kept repeating. "You'll have to speak up louder."

"I want Jack Krazowski!" I shouted.

"She wants Jack Krazowski!" he shouted. There was a lot

of male laughter. I was getting ready to hang up in embarrassment.

"Hello," he said. "Don't mind them."

"This is Janie Lewis, from the bookstore," I said.

"I know that. When are we going to dinner? How about tonight?"

"That would be fine. Actually, I've been . . . it will be nice to talk to you."

"I'll be over in about an hour," he said. "I'll shave and put on a suit so you won't be ashamed of me."

"I look forward to it," I said, feeling better.

"I'm glad you finally got around to calling," he said. Was he laughing? I couldn't tell.

When I looked for him in the dorm parlor, I skipped right over him at first. I looked at the boys lounging self-consciously against armchairs and walls, huddling together in groups. One of these boys I recognized as a new Deke, who'd pledged in January. Jack, in a dark suit, turned from the window where he'd been standing. He'd been there all the time, but I had been looking for a boy, not a man.

"I didn't recognize you, all dressed up," I said, hurrying along beside his long-march strides into the early-spring evening. The new Deke looked after us. I supposed it would get back to Graham but I didn't care.

"It's only my charisma," said Jack. "You'll get used to it."

He took me to a steak house on the highway. None of the Greeks ever went there. Everything seemed strangely and pleasantly adult. Jack had borrowed a car, a pedestrian black Plymouth with the radio missing from the dashboard.

"What did you want to talk about?" he said.

"Oh nothing. Everything. I just feel I can be myself around you."

"Can't you be with your other friends? Your friend that had the birthday, for instance?"

"Oh God!" I laughed wildly. Then I amended, "It's just

that . . . with a lot of people, I seem to be able to present only certain sides of myself. But with you, I can just let go."

"Knowing what I think I know," he said, "I'm not sure that's a compliment from you."

"What do you mean?"

"Oh, let's pass on that one. If you don't know, it's because you don't want to know yet. Besides, I'm glad you called." He reached over and tapped the back of my neck lightly with his finger, and a queer thing happened to my stomach.

The atmosphere of the steak house had a liberating effect on me. It seemed we were decades away from the college campus. Sitting across from each other in the dark little restaurant, eating our charcoaled steaks and drinking our beers, we might have been two highway travelers going anywhere. "I haven't felt so relaxed all year," I said. "If you only knew how much time I spend talking about nothing with people I don't even like."

"Why do you do it?" Jack asked, watching me closely. The way he had tapped my neck in the car: I hoped he would touch me again.

I said, "When I was growing up, all my friends belonged to a country club. Or, rather, their parents did. This club had the only swimming pool in town. There was another place, a sort of walled-in lake, but a girl had been molested there—a bunch of local hoodlums stood in a circle around her and made her let them feel under her bathing suit—and my mother wouldn't let me go. I was allowed into the country club pool, as a guest, twice a month. Once, a friend tried to sneak me in a third time and the lifeguard caught us and made me leave. My friend decided to stay on. I remember she gave me this sort of pitying look through the fence and said, very cool and sweet, 'We'll have better luck next time, Janie.' I walked back home, over the golf course, and I felt so ashamed."

"It was your so-called friend who should have felt ashamed," said Jack. "Did that ever cross your mind?"

"No, I guess it didn't. Not until now. How funny that it shouldn't have, until now."

"That's because you're in a rut," said Jack. "Do you want to be accepted by people just because they remind you of those rich kids in your hometown? Shouldn't you ask yourself, first of all, whether you accept *them?*"

"I don't know," I said. "It's not that simple. These people do have something. This kind of unshakable quality. I'm so . . . shakable. There's a mystery about these people I need to decipher."

"Mystery!" scoffed Jack. He drummed his long fingers on the checkered tablecloth.

"You have wonderful hands," I said, wanting an excuse to touch him. "Have you ever taken piano?"

"Coal miners' sons aren't in the habit of taking piano lessons," he replied, and I hated the smugness in his voice.

"Why do you play up your proletarian role?" I said.

"I don't know. Do I play it up? Perhaps it's my Budapest defense. Do you know chess? No? I'll have to teach you. It will develop your unshakable powers." He picked up my hand.

"What is a Budapest defense?" I said rapturously.

"A gambit. A sort of counterattack. Get them before they have a chance to get you. You of all people ought to understand."

"I wish you would teach me," I said. "Chess, I mean. No, I don't. I wish you could teach me everything." I did not have to ask myself whether I accepted Jack. There were other ways of knowing.

"Janie," he said. "Too bad we didn't meet earlier."

"But we've got now," I said recklessly. "We've got two more months." I pushed it too quickly, promising more than I was sure I could give.

"We have, if you want it," he said, looking at me carefully.

As soon as we got back to the car, in the dark parking lot behind the steak house, we began kissing. Now and then, a car or a truck would hurtle down the highway, beaming its headlights momentarily on the tall yellow grasses growing wild. Then there was darkness and the stars scattered liberally across a black sky. Suddenly the world was so much bigger. Jack and I existed alone under that sky. We were members of the universe, and anything smaller was a bore.

But when we drove back again, into the lights of the town, and saw students coming out of the movies in pairs, and convertibles skimming around corners, my old paltry fear returned. Jack asked whether I would like to stop off at Harry's, a popular campus hangout, for a cup of coffee, but I said no. I was afraid for his charisma, under the fluorescent lights. It might dissolve, and I would be stuck in Harry's with a coal miner's son and his Budapest defense, and I was not ready yet. He seemed to understand, and drove me to the dorm.

At the front door, he took me by the shoulders and looked searchingly into my face. "Janie, there isn't unlimited time for all there is to do," he said. "Don't waste it. Don't be afraid of doing what you want."

"I enjoyed the dinner," I said, in a turmoil.

He sighed. "Well, you call me when you want another one," he said. "Only it probably won't be steak next time. I'm a poor man, remember."

The spring went quickly, like a 33 record somebody had turned up to 78. Graham became hyperattentive. He'd obviously been told of my stepping out by the new Deke trying to score a few Brownie points. Graham didn't pry. That was not his way. He asked me to accept his pin. I had hoped for this for a long time; it had seemed the answer to so many things. With a dry mouth, feeling a stranger to myself, I accepted the pin in an impressive candlelight ceremony. The brothers stood in a circle around us. Even Suzanne Pinkerton came up to me afterward and took my hand and said, as though she meant it, "I'm so happy for you, Janie."

I saw Jack only once more, at the bookstore. I had gone there to browse, hoping I might meet him.

"That's an elegant pin you've got on," he said, looking straight at my eyes and not at the pin. "Does it mean you're engaged?"

"Not exactly. Kind of engaged to be engaged."

"Hmm. What are those, rubies?"

"They're not tin," I said, without thinking, and could have bitten off my tongue.

"No, I can see that," he said quietly. A remote look came into his face. I remembered how we had kissed under the stars. It would be unthinkable, never to do it again. And yet his remoteness clearly proclaimed we wouldn't.

"Oh well," I said, "things happen. But they also unhappen. Will you be back in the fall?"

"I'm finishing up in June," he said. "I get my law degree in June. Then back to West Virginia, to study for the bar."

"Oh." There was nothing else I could think of to say, yet there was so much going on between us.

He broke the silence. "Well, take care, Janie." Then he went out of the bookstore, bouncing up and down on the balls of his feet, in his long-march style. I had an impulse to run after him. But what would I say when I caught up with him?

After finals, Graham gave a houseparty at his parents' summer cottage at the beach. There was much beer-drinking and water-skiing and necking, and I was so integral a part of the group that I found I could dispense altogether with my Mary McCarthy smile. I shared a bedroom with Suzanne Pinkerton and was able to penetrate her mystique at last. She worried terribly about her small breasts and had sent off secretly for a chest developer, which she used morning and night. She slept with a yellow rabbit, whose fur had come off in patches, which she'd been given as a child. She confided that she was not really in love with the boy who was her date for this houseparty. "There's someone . . . he's in Maine . . . in some ways he reminds me of you, Janie."

"Oh? In what ways?"

"Well, he's real smart, like you . . . and at first he seems, you know, kind of critical. But after you get to know him, he's a wonderful person."

We were lying on the beach one morning, doing our nails

from the same bottle of polish. She said to me, "Marietta Porter is transferring to William and Mary in the fall. There'll be a vacancy at the Chi O house. I could speak to the others if you're interested, Janie."

I was lying on my stomach, listening to the dull, even plash of the sea at low tide, watching Suzanne's polish harden to a fine porcelain sheen on my fingernails. I pretended Jack Krazowski was within listening distance, hearing me utter the finale to that wasted year. But no one was listening as I thanked Suzanne and explained about that clause in my scholarship. No one at all, not even the Spirit of the Times, who had turned her back on us to scan the horizon. There were new things on the way for people to join or to be angry about. The sixties were coming.

Suzanne said, well, she hoped I'd come around to the house and have dinner sometime, she hoped we could get to know each other better. Then she started on her second coat of polish. I lay there beside her, staring at my own nails, getting angrier by the minute because I couldn't love them, even now that I'd made them love me.

Then the boys came back, carrying their surfboards, waving at us while they were still some distance away. Without my glasses I was not sure which of them, in their look-alike plaid bathing trunks, was Graham. The closer they came, the angrier I got, not with the deflected anger that went into the columns of "Without Restrictions," but with a deep, abiding, central anger at the real culprit, the crass conformist who'd been harboring inside the rebel all along. I dug my nails into the sand, ruining the careful polish job. What was the proper procedure for returning a fraternity pin without hurting anyone's feelings?

I don't remember the actual returning of Graham's pin. He must have been hurt, or baffled at the very least. What happened to him later I don't know.

The fall of my senior year I spent ministering to the almost constant anger of a new man, a young psychiatrist in the blackest depths of his training analysis. We spent most of our time together confusing me with his mother. In the spring I rallied and helped to found a new literary magazine on campus. It was called *Shock!!!* and had one triumphant issue before being quashed by the local postmaster. Then I graduated, with no *laudes,* and went out into the world, where I found new people to love and plenty of new things to be angry about.

But ever since the Angry-Year, I have reserved my most energetic fury for the Culprit. Though her powers have diminished as I've grown more sure of mine, she still keeps quarters for herself in some unreachable part of my psyche. She bores from inside at the braver scaffoldings erected by my imagination, and her favorite trick is posing as other people whom I hate until I realize I'm hating myself. She is forever trying to constrain me to the well-trodden paths of expression, even as I write this story. For every mental mile I succeed in traveling without her restrictions, she leadens my heart with her ceaseless plaint: *What are the others thinking? What will others think?*

A Cultural
Exchange

Once I was twenty-one and terrified I would not get the most out of life. I wanted to marry, to travel, to be a writer. Not in that order; not in any order. Perhaps I could bring everything about simultaneously, without having to make any bridge-burning choices. The truth was, I was a person who had spacious ideals, but who was rather timid when it came to facing unknown space.

I went to Copenhagen on a freighter. It was October, the worst month for storms, and I stayed flat on my back in my cabin for most of the trip. The stewardess brought me oranges, and, in my good moments, I sat up and continued work on the long letter I was writing to the man I intended to marry one of these days.

After a week in Copenhagen, I decided to stay for the winter. I wrote to Barney, my intended, that I had "fallen in love with the Danes." Let him worry a little about the ambiguous plural. The real reason, though I couldn't have told you then, was that traveling wearied and depressed me. I found it hard to concentrate on the pure experience of another culture, when I was feeling self-conscious about eating alone, or trying to dissolve little grains of Woolite in a hotel basin that leaked, or constantly being surprised by one more expense I hadn't counted on.

I went to the American Embassy, and the cultural attaché gave me the name of a widower in Klampenborg who took out a lot of books on American culture from the USIS library. "He's not running a boardinghouse or anything, mind you, but he did once say that his family has shrunk and he has too much space and he had been entertaining the thought of taking into the house a well-behaved young person, someone who could help improve his son's English."

And so, on Sunday afternoon, I found myself aboard the electric train, shuttling outward from the city. A rush of cold air came in at each stop: Nordhavn, Svanemøllen, Hellerup, Charlottenlund, Ordrup ... The names of these suburbs vibrated with the secrets of the country I was now going to discover. Secure that I was being met at the end of the line, I could concentrate on the essences along the way.

I saw him before he saw me. He was clearly a gentleman in the old tradition, the way he stood on the station platform, proud and rather aloof, in his chesterfield, his gray-gloved hands on his walking stick. A real patriarch. Then I shrank back as he scanned the windows of my car. But not before I caught the naked wistfulness that played across his features. "We shall look each other over," he had said on the phone, in precise Oxford English. But I had seen, in that eager, lonely look, a predisposition to welcome whatever stepped off the train.

I did just that, pulling up the collar of my polo coat to have something to do with my hands. There was no point in pretending to look up and down the platform, for he was the only person waiting. "Mr. Engelgard? I'm Amanda Sloane. How nice of you to meet me at the station." ("... *a well-behaved young person* ...")

"Rolf Engelgard. It is my pleasure." I could see he was as pleased with my appearance as I had been with his. "I live only there, but first we shall walk a little." He pointed to some white apartment buildings on the slope of a hill. Beyond their flat roofs stretched the glassy gray smoothness of the sea, its horizon topped by a small, misty slice of Sweden. "Are you hungry?" he asked. "Maybe you would like to eat first."

"Oh, I had a late breakfast."

"In that case, we shall wait a little. Would you like a ride into Dryehavn, the King's deer park and hunting lodge? It is lovely just now, before the frost comes. We will lunch after. How would you like that?"

"I'd love it, but I hadn't meant to take up your entire Sunday afternoon."

"Time is something of which I have plenty," he said, taking my arm. "So! First a ride into the park, then lunch at Ryttergarten, then I show you my big old flat. Have you learned any Danish yet?"

"Just *tak*. And *tak for sidst*, and *tusind tak*, and *mange tak*. The people here all speak such good English that it makes me shy. Nevertheless, I'd like to try to learn enough to make myself understood. . . ."

He stopped suddenly. We were mounting a rather steep cement upgrade, away from the Klampenborg station into a leaf-strewn park. His handsome old face went very pale. "I am sorry," he said, breathing very fast. "Last winter I had a little bronchial ailment and still find myself short of breath. It is such a nuisance." He spoke lightly, with an ironic lilt, but his blue eyes were hard with fury. He stood for several minutes, leaning heavily on his stick, glaring at the clean October sky, as if cursing some Viking deity up there.

"We're not in any hurry," I said tactfully. "That's why I like it here. Everyone takes his time."

"The Danes are downright lazy." He started to walk again. "I am a Norwegian. My parents came here when I was a boy."

"What are Norwegians like, then?" I wanted to win his approval.

"Fierce, proud, hardworking. The Danes have a sense of humor, but the Norwegians work harder. My elder son, for example, is Norwegian to the core. My younger, who lives with me, is typical Danish. Almost thirty and still a student."

"And what does your older son do?"

"A lawyer in Copenhagen. We don't speak of him, please."

"Of course," I agreed, embarrassed by the unexpected rebuff. "Where is your car parked?"

"I have no car. They are very dear in this country. I always ride a bicycle until this drat illness."

"Oh, I thought you said something about a ride in the deer park." Eccentric, I was thinking; a bit senile. . . ?

"Ah!"—he now smiled broadly for the first time—"we are in the deer park. Look." He pointed with his stick toward a hill crowned by a small castle, behind which the early-winter sun was already setting at half past one. "We *shall* ride to the King's hunting lodge." He looked down at me, quite pleased with himself. "You wait here, please." He crossed the road and spoke in Danish to a hack driver who stood beside his horses, drinking a bottle of beer.

Soon we were sitting side by side in the open carriage, our legs wrapped in blankets. The driver trotted his pair of bays along the curving path of the woods, where deer grazed close enough for us to see their eyes blink. Engelgard was watching my face avidly for every reaction. "I am so interested to know what you think, all your impressions, Amanda. May I call you Amanda? This will be a new experience for me, too. I have never taken in a lodger. Ever since my wife died, Lars—that is the son who lives with me—has been urging me to let one of our unused rooms. It is such a big flat. It contained twenty-one years of our busy married life, the growing of two boys. I told Lars, 'Whoever comes to live here, *if* I shall find such a person, shall be treated like family.' I could not have it any other way. I wanted a young person. They are more adaptable and straightforward. You come from the southern part of the United States. Wait, let me guess where. One of the Carolinas."

"North Carolina," I said, amazed, "but how could you tell?"

He smiled radiantly. I suddenly saw how good-looking he must have been as a young man. "I was not manager of Thomas Cook and Sons for thirty years without knowing some Americans. Also I have made a study of American dialects. Languages are my hobby. I speak twelve. Would you like to bet: before you leave us, I shall be able to speak like a—what would you call a native of North Carolina?"

"Well, a lot of people say Tarheel."

"Tarheel! How delightful! And what is the origin of the term?"

"I'm ashamed to say I don't know."

"Never mind, we shall find out. We have plenty of time during these long winter months. I must teach you about North Carolina; you shall show me the Danes." He rubbed his gloved hands together and chuckled. "It will be so good to have interesting conversations with someone young and vital. Poor Lars is at the university all day."

The horses had slowed at the top of a hill. The driver turned to Engelgard and said something in Danish. He replied. When speaking the Scandinavian tongue, his deep voice went up a pitch; he glided softly over the diphthongs, as if he were afraid of mashing them with his strength. *Wait a minute, wait a minute,* the Voice of Experience was warning me, though I hardly ever listened in those days. *Having a fatherly, interpretative landlord your first uncertain winter abroad is one thing; getting involved in the needs of a lonely, authoritative old widower whose moods go up and down like a seesaw is something else.*

"Look there, Tarheel. Have you ever seen so many deer in one place?"

I was already phrasing its beauty in a letter to Barney: the tough, bare lines of the royal hunting lodge; the vast and peaceful sward where hundreds of deer grazed within touching-distance of the Sunday strollers; the whole thing bathed in the russet glow of this uncanny early sunset. I was so excited about being somewhere foreign, at last, and how I would write about it, that I grabbed Mr. Engelgard and committed myself in a rush of exuberant gratitude.

"You certainly do know how to give things a lovely beginning," I said.

He looked studiously at the crowds of deer and people. A tear detached itself from his eye and rolled down his bony cheek.

"How many deer are there in all, I wonder," I went on, pretending I hadn't seen.

"The guidebooks say two thousand," replied the ironic, lilting voice, "but I should think many more than that, myself."

I moved into the enormous, rather dark old flat on Wednesday. Its one advantage was its view of the sea. My room had been Mrs. Engelgard's studio, where she did illustrations for women's magazines. Framed originals of these hung three and four deep on every wall. They showed people wearing slightly out-of-style clothes kissing under leafy trees, little children sitting alone in corners, a girl in an evening dress running away from a gloomy old house, her evening cloak streaming behind her.

Mr. Engelgard had spent all of Monday and Tuesday going through the big oak wardrobe, transferring her things into cardboard boxes. The project was still unfinished when I arrived in the taxi.

The old man had taken the train to town, to do some shopping. It was Lars, the perennial-student son, who helped me settle in.

"All these clotheses shall go away," he said, removing from the floor of the wardrobe several pairs of small walking shoes with mud still caked to the heels. He dropped them gently into the cardboard box. "Poor Father. He worked all day and didn't get nowhere. He spend all the time looking at the things. He loved her so much."

Lars was not a bit like his father. He was short and round, like a troll, and had bright red cheeks and a scruffy beard. His English was as rapid as it was incorrect, for he never paused to search for a word, simply filled in the nearest thing handy. He had switched majors several times and was now in zoology at the University of Copenhagen. "I should have finished my *eksamen* last year, but father went poor and I stay back and take care of him."

"He said he'd been sick." I began hanging my miracle-fiber outfits in Mrs. Engelgard's wardrobe. I decided to keep Lars's physical description vague in my letter to Barney.

"At night, you hear him. He searches for breath. It break

your heart. I sleep in the bed with him. He is unwilling to sleep alone since she die. We hope you shall join us for our supper to-night. Gudrun will cook yellow bean soup. It is gorgeously good, I can tell you. Gudrun is our housekeeper. She is a jolly tart. In the evening she works under the bar at the hotel across the street."

"You mean behind the bar, I hope."

"Behind the bar. You will help my English. It is killing Father. Only, if I wait till I have the right word I never get my thing said. Is better to crash on, don't you think? He who hesitates is last."

"Lost," I corrected, laughing. He would be the brother I never had.

"Lost. Oh, you will be wonderful to have around. And look you—" He walked briskly across the cluttered room to the French doors and pointed proudly to a slab of frozen earth outside. Several twiglike plants, quite dead, stood stiffly erect. "Our garden. In spring, you shall have vegetables and flowers rising out there."

"But I'll be gone by then. I'll go to Paris in the spring."

"Ah, Paris. Yes. But now we enjoy the long Danish winter."

Mr. Engelgard came home long after dark, his arms full of parcels and books checked out of the USIS library. He breathed as though he might collapse any minute. Lars and I were sitting on the sofa in the living room, looking at their family album. "Welcome to our house, Amanda," he said. Then, when he caught his breath, "What did the governor of North Carolina say to the governor of South Carolina?"

"At least I know that one. 'It's a long time between drinks.' "

"Right you are. But watch out: in future they shall not be so easy. I have been to your Embassy and wiped out the Carolina shelf." He dropped a package as he was trying to show me a book, and cursed in Danish. "Lars, do you think you might help me?" he said petulantly to his son.

Lars jumped up at once and took all the parcels. The cork of a wine bottle poked out of one. "Lucky *that* did not drop," he said roguishly, and disappeared into the kitchen.

"Well, now," said Engelgard, slumping heavily into an armchair, "has Lars shown you where to find things? I see he has lost no time in dragging out the family album. Actually I planned to show you it myself, a bit later on, after dinner some night, when you know us better and the pictures mean something. Poor Lars lacks a sense of occasion, but he means well. Do you like your room? It was my wife's studio."

"I love it. All those paintings. The sea outside. All I need now is a typewriter."

"Yes, you are going to begin your writing career. I shall call a man I know about renting you a machine. My wife worked long hours in that room. Late into the night sometimes. Of course, you must feel free to change things around, though personally I think everything looks so appropriate as it is."

"Oh, I wouldn't dream of changing anything," I heard myself declare. All afternoon I had been looking for corners and drawers where I could stash the cactus plants and odd knickknacks whose value must lie in personal meanings for some family member.

"No, I thought you wouldn't," he said, rewarding me with his smile. "Ah, Lars, my boy, here you are. I thought of a perfect nickname for you today, since we will be speaking more English in this house now."

"What is the name, Father?" Lars asked cheerfully, entering with a tray of drinks. There were two whiskies and some strange, yellowish, oily mixture in a wineglass, on whose bottom bounced a disconsolate black olive. "I have made Amanda a martini, just like in America, so she feels at home."

" 'Frowsy' is the name I have chosen," said Engelgard. He turned his head at such an angle that his son could not see his broad wink to me.

"Hmm. It sounds all right. What do it mean?"

"What *does* it mean. Well, the nearest translation would be—" He was shaking with barely suppressed mirth. "Let's see,

Amanda, wouldn't you say the nearest translation of 'Frowsy' would be 'an American nobleman'?" The old blue eyes coaxed me to be an accomplice.

"Well, yes. I guess that's as good as any," I said. I took a sip of my "martini." Lars had made it with sweet vermouth.

"Frowsy," repeated Lars, rather pleased. "I am Frowsy. How is your martini, the way you like it?"

"Let us drink a toast to the newest member of our family," said Engelgard, raising his own glass, sparing me the necessity of speaking a second untruth.

The next morning, Mr. Engelgard picked up the telephone and spoke familiarly in his musical Danish, and within a few hours a blue portable typewriter was delivered to the flat. We set it up on a large table in the center of my room, and drank a toast to it from Engelgard's schnapps bottle. "When you are a famous writer and they are giving you a cocktail party in a New York skyscraper, go to the window and look out and remember the day we launched your career with a rented typewriter," said the old man. "And remember me a little." Then out he tiptoed ceremoniously, making way for the Muse, and I rolled two sheets and a carbon into the machine and began typing rapidly, knowing he would be listening in the next room.

"Your move, my dear," said Engelgard. It was Saturday night.

Apathetically I moved my queen into the diagonal line of fire from his bishop. My head hurt. *Jeg har en dundrende ho-vedpine*, according to my Danish phrase book, which was the last thing I needed with eloquent Mr. Engelgard. I have a splitting headache. Outside, the ocean crashed. Frowsy had telephoned from town to say he had run into his brother, Palle, in the bookstore and they would dine together. Englegard had been in the bathroom having a coughing fit when the call came, and I had to relay the message. He glared at the telephone, then smiled dotingly and asked would I like a game of chess. I had thought of going into Copenhagen on the train, sitting for an hour or so in a place where students hung out. But somehow I had slipped into this role of the dutiful daughter, so of course I couldn't go. He'd feel so abandoned, with Frowsy gone as well, to eat with the son of whom we didn't speak.

"Amanda, you aren't keeping your mind on the game. Is something the matter? I never saw you give up your queen without a bloodbath."

"Sorry. I think I'm coming down with something. Do you hear a sort of echo in the room? When I woke up today, my throat was kind of scratchy."

"Why did you not say something?" He came around and felt my forehead. He cursed in Danish. "But, my child, you have a fever! We shall have to move quickly if we are to rout this Danish cold. He hangs on and on and sucks your vitality. That is how my illness began. You must go to bed this minute. That is orders." He looked almost pleased.

"But we haven't finished our game," I said, torn between wanting the eventfulness of a sickbed bustle and feeling trapped, here in this overcrowded flat, with a lonely, autocratic old nurse whose dead wife's apron still hung on the hook behind the kitchen door.

"I would have demolished you in three more moves. See? I take your queen and that leaves your castle defenseless. He cannot budge because he is blocked by your pawn. I take your castle and what stands between me and your king?"

True to his diagnosis, I had contracted the genuine Danish cold. For three days I perspired under the eiderdown, feverishly imagining what kinds of stories had gone with the framed illustrations on my walls, sneezing into Mr. Engelgard's best silk handkerchiefs, which he then boiled, along with the ones he coughed into, in a cooking pot on the back burner of the stove. I ate the oysters he ordered from the hotel across the street. I drank his toddies of whiskey, sugar, and hot water. I slept and dreamed of North Carolina and woke to hear the Danish wind howling and the waves lashing against the strand. Mr. Engelgard pulled up a chair, propped his feet on the foot of my bed, and told stories about the German occupation of Denmark: how, just here, on Strandvej, the Underground had smuggled the Jewish population in fishing boats over to Sweden; how every Danish wife practiced passive resistance by staring at the crotch of every German soldier she passed. And he told me how he and his wife had ridden their bicycles to Rungsted to have tea with Baroness Blixen.

"You had tea with Isak Dinesen!"

"Certainly. My wife illustrated some of her work. If you are a good girl, Amanda, and write very hard, I shall take you to visit her in the spring."

In those days, I kept carbons of all the letters I wrote. I found I could express things in the unselfconscious flow of a letter that simply evaporated when I sat down, consciously, to write a story. But as I reread these carbons now, in my study in upstate New York, I find that I was then so busy creating experiences that I missed the reality.

Dear Barney [Barney's sons in North Carolina must be teenagers by now],

Outside: the howling northern wind. Four hours of daylight. But how I love it, here among the lovable Danes, fantastic schizophrenic race of Peter Pans, telling macabre jokes one minute and shooting themselves the next. [Who on earth was I referring to?] For twenty-five dollars a month [I'm sure it must have been more] I have a perfect setup, a beautiful room overlooking the sea [well, their living room did], very near to Isak Dinesen's house. My landlord is a very close friend of hers and we will dine there next week. Engelgard is a real aristocrat, but he hates being old. His son Lars is a very attractive Dane (don't worry, my American heart belongs to you—eventually). Lars, who is studying zoology at the University of Copenhagen, was showing me the Engelgard family album and there was this picture, browning at the edges, of Mr. Engelgard as a young skier, framed against a Norwegian slope. He was incredibly handsome, a Viking Romeo, cheekbones like brackets (they still are) and a wonderful rakish grin.

After supper the first night I came here, my proud silver-haired host arises from the table (we had yellow bean soup, fried octopus, and Liebfraumilch in my honor) and goes over to the old upright piano with his dead wife's picture on top and proceeds to play and sing in a deep, rich baritone, pausing, however, for shortness of breath, "Nothing could be finer than to be in Carolina in the mor-or-or-ning ..." I almost cried. And did you know (I didn't) that the reason we are called Tarheels is that General Lee said of the N.C. Regiment, "Oh, they'll stick. They've got tar on their heels."

"I think I'll get dressed and take a walk down Strandvej," I said on the second day I had been out of bed. We were having the lunch he'd made: black broth, sardines on toast, and Carlsberg Elephant beer.

"You'll do nothing of the kind," snapped Engelgard.

I burst into tears. It was partly out of frustration over being cooped up so long. But also I knew that my own fear of his displeasure was creating a formidable barrier to my freedom.

"Amanda! Dear me!" He came to me quickly, laid his trembling hand against my face. "Oh, I am sorry. I did not think. Maybe I am so afraid of losing things that I hold on too fiercely. You are of course free to walk at any time you wish. I know what, we will go together. I, too, could use some fresh air. This musty old flat. I could show you the fishing boats, then we will have a little something at the hotel. But you must bundle up snugly. Wear those long black stockings I teased you about."

It was a release to be outside, chaperoned or not. How much I'd missed the sense of just going someplace. The sea was calm and Sweden was clear today. We walked slowly because of his shortness of breath. Gulls dipped, squeaking, up and down in the sky.

"Are things okay between us, Tarheel?" He looked very fit, wearing his chesterfield and a dark-blue woolen scarf knotted high on his neck. His cheeks were pink. Since I had been ill, he seemed to have gained in strength.

"Of course." Tomorrow I would get up early, take the train into Copenhagen, spend the day on my own. It seemed a point of honor to do this, even if, when tomorrow came, I wanted to snuggle in bed. If I didn't get out and go somewhere, I would have nothing to write about.

Sitting in our usual corner in the hotel bar, we drank hot rum. Outside the picture window, the early-afternoon sun was setting. "So you don't think I am a mean old man," said Engelgard.

I said don't be silly.

"Palle, my older boy, the lawyer, you know"—he began suddenly, wiping his lips with the napkin—"after my wife died, I became very morbid. Possibly a bit irritable and demanding. I felt Palle neglected me. He would arrive only to change into clean clothes, then back into town. Sometimes he stayed out all night! One day, we had a showdown. I don't wish to hold a postmortem, but I said, 'As long as you live in my home you behave like a proper son and show some consideration.' He said, 'Very well, Father, I will not live anymore in your home.' And he was gone. He packed his things and moved out the very same night! It shows a certain strength of character, don't you agree? But also a hardness of heart. I haven't seen him since. I keep thinking for a while that perhaps he would ring me up on the telephone. He did not ring. I send Frowsy to find out if he was all right. They have dinner in town now and then. Frowsy will not say if he speaks of me. Sometimes, I confess it, I feel downright sorry for myself and get a bit crotchety. You do forgive me, won't you, for today? You are free to come and go as you please."

"There's nothing to forgive. You were concerned about me. I appreciate having you in my life."

"Honestly?" he asked eagerly.

"Honestly. I'm sure he'll come around. You'll make up."

His face went hard. "You mistake me. It is too late. He will be sorry one day, possibly, but it is over for me."

I took the ten o'clock train to Copenhagen next day. Mr. Engelgard said, "I think I might straighten out your bookshelf while you are in town. You can't want all those dusty foreign books. I shall leave you some space to put in your own, as you buy them."

I nodded agreeably, rather than say I had no intention of accumulating a lot of heavy books to cart around Europe when I went on the road again.

As I crossed the big square in the center of Copenhagen, in bright winter sunshine, I felt like a racehorse being given his head after weeks inside a stable. I strolled down Stroget and looked in the shops. I bought some stretch ski pants for myself, a package of Viennese coffee (his favorite) for Mr. Engelgard, and a new science-fiction anthology for Frowsy. Then I wandered down to Nyhavn, to the port area, and watched the fishwives scream their wares. At a fruit stand I bought a red apple, which I ate ceremoniously while exploring the narrow streets and feeling super-conscious of being in Copenhagen. I played a favorite game with myself, in which I imagined my every action being observed by some person at home. Today it was Barney who watched me munching the apple and trailing my fingers along old walls.

In the late afternoon, I came across a restaurant on the corner of two streets. It was crammed with young people. I went in and ordered a beer and looked helplessly around for somewhere to sit. A handsome young Dane with gold hair and the proverbial sucked-in cheeks waved at me, as though I'd been expected. I sat down with him and his friend, a black man in a dapper tweed suit. Their names were Niels and Jean. Niels was a painter; Jean was a journalist from Marseilles. Their English was rudimentary, but they shared what they had with me; every now and then, some enthusiasm would get the better of them and away they would go, into a fluid, gesticulating French. Niels said he had met lots of American girls seeing the world. "Why you all the time climbing for something?" he asked. "Why is American women so"—he erupted into French, gesticulating to Jean, who supplied him with the word he wanted— "ambitious? You are never in the place where you are, always looking into distance of where you aren't."

"I'm not like that," I said, remembering my pure present-time joy of walking in Nyhavn with my apple.

"May we buy you another beer?" asked Jean, in heavily accented English.

After several more beers, it became easier to communicate. We gestured and laughed a lot and language seemed a silly barrier. We were all young, that was the point. Then we were in another restaurant and I was insisting on buying them both supper, for Niels had explained they could not afford to have more than soup. I told them they could take me to see Christiansborg Castle in return; I was afraid to go by myself in the dark. Then, magically, we were there, a sliver of moon tipped over our heads, our giggling ringing out over the silent battlements and turrets. A palace guard appeared out of the shadows and told us we had to leave. We went to another place and drank more beer and I missed the last train to Klampenborg. I thought this was funny, but Niels and Jean exchanged a look of irritation. "Well, I guess you stay at my place and go first thing tomorrow," said Niels. Our camaraderie was strangely muted as we went through the cobbled streets to Niels's place. Jean and Niels slept on the floor of the living room, giving the bedroom over to me. The sheets were not clean. I heard them giggling together during the early hours of the morning. I slept badly, dreaming that Mr. Englegard came with the police and dragged me into the public square where two fishwives dressed like Nazis flayed me with wet flounders.

When I returned to the flat in Klampenborg, I found it ominously silent. The door to the bedroom Mr. Engelgard shared with his son was closed. As was the door to the living room, where I had spent so much time with the two of them. I went into my room and dropped the packages on the bed. The bookcase had been straightened and some Penguin paperbacks put in. On the table, next to the blue typewriter, was a note from Frowsy.

> Dear Little Sister
>
> If you look you out of the window you shall see a little some thing that look like *oil* on the sea, around the edge. That is ICE!!! Father is not himself today and if I was in your shoe I would leave him be. He is an old man and his moods are his privaledge. He worried for you all the night and though I say dont wait up he must. I come and explain this evening.
>
> "Frowsy" (American Nobleman)

I did not see Mr. Engelgard for one week. He stayed out of my way and I stayed out of his. Frowsy would come to my room after supper (I was no longer invited to share their meal with them) and we would read our separate books (he was studying for his exams) and talk, after his father had gone to bed early.

"But he said I was free to come and go as I pleased," I protested. "It's unfair! I am an adult, not a child." I told Frowsy the truth, how I had missed the train. For some reason, I felt it necessary to clear my virtue. "Those two weren't even interested in me!" I said.

"Then they was fools," said Frowsy humorously. "I understand perfectly, but Father is the older generation and also Norwegian. That make a difference. We just have to wait till he get over his fury."

I gave him the Viennese coffee to give to his father. Later I saw it, still sealed, placed on my new kitchen "shelf." For now, by decree relayed by a reluctant Frowsy, I was no longer welcome in the living room—that was for "family." One night, when brewing coffee for myself in the kitchen, I discovered I'd run out of sugar. Furtively, I reached for their sugar on the next shelf. Old Engelgard had foreseen this. Their package had a homemade label Scotch-taped to it: ENGELGARD. DO NOT USE! How small-minded could you get, I thought, outraged. I do not have to be a paying prisoner here.

I went into town to American Express and signed up for a bus tour leaving for Spain the week after Christmas. Meanwhile I would sweat out my exile. My rent was paid for the rest of November, and I couldn't leave Denmark till Christmas, because my mother was sending a Christmas box and she'd be hurt if there was no place to send it.

I took long walks in the deer park during the day, to avoid bumping into Mr. Engelgard in the hallway. But the deer were gone. Then I'd come back, furtively make myself a sandwich, and slip off to my room, where, behind the closed door, I would type madly: letters to my mother, to Barney, to old school friends, sometimes just tirades against "the old tyrant," which I would later tear up. Let him think I was writing a great novel. I knew he could hear me. I could hear him, coughing in the next room.

A week before Christmas, he was listening to some carols on the radio. I was in my room, waiting for his next cough. It came. Suddenly, I coughed, too, after he'd finished. I heard him turn down the volume of the carols. He coughed again. I coughed back. Then he called out tentatively, "Amanda?" I combed my hair and went at once to knock on the living-room door.

"Come in."

I opened the door. He was sitting in his chair by the fire, his Norwegian blanket wrapped about his legs. He was holding out his arms to me. I went to him and knelt down beside him and bowed my head in his lap. I cried loudly and he raked my hair with his fingers.

"Oh, no, it is not easy, loving people," he said. "Look, Tarheel, can you forgive a selfish old creature?"

"Me, me," I sobbed. "I'm the one. I should have telephoned. But then it was so late. Oh, it was so sordid. I had to spend the night with awful people."

"Yes," he crooned, some of the old authoritativeness creeping back into his voice. "You *should* have called. I was worried sick. If you are going to be a great writer, little Amanda, you must learn to imagine the feelings of others."

Dearest Barney,

This will be the last communication from Denmark. Friday I take the *solbusen* (means "sun bus") bound for Barcelona via Hamburg, Strasbourg, Colmar, Besançon, Valence, Provence, and the Pyrenees. . . . Christmas among the Danes was the best ever. We stuffed ourselves and lay about in alcoholic goodwill. Father Engelgard had placed the almond in my dish of rice porridge, and so I got the *mandelgave* (almond gift): an aquamarine pendant, set in antique gold. It belonged to his wife. I have not had the heart to tell him I'm leaving yet, but I must do it tonight. It will make him sad and that will make me sad.

"What clever clotheses you Americans have." Frowsy was helping me pack. "In and out of suitcases, yet they never bend."

"Wrinkle," I corrected, pinching him playfully.

"Wrinkle. You have been a good thing for me and my English. But why did you wait so long to tell us you were going?"

"I thought it would be easier."

"Easier for you, maybe. For me, I don't mind. But older people need time to make their brains say yes. It is exactly the way Palle left. Good-bye. Crash. You should have said sooner."

"Oh dear. I've done the wrong thing again." I was angry at Engelgard for refusing to come out of his room and making me feel guilty. "I hate myself," I added, wanting to be told I shouldn't.

"Oh, you are young. You live a little more and change."

Later that morning, the morning I was to leave, a man with a mop bucket and rags and brushes arrived at the flat. He wore white overalls and went straight to work, cleaning.

"Who on earth is that funny little man in the kitchen?" I asked Frowsy.

"Oh, it's Jacobsen. Father asked me to call him for this morning. He comes sometimes when Father wants to spring-clean."

"But it's not spring."

There was an hour to go before my taxi came. Engelgard's bedroom door was shut. When Jacobsen had finished with the bathroom, I went in and took a long bath, soaking and steaming, wanting to be gone. There was still the painful good-bye to have out with old Engelgard.

I had dressed in the pants and sweater I would wear for traveling, and was crouching before Mrs. Engelgard's too-low mirror, combing my hair, when Mr. Engelgard knocked once on the door and called my name. This was it. We would probably both bawl. I opened the door, smiling sadly.

He was dressed in the suit he'd worn the day we met. I had my mouth open to compliment him on his sense of occasion. How nice he looked, with the dark ascot tucked inside his woolen shirt.

"I will appreciate it," he said in his Oxford English, pointing across the hall, "if you will return to my bathroom and wash away the ring you left in my bathtub. I do not feel I should have to do that for you. Especially when the place has just been cleaned by Jacobsen. I want every trace gone, please."

Then he turned and walked back to his room and slammed the door. I never saw him again.

For several Christmases, Frowsy and I exchanged cards. The Christmas after I left, he became engaged to a fellow student, named Birgit. The next Christmas, Birgit had found another. And the following Christmas he wrote, "Father did not make it this year."

Barney also found another, and, I must say, reading over those old carbons, I don't blame him. I also found somebody, and lost him, and found another. Fifteen years passed and my husband and I were staying in the finest hotel in Copenhagen. I am sure the basin did not leak when one tried to dissolve Woolite; I was not there long enough to find out. I looked in the phone book and there was the name, ENGELGARD, and the same address my mother and Barney had written to, during that other winter.

When I said, "Lars?" he didn't know who I was, but when I said, "Frowsy," he cursed in Danish and said, "Amanda, you come out here at once! This minute, do you hear me?" My husband and I took the train through the autumn suburbs and I found my way from Klampenborg station to the flat as if I'd been gone but a few hours.

The man who opened the door was neither short nor round. He no longer looked like a troll. He had shaved the scruffy beard and his hair was golder than I remembered. How could he have grown taller? He was almost thirty when we met. Then I realized it was because he no longer stood next to his father. At first he was terribly nervous. When he handed us our coffee cups, his hands shook. For the first half hour, he addressed all his remarks to my husband. But then he saw me looking around and he said, "You like the way I have decorated. After Father died, I got rid of the old things." He had a slim brown cat who arched her back as he stroked her. "Father would never let us have animals," he said. "One of these days, I may get myself a wife, too, who knows?" Then he laughed like the old Frowsy.

The three of us drove in his new car to Rungsted, along the road that runs by the sea. "So," he said to me, obviously enjoying himself behind the wheel of this sleek machine, "you have become a writer, Amanda, and I have become a zoologist." To my husband he said, "Do you know, if it had not been for your wife, I would have failed those exams. My father was ill and I could not study in bed beside him, and she let me use the table in her room and made coffee when I became sleepy. She rehearsed with me all the bones in the body of a dog, sometimes till three or four in the morning."

"How funny!" I said. "I had forgotten completely about all that. I have been telling Jim what an awful spoiled thing I was."

"Amanda is frequently too hard on herself," said Jim.

We walked through the woods to visit Isak Dinesen's grave. The long, rectangular stone was set flat, under a very old and noble tree. Some beechnuts had fallen on it, near where her name was carved—KAREN BLIXEN—and I put them in my pocket as talismans to make my own writing nobler.

"I tell you something funny," said the attractive Dane, who had at last come to look like my false descriptions of him in letters to Barney. "I don't mean it is funny, but it is typical of Father. The only time he ever mentioned you again was when she died. When he saw it in the newspaper, he got very pink—you know how he went, Amanda, when he began to be furious—and he said, 'Good, good, that will show her. It will be in their newspapers, too, and she will read it and regret she was a poor Tarheel who could not stick and will never meet the greatest writer in Denmark. She will be good and sorry.' I hope you don't mind this little anecdote."

"How could I mind," I said, "when it is so like him?" And with love's delayed reaction, I wished with all my heart that the old man could hear me say it: "I am sorry."

"It is the quirks we come to miss most in our dead," mused our host philosophically, as we walked through the sun-touched woods, back to the car. "I wonder why this is?"

I wondered if I should tell him how much better his English was.

Author's Note

In the old days, storytellers began by invoking the help of their Muses. "Begin it, goddess, at whatever point you will," Homer modestly bids his Muse at the start of *The Odyssey*. In the same spirit—because I wanted guidance—I invoked Mr. Bedford to lead me through the short novel that would bear his name. Now that I am putting his story together with some companions, all of whom had their respective Muses, I feel compelled to acknowledge this welcome band of inspirers who have appeared to me over the years in the most unpredictable disguises.

Mr. Bedford's was the most striking epiphany; so much so that I have since claimed him as my mascot. I collect his images and place them at strategic points around my study, to remind me of the valuable lessons I learned while writing his story, and to warn me against the precipitance that his serene nature deplores.

A few seasons ago, I was in the throes of that occupational malady popularly known as "Writer's Block." Now, Writer's Block has many forms, possibly as many as its antidote: Inspiration. Writer's Block does not mean necessarily that you sit down wordlessly in front of your "cold altar of a typewriter," as Constance LeFevre does at her lowest point in "Amanuensis." Perfect wordlessness may be one of the malady's most honest forms. There is a spiritual purity about that, like the Dark Night of the Soul. No, I was being driven, at the time, by one of the insidious forms of Writer's Block to which my industrious, ambitious nature is prone: Emptiness disguised as Wordiness. And

I had perpetrated over a hundred pages of "a novel" before I understood that my characters had no reason to be in the same book with one another.

I entombed them in a file folder, which I hid from my sight. That evening I watched an English play on television. Later the same night, I had a short dream. I was rushing to catch a flight from England to the United States, but I needed someone to take care of my cat (who, for some reason, had to stay behind in England). And then there suddenly appeared a woman I had known years ago, while working in London, and this woman said she would keep my cat for me if I invited her to come and visit me in the United States.

All the next day, I was absorbed by this dream. It had set me to thinking about that English period of my life, which was in so many ways synonymous with Youthful Expectations—and Dreads. I got out my old journals and browsed for a while in the early 1960s, and that's when I came across the story of Mr. Bedford, as told to me by the very woman who had appeared in my dream.

The next day, I began to write. Because I wanted to write in order to recapture and understand, not because I felt I ought to be writing. I wanted to live in that English time again—but with the perspective that time and distance *and imagination* can bestow. There were memory gaps, but I would fill them in with fiction, which, as every writer knows, is often the best way to get at the important truths that lie buried beneath "what really happened."

Chastened by the recent shame of my hundred empty pages, I resolutely set my pace to one of which Mr. Bedford would approve. I wanted to *find* my story in all that past material, rather than snatch and grab from the material and *impose* a story. That was when I bought my first Mr. Bedford icon and placed it on my desk between the rock from D. H. Lawrence's grave and the beechnut from Isak Dinesen's tree. Go slowly, I told myself: this is a quest, not a race or a contest. And, though the little novel was completed in three months, I will always remember it for the leisurely mood and the sense of discovery that accompanied its progress throughout.

The final proof of its integrity, it seemed to me, was its unpopular length: too long to be a story; too short to be published by itself as a novel. However, just as in the old fable about the race between the tortoise and the hare, "Mr. Bedford" gets there in the end.

Some of the other Muses who inspired stories in this collection have histories too personal for me to elaborate on. It would be fun to tell you how an object left behind in a closet by a houseguest led to my writing "A Father's Pleasures," but I really oughtn't. Nevertheless, I am indebted to that interesting object and its owner.

Likewise, "Amanuensis" would not have come into being had not a certain person suggested herself as a candidate for mine, leading me to imagine all the comforts and drawbacks of having such a person in the house. And Charles St. John, in "St. John," was not the first writer to discover he had a double in town.

Anonymous Muses, you know who you are.

The Muse of "A Cultural Exchange" was Revision, frequently passed over at acknowledgment time because of his low-key and undramatic nature. Most writers have stories that they cut their teeth on, and this was one of mine. Denmark was the first foreign country I lived in, and, full of my adventure, I began writing this story while I was still living it. (It was quite a different story from the one in this volume.) Then, many drafts and some years later, I revisited Denmark and saw the larger landscape and some of the eventualities that had surrounded young Amanda during her sojourn with the Engelgards in Klampenborg, and when I returned home, I got out the old folder, unclipped the yellowing rejection letter from Roger Angell at *The*

New Yorker (which began "I am sorry to disappoint you again ..." and ended with "... but you get better and better"), and fussed around with the story until Revision showed me what I had been trying to say.

I think it will be okay if I tell about the housepainter and his little girl, the Muses of the final version of "The Angry-Year." That, too, was a story that had languished in the limbo of its file folder with a yellowing rejection (from another magazine) clipped to the top. The story was lively and well written, said this rejection, but ... well ... it was 1968 and sororities were anachronistic. If only I could *take out* the sorority parts ... but then, of course, there wouldn't be a story. So sorry. Try us again.

Then we decided to have some downstairs rooms painted.

The first day the painter came, I suspected he was not very impressed with the way the woman of the house spent her time. She was supposed to be a writer; why, then, did she wander around the house so much? When he painted, you could hear the steady *slush-swish* of his brush; but where was the steady sound to prove that I was working?

The second day, he showed up with his three-year-old daughter. "Her mother has some important errands," he explained, smiling in anticipation of the nice surprise he had for this restless, childless woman. "And I thought *you* might enjoy playing with her for a while."

I know what I probably should have done. But the child looked so delighted at the prospect of our playing that I didn't want to be the one to spoil adults for her. So we spent the morning on the floor with crayons.

The next morning, however, I was already fast at work, typing loudly and steadily, when he came. "The Angry-Year" needed a new perspective—I was old enough now to look back with a motherly glance on Janie's social agony and see both the humor and the cause of it—but, except for the silent pauses necessary to find the right words for this new material, the rest of the story had held up pretty well and could be fed into my machine more or less intact. Thus I was provided with two full working days of fuel for my typewriter, whose noise convinced the man downstairs I was a genuine writer and not someone on the lookout for a baby-sitting job.

(There was a bonus, too. It was no longer 1968; sororities were part of the scene again; and magazines were interested in printing stories about them.)

Though Muses do not walk into my dreams every night and announce, "Look here, I'll take care of your living creature if you'll put my story into your next novel," as the "Mr. Bedford" lady did, I am delighted to be able to report that these things do happen. And, even when they aren't happening, which is most of the time, I believe the air around us is thick with what Henry James called "the virus of suggestion." Sometimes it's enough just to keep your eyes and ears open, and answer the door; other times, you might have to exert more energy and go digging into closets. But, "Try to be one of those people on whom nothing is lost!" James advises, and, just as I've taken Mr. Bedford as my official Writing Mascot, I've made those words my motto.